BLOOD FOAM

BLOOD FOAM

A LEWIS COLE MYSTERY

BRENDAN DUBOIS

PEGASUS CRIME
NEW YORK LONDON

BLOOD FOAM

Pegasus Books LLC
80 Broad Street, 5th Floor
New York, NY 10004

Copyright © 2015 by Brendan DuBois

First Pegasus Books cloth edition June 2015

Interior design by Maria Fernandez

Library of Congress Cataloging-in-Publication Data is available.

ISBN: 978-1-60598-790-3

10 9 8 7 6 5 4 3 2 1

Printed in the United States of America
Distributed by W. W. Norton & Company

To the memory of Jeremiah Healy III

BLOOD FOAM

CHAPTER ONE

On a Sunday in the third week of November outside my half-burnt home on Tyler Beach, N.H., while attempting to nail a heavy blue tarp on a gaping hole above the shuttered front door, I learned quite the important lesson: the bright decal on folding stepladders that warns you not to step on the very top is there for a reason. I was reaching up to nail a flapping corner, hammer in hand, feeling the stepladder shaking under my right foot, and I just wanted to get the damn thing fastened, when the ladder disappeared from under my feet.

So I was airborne.

Damn.

I didn't have time to think of much as I fell, only knowing that it was going to hurt like hell when it was over and done.

True.

I hit the ground flat on my back, and the pain just exploded from the top of my spine to the base. Being that it was my house, there was no shrubbery or lawn or anything soft to land on, just rocky soil with a few tufts of grass here and there.

As I was trying to determine quickly just how much I had hurt myself, something heavy slammed into my forehead and bounced off, which led to a set of muttered curses.

My flying hammer, which decided to land where it would have the most impact.

Not my best of days.

I decided not to move and let the pain dull and sort itself out. My previously injured right leg throbbed some as well, just to make sure it wasn't feeling left out. My point of view was the cold gray November sky, the stone steps leading into my house, and the burnt wreckage of my home, which had first been built in the mid-1800s as a lifeboat station for the U.S. Lifesaving Service. The station was reconstructed, expanded, and when the Coast Artillery Station nearby on Samson Point was activated, it became officer's quarters. After the station closed, the building was transferred to the Department of the Interior, and after the government—which nearly killed me a number of years ago—pulled some strings, the title became mine.

After moving in some years back, I filled my new home with antiques, books, and old Oriental rugs, and made it a refuge from whatever passed as the world out there, as I sorted out bad dreams and memories of my time as a research analyst in the Department of Defense. Eventually my life had settled into a pleasant routine of reading, writing, spending time with a few friends, and being a part of Tyler Beach and getting involved in a few interesting matters.

A couple of weeks ago, however, the routine had been disrupted—which is like saying the Civil War was a bar brawl that got out of hand—when I tried to track down the man who had nearly killed my best friend some days earlier. While I was trying to find out who he was and where he was, he and his friends had tried to discourage me by burning down my house.

I took a deep breath. The pain in my back was starting to ease, but the thump from the hammer still hurt like hell, and my right leg was still making its wounded presence known.

There was a crunch of gravel as somebody came down the rutted wide trail that served as a driveway for what was left of my home. I took another deep breath, tried to move, winced.

More footsteps. It had been just over a week since I had gotten back home and thought that things were settling down, but maybe other people with long and hard memories had other thoughts. My 9mm Beretta was secure in my rental Honda Pilot, parked up at the other end of the driveway, and the only other weapon I could think of was my vengeful hammer. I moved my arm, winced again, and the footsteps stopped, replaced by the familiar voice of a woman.

"Lewis, are you all right?"

I shifted my head, smiled up at Paula Quinn, assistant editor of the *Tyler Chronicle*, one-time lover and dear friend. She had on a tan trench coat, belt tied tight around her slim waist. She wore thin black leather gloves and her blond hair was cut short and styled, but still her prominent ears stuck out, highlighting her pug nose. A black leather purse was over her left shoulder.

"I've been better."

"What are you doing down there?"

"Conducting an experiment in gravity," I replied. "Trying to see if I can still do outside work with a ladder flying away from underneath my feet."

She squatted down, smiling. "Looks like the experiment failed."

I sat up, grimacing. "Nope, it was a success. I learned outside work does in fact require a steady ladder."

"Help you up?"

"Please."

She grabbed my right arm and helped me up, my right leg still aching some, and she said "Your forehead . . . hell of a mark there."

"Craftsman hammers. What can I say?"

"Hold on." She unsnapped her purse, reached in, and took out a blue slip of tissue. She moistened it with her tongue and gently pressed it against my forehead. It hurt some, but I didn't mind. She pressed it two more times and then rolled it into a ball and stuffed it in a coat pocket.

"There. I think you'll live."

"Glad to hear it, Florence," I said and got a smile in return.

I led her over to the stone steps and we both sat down. I stretched out my right leg. It had been weeks since the arson at my house, yet there was still the sooty smell of wood and other items burnt and then wetted down. Paula gently pushed her body against mine, and then withdrew.

"Oh, Lewis. Your poor house."

The wind had come up and the top right corner of the blue tarp was flapping hard, like it was the banner of some abandoned ship. The two-story house was now basically one story and a bit. Most of the roof had collapsed, crushing my bedroom and upstairs study. The kitchen was also a mess, but the Tyler firefighters had managed to get the fire under control before it took out the downstairs living room and the rest of the house. Near the house was a small outbuilding that had served as equipment storage during my home's life-saving days and, until recently, had been my garage.

That building was a flattened mess, burnt timber, shingles, and broken wood, all tumbled upon a hunk of metal and melted rubber that had once been my Ford Explorer.

"Yeah," I said. "My poor house."

She craned her head to watch the tarp flap away. "I'm sorry to ask this, but I don't understand why you're doing this all by yourself. Shouldn't you have gotten a settlement or some sort of payment from your insurance company?"

"Well . . . the insurance company is conducting due diligence. They don't like the amazing coincidence that someone burned my house down and then, a few days later, I was arrested at the scene of another arson up in the lakes region. Too many questions on their part, not enough answers or funds on my part."

"I thought those charges had been dropped."

"They were."

"For lack of evidence, right?"

Which was true, if one didn't look too closely at the fact that someone had broken into the secure State Police crime lab and spirited away everything connected to me and that arson prior to trial. The State Police detective in charge of the case thought it was my doing, which was hard for them to prove, since I'd been handcuffed to a hospital bed at the Dartmouth-Hitchcock Medical Center at the time.

Justice sure does move in mysterious ways.

"You got it. No evidence. But still lots of questions, and the insurance company is dragging its clumsy feet. So in the meantime, I'm trying to tighten up the ol' girl before we get heavy rains."

"What's the prediction?"

"Locally, everything's fine for the next day or two. It's what's coming up the coast later that's bothering me."

"And what's that?"

"A tropical depression off the Florida coast," I explained. "Might turn into a tropical storm . . . might even turn into the last hurricane of the season."

"I see." She looked up again at the flapping corner of the blue tarp. "Then it might come up the coast and soak everything in sight."

"That's what I'm thinking."

She nudged me with her elbow. "Then let's finish the job. I'll hold the ladder if you'd like."

"That'd be great."

We both got up and I grabbed the stepladder, put it back where it had been, and then recovered my wayward hammer. "No hard feelings, eh?" I asked, as I slipped it through a belt loop. Paula stood near the ladder, holding it tight, and I scrambled up. I got to the top, retrieved the hammer and a couple of nails from my jacket, stretched up again, and in a few minutes the job was done.

I slowly took my time climbing back down, and when it was safe Paula removed her gloved hands from the ladder and slowly clapped. "Well done, friend, well done."

"Thanks. Up for something warm to drink? Coffee? Tea? Cocoa?"

She glanced at my house. "Really? Your kitchen still up and running?"

"My kitchen is a hazardous waste site, Paula. I was thinking about across the street."

A smile, and she slipped her arm through mine. "That'd be great." She paused and said "Quick question, though. I thought you were going back to work at *Shoreline*, as their editor. What happened?"

"I changed my mind."

"Oh. How did they handle that?"

"They told me they weren't happy, and if I didn't take the job they'd ruin my life."

We started walking. "What then?"

I glanced back at my house. "I told them they were too late."

About ten minutes later we were across the street at the Lafayette House Inn, one of the few remaining grand hotels in New Hampshire. It's nearly two hundred years old and was so named because the Marquis de Lafayette, during his famed tour of the young United States back in 1824, stopped at the place for a drink or three. It's changed a lot since then and has managed to stay alive during recessions, depressions, and the death of tourist excursion trains and the rise of the automobile.

Paula and I took a seat in the lounge, where we had a great view of the Atlantic Ocean, the small lawn in front of the hotel, and the parking lot across the street that stored the vehicles of its guests and my own rented Pilot. There was a splotch of blue that marked where I'd once lived, and I saw a Tyler police cruiser slowly roll into the parking lot; then two officers came out, chatting, looking down at my crumpled home.

There were only a few boats out in the ocean, fishing vessels it looked like, and the rocky lumps that marked the Isles of Shoals. The cops got back into their cruiser and left. We both went with cups of hot cocoa, and it was nice and relaxing to be with Paula, after all that had gone on during the past couple of weeks. We talked some about local politics and the recent presidential election.

Then she looked at me and tried a smile, and started weeping. Not a bawling or a loud wail, but eyes welling and filling up and tears rolling down her cheeks.

I put down my cocoa, reached over, touched her wrist. "Hey, what's going on?"

"Oh . . . Lewis . . . I need your help."

I squeezed her wrist. "You just helped me nail a piece of tarp to the roof of my house. I owe you one."

Paula sniffled, attempted a smile, failed. She lowered her head, took out a few more pieces of tissue, tried to clean up some. "Lewis . . . it would take me a year of working at your house to even out what I'm going to ask you to do."

Another squeeze of her wrist. "Let me decide that. What do you need?"

She crumpled up her tissues, tossed them on the white tablecloth. "It's Mark."

Mark Spencer. Lawyer, town counsel for Tyler, N.H., and Paula's fiancé . . . if that term is still being used.

"What about Mark? What's up?"

"I don't know where he is. He's missing."

"Missing? As in gone?"

A quick nod. "Oh, God. It's been three days. . . ."

"Paula . . . how? I mean . . . he works for the town. Did he take an unplanned vacation?"

She shook her head. "No. Yesterday we had a date to go for a drive up north, check out a couple of ski condos that we might rent the week after Christmas. But two days earlier . . . nothing. Didn't return my phone calls, to his house or his cell, and didn't reply to my texts. My e-mails, too."

"His co-workers know anything?"

"Not a damn thing. Besides the work he does for the town, he belongs to a small firm in town, Adams & Lessard. The office manager, the two partners . . . I've talked to them all. Nothing. He left work three days ago, and that was that. In fact, they're pissed at him for leaving without saying anything, because there's a bunch of work they're trying to get done before Thanksgiving."

"You check out his home?"

Another nod. "Sure. I went over yesterday, thinking he was sick. Nobody was there, none of his neighbors saw him after he left for work on Thursday."

"Is there a favorite B&B or hotel in the area he might go to if he's feeling stressed or something?"

"None that I can think of."

I made a circle at the top of my cocoa cup with my finger. "I need to ask you something."

"Go ahead."

I paused. Some time ago, Paula and I had had a brief yet intense relationship, soon after I had moved here to Tyler Beach. We had been close friends ever since, with a few sparks flying here and there. But a number of weeks ago, she had nearly been killed while covering an anti-nuclear demonstration in Falconer, and during that moment of crisis she had expressed her undying love to me. And then she had a change of heart, or snapped out of it, or something, and the moment had gone, until I saw her a few weeks ago, wearing a diamond engagement ring following a vacation trip out west with the lucky counselor.

Enough of the pause. "You guys doing all right? Any fights or spats lately that got out of hand?"

She shook her head. "No. Nothing like that."

"Either of you having cold feet about getting married?"

Another shake of the head.

I said "All right. Had to ask. Is his car still at the condo lot?"

"No, it's not."

"Family?"

"He has no family, either here or in Vermont, where he's from. His parents died when he was young; and in the time I've known him, no mention of any brothers, sisters, or cousins."

Outside, the sky was darkening. It was late afternoon, and by five it would be pitch-black out there. Part of the charm of living this far north.

"Paula, have you gone to the police yet?"

She sighed, ran a hand through her hair. "I've talked to Captain Kate Nickerson. She's been assigned detective duties since Diane Woods got injured at the anti-nuke demonstration. She was polite, but she admitted right up front that there wasn't much she could do. I'm not a spouse or relative. There's no evidence of foul play. She took a missing-persons report, but I could tell her heart wasn't really in it. He's of legal age . . . and as she said, it's not against the law to decide to take a few days off."

"Hell of an answer. He is the town counsel, after all."

"Sure, Lewis, but this is still small-town New Hampshire. We like the live-and-let-live attitude; and if Mark is out on a bender with a flight attendant or a lonely housewife, why should anyone care?"

I had met Mark Spencer a few times in my dealings with Paula and other members of the town over the past year or so. Based on his professional attitude and approach, I would guess the only bender he had ever experienced was dislodging a stubborn spoon from his dishwasher.

"You care," I said. "That should be enough. All right, I'll give you a hand, see what I can do to find him. I'll give it my best shot, Paula."

She sniffled once, her eyes wide with shock. "Just like that?"

"Yeah, just like that. What, you think I was going to haggle with you, or tell you not to worry, or anything like that?" I glanced at my watch. "It's getting late. I have an appointment tomorrow morning . . . any chance you and I could get together, say at eleven A.M.?"

"That's my morning deadline, but I'll break it."

I finished off my cocoa. It tasted pretty damn good. "Glad to hear it. I want you to bring me a copy of the missing-persons report, his date of birth and Social Security number if you have it. Give me a spare key to his condo so I can check things out. I'll talk to his neighbors, the town manager, and his law-firm folks, see if I can get a lead on something. I'll even meet up with Captain Nickerson. In the meantime, relax . . . take a deep breath . . . maybe take a hot bath. And then I want you to think back on anything odd or unusual that might have happened to Mark within the last few days."

"Like what?"

"Unexpected absences before he went missing. Hang-up phone calls. Anything that might show he was being harassed, or got someone's attention. Any strange remarks that seemed off the cuff but might mean something later. Okay?"

"Yes, yes, of course."

The waiter came by, dropped off the bill for our two cocoas. Damn. At six bucks each, no wonder it had tasted so fine. I took out my wallet and carefully laid down a ten and a five.

"But, Paula . . . just to be very clear on this, I don't have a private investigator's license. I don't have a job with *Shoreline* anymore, meaning I can't snoop around pretending I'm doing a column. It's just . . . me."

She opened her purse, took out her car keys, and her face firmed up. "You'll be plenty. I've seen what you've done here in Tyler over the years. You've always been much more than a magazine columnist, Lewis, and lately—much to my surprise—you've been open about your previous work at the Pentagon. So I know you're skilled in a lot of things. But most of all . . . I trust you."

Paula's eyes teared up again. "You said you're going to do your best, and I know you will."

Outside, it was chilly and I could spot the bright sparkling dot of light that was Venus in the western sky, just over the flat marshes of Tyler

Beach. I walked Paula back to her car—a cute little Volkswagen Beetle that was light blue—and she kissed me on the cheek after opening the door.

"Lewis . . . thanks so much. I feel a hundred percent better than I did when I came here."

"Must be the fine cocoa."

"Doubtful." She looked past me, down the rugged path that led to my dark house. It didn't look like a house: it looked like a cardboard model that some child had stepped on. "Your poor house," she repeated. "What are you going to do?"

"I'm going to hope that tropical depression doesn't become a storm, and hope the insurance company puts away their persecution complex about me and cuts a hefty check in my name. In the meanwhile, I've paid for some old lumber from the 1800s and, with the original blueprints from the Tyler Historical Society, hope to be able to move back in before December. I got a local contractor raring to start work, as soon as I can give him a hefty down payment."

"So, where have you been spending your nights?"

"As a guest of the Lafayette House, where else."

That got me a laugh and another kiss on the cheek, and I stood still in the hotel's parking lot until I saw her Volkswagen start up, leave the parking lot, and drive down Atlantic Avenue.

Then I turned around and trudged down to my home.

When I got back to my earlier work area, I unlocked the front door and shoved it open by slamming my hip into it three times. With most of the second floor resting on the first floor, frames and such had shifted. With the door open, I was greeted by a blast of cold air and the stench again of burnt wood and wet items. I put the ladder and tools away, tried not to look too hard at what remained of my living room and the kitchen beyond it. At least the dark covered most of the depressing details.

I grabbed a rucksack and flashlight, and it only took two attempts to slam the door shut. I went back up the driveway, switching on the flashlight. It was getting dark pretty quick. At my rented Honda Pilot, I opened up the rear hatch. My Explorer was back under what was left of my garage, and since my homeowner's policy was with the same carrier that provided me with car insurance, I was still waiting for a settlement from that end of the insurance universe as well.

With the Pilot's hatchback open, I tossed my rucksack in and then followed it in, crawling over a foam mattress pad and open sleeping bag. The windows in this part of the Pilot were covered by taped-up newspaper, and after putting on a headlamp, I pulled the rear hatch down, it thumping satisfactorily in place.

"Home, sweet home," I muttered, "once again."

There were some clothes dumped in the front passenger's seat and, with the rear seats folded down, I had a reasonable amount of space. I stretched out, winced at the pain in my right leg, and opened up a small cooler. Dinner tonight was a steak-and-cheese sub, about four hours old, still fairly warm having been double-wrapped in foil, accompanied by a take-out salad and a bottle of Sprite. I ate quickly and then cleaned up, and then went back outside, to a row of boulders that marked the farthest end of the parking lot. There, I did some personal business, brushed my teeth, washed my face and hands with cold water, and then went back to the Pilot.

Across the street, the bright and warm lights of the Lafayette House were beckoning to me. It was easy to imagine a warm room, hot shower, and gourmet meal, and then snuggling up in a wide soft bed. And after the fire and after I had come home, I had indeed spent a few nights there, but realized that spending more than a week as their guest—with no income stream from my previous job as a columnist for *Shoreline* magazine—meant I'd be in debt up to my tired eyeballs in no time.

So in the language of the time, I downsized. I understand from the *New York Times'* editorial pages that it's been quite the fad lately.

I wormed my way back into the rear of the Pilot, stretched out, and draped the sleeping bag over myself. With the headlamp still on, I picked up a thick volume of Rick Atkinson's majestic three-book history of the United States Army in Africa and Europe during World War II and opened up the pages.

As I read, I was nagged by two little things. One was that I sort of had stretched the truth when I told Paula I was a guest of the Lafayette House.

All right, to be specific, I wasn't a guest of the Lafayette House building, but I was indeed a guest of their parking lot.

And the other thing . . . well.

I turned another page.

I had promised Paula that I would locate her fiancé, the town counsel, Mark Spencer.

But I didn't promise that I'd bring him back to her.

For I was fairly certain he was dead.

CHAPTER TWO

The next morning I drove about a half hour up the coast, to the Porter Rehab and Extended Care Center, where I had my appointment in Room 209. The room was wide and well lit, and it had a nice view of the neighboring McIntosh Air Force Base. Inside, my best friend, Detective Sergeant Diane Woods, was sitting up and sipping a glass of orange juice through a straw. Her hair had been freshly washed, and the IV tubes and other wires had been removed. Two weeks earlier, she had been in a coma; a week and six days ago, she had woken up.

She had on blue pajama pants, slippers, and a flowered top, and she smiled widely as I came in, her voice still hoarse from having a breathing tube stuck down her throat for weeks. "Hey, you bad man, how are you?"

"Doing fine. And you?"

She put the orange-juice glass down on a nearby rolling table. "Still look horrible, don't I."

Which, unfortunately, was true. While most of the abrasions had healed, her eyes were still swollen, like she had gone twelve rounds with an Olympic-class boxer while sitting down in a reclining chair. The skin around her eyes was a ghastly shade of black, blue, and green.

I went to her, kissed her forehead. "Beauty's only skin-deep, haven't you heard?"

She patted my hand. Hers was covered with needle marks and sticky adhesive-tape remains. "Yeah, but as you know, ugly goes right to the bone."

"Which means you have nothing to worry about. C'mon, we're wasting time."

Diane frowned. "You're a mean man. I've already got a full day of PT and OT ahead of me. And did I tell you . . . you're a mean man."

I pulled her table away, took a hand. "I'm indeed a mean man, who also remembers your doc saying that any extra PT on your part will help. So let's shake a leg, get up for a stroll."

A few minutes later, I got her up and out of bed and, using a walker, we got out into the wide hallway of the second floor. We bore to the right, and Diane made good progress, holding on tightly to the two handles of her walker. It had two large wheels up forward and two smaller ones at the rear, and had a square center that served as a seat.

The place was quiet, with large single rooms on either side of the hallway and a nurse's station in the center. Besides the resident rooms, there were larger rooms designed for physical therapy, where therapists put patients through their paces by lifting weights, stretching, or using exercise gear. There was also a mock-up of a car and an apartment for occupational therapy, where patients could re-learn how to get along back at home with either an injured limb or an injured brain.

She looked firmly ahead and said "You look to be moving well."

"Why shouldn't I?"

"Because a little birdie told me that you'd been shot in your right leg."

"Some little birdie."

"True, though, isn't it?"

"Well . . . yes."

Diane said, "You don't seem too upset about it."

I shrugged. "Not much to complain about. It was the proverbial flesh wound. Plus, I shot him first."

She slowly moved her head in my direction. "I'd like to remind you, Mister Cole, that even though I'm moving as slow as a three-legged turtle, I'm still a sworn police officer for the State of New Hampshire."

"It was way out of your jurisdiction."

"But your home is in Tyler Beach."

"Still is," I said. "It's not moving any time soon."

"But you're okay?"

"Fit as a fiddle that's missing a string or two, and that's been dropped on the ground a couple of times."

She kept quiet, and the hallway emerged in a spacious sunroom. There were large windows overlooking a grove of evergreens, with comfortable chairs and couches and two bookcases. She went to the near chair and locked the front wheels of her walker, and I took an arm and helped her down. I sat next to her and squeezed her hand, and she squeezed back.

"What's going on with your house?"

"A bit of good luck last week," I said. "Got my building permit from the town. With the old lumber I've bought, I'm two thirds of the way there. Unfortunately, the last third involves labor and money, of which I have none. The money's not there, and the labor's not moving until the money comes in."

"Insurance companies suck, don't they."

"Right now, no argument from me," I said.

"And why are you still living in your car? You can still hang your hat at our place. Unless you think Kara will be overwhelmed by your masculinity and jump your bones."

"I don't think I'm whelming, either under or over. And I don't want to be underfoot."

"If you need some funds to rent at the hotel, we could—"

"No. Kind and gracious offers, both of them. But I'm doing fine. I also like being near my house in case somebody gets the urge late at night to break in and strip out the copper plumbing. But enough about me . . . how are you doing?"

She moved one leg and then another out away from her chair, moving slow, like she was afraid she wouldn't be able to move them back again. "Progressing. The doc . . . he has a good flowchart of how to work my muscles, how to get back into shape. There's a definite timetable, and I'm ahead of schedule. But the muscle between my ears . . . that's proving more of a challenge. My mind . . . it gets fuzzy sometimes. I get up and walk to the bathroom, and I forget about a second later why I got up. I read the newspaper, and the words seem to float right off the page. And I get scared sometimes . . . which is not like me. But hey, some good news, like you. *Miranda*'s out of the harbor. Last boat taken out for the winter."

"Good for you. How's Kara?"

"About that close to getting fired for spending so much time here. But she's still doing fine."

"Wedding still on for next June?"

"Even if I'm dragged in on a stretcher after a relapse, yeah, still on. And a little birdie also told me that Paula Quinn has been seen in your vicinity. What's going on with that? I thought she was engaged to our illustrious town counsel."

"I'm surprised your little birdie can fly, with ears so large," I said. "She has been seen with me, she's still engaged to Mister Spencer; but . . . has your little birdie told you the news about him?"

"Not a thing. What, is he getting disbarred for having a sense of humor?"

"Not quite," I said. "He's gone missing, and I don't mean overdue getting back from picking up his dry cleaning. For three days, he hasn't been seen at work or at his home, and he's not answering his cell phone, e-mail, or texts. No threats, no bloody crime scene at his office or condo. And supposedly nothing unusual or odd happening in the last several days to raise questions for Paula."

Diane gingerly moved her legs back closer. "Paula gone to the local cop shop?"

"She's seen Captain Nickerson. But you can imagine the response."

"Sure," Diane said. "He's an adult and it's not against the law to disappear. The fact that he's town counsel . . . well, Kate's probably taken a report and that's about it."

"I understand that."

"So. What did you promise Paula?"

"What makes you think I promised her anything?"

"I know you fairly well, my friend. When does your search begin?"

"Later this morning," I said. "I'm going to ask Paula for a complete debrief, get a meeting with Captain Nickerson, talk to co-workers and neighbors. The usual."

"Three days, eh?"

"Yep."

"He's probably dead, you know. Had a bit to drink, drove his car into a river or pond. Or parked his car at a store somewhere, hit-and-run driver takes him out, propels him into a wooded area. Or maybe some past client with a grudge and a lack of conscience decided to settle some obscure score."

"Probably. But I'm still going to look for him."

She brushed my hand with hers. "Of course you will. Good luck, then. . . . Tell you what: in between those torture sessions they call PT, I'll reach out to Captain Nickerson, let her know you'll be by in a bit. How does that sound?"

"Sounds great."

"Fine," she said, reaching up to grab her walker. "Now escort me back, before we encourage the gossips about all the time we're spending together here alone."

I helped her up, and she unlocked the wheels to her walker. Before we left, I said, "Diane . . . your dreams. Any of them have to do with Curt Chesak?"

She started moving out of the sunroom, and I wondered if she hadn't heard me, when she said, quietly, "Same dream, most times. Curt Chesak is coming after me at the nuke plant demonstration. I can't move. It's like my feet have been buried in the ground . . . and he raises up that lead pipe. He hits me again and again . . . and in the dream, I don't faint or lose consciousness. The lead pipe comes again and again. Covered with blood. My hair . . . my brain . . . I just stand there and take it and take it and take it. . . ." And in her last sentence, her voice rose higher and higher.

I took her near arm. "About Curt Chesak."

"What about him?"

"You never have to worry about him, ever again."

She slowed the walker down until it came to a stop. "I'm still a fully sworn police officer in the State of New Hampshire."

"I'm sure you are," I said. "And I'm still your fully sworn friend. Curt Chesak is gone. Period."

Diane didn't say anything more as we went back to her room, but as I helped her back into her hospital bed, she raised up her battered head and kissed me firmly on the lips. Her lips were rough and chapped, and she had sour breath, and I didn't care one bit.

A half hour later, I was at the offices of the *Tyler Chronicle*. It was located in an office building adjacent to the small Tyler town common, right in the center of town. I parked next to the building and strolled through the front door. Once upon a time, I would have been greeted by a receptionist who would take classified ads from walk-ins. But with the rise of the almighty Internet, classified advertising had collapsed, and the newspaper could no longer afford the expense of a receptionist.

I went around the empty counter, into the main office. There was the sound of rumba music and a rhythmic *thump-thump-thump*. Last year, in a desperate measure to keep the newspaper alive, the *Chronicle*'s owners had given up half their office space, and that new space had been turned into a dance studio.

Thump-thump-thump.

A tired-looking Paula Quinn got up from her cluttered desk, manila folder in hand, and motioned me to follow her. The rest of the office was empty, save for one young man with a Vandyke beard and a stud below his lower lip, pounding away on a laptop. There were four other empty desks. At one time, near deadline, reporters and local town correspondents would have occupied the desks; but with the ability to file their stories from home, from inside a car or a town hall lobby, the *Chronicle*'s offices were mostly empty, day to day.

It was no doubt more efficient, but it was still depressing to look at.

Paula led me into a small conference room and shut the door. She had on khaki slacks and a black turtleneck sweater. There were coffee stains on her left leg and crumbs on her sweater. She sat down at a round table and I sat across from her, and she slid the folder over.

"Here you go," she said, voice wavering. "A copy of the missing-persons report, his résumé, recent photo. I can't think of anything else."

I opened up the folder, flipped through it. Birthplace of Trenton, Vermont. Local schools. New England College of Law. A couple of law internships, then arriving in Tyler and joining the firm of Adams & Lessard. Date of birth showed he was two years older than Paula, and his Social

Security number was 520-54-1959. Hair black, eyes blue, five feet eleven inches tall, 170 pounds. No distinguishing scars or tattoos. The photo was a color headshot, taken in the summer, wearing a lime-green polo shirt, big smile, short black hair, and with a golf club over his shoulder.

"Where was this taken?" I asked.

"During the Tyler Beach Chamber of Commerce invitational last summer."

"Nice."

I closed the folder and she passed over a key. "His condo. The address is Twelve Rockland Ridge. Unit 4. I have some time this afternoon if you want to go over."

I took the key, pocketed it. "No offense, Paula, but I'd rather go myself."

"But I can explain and—"

"It's better if I see things by myself, with a fresh eye. If I have any questions, I'll get back to you. All right?"

She nodded quickly. "I understand."

A knock on the door, and the bearded young man with the stud below his lower lip appeared. "Paula, my story's filed. And I need to get out . . . can you give my story a look-see?"

"Sure, Jonah," she said, standing up. "Lewis?"

I picked up the folder. "I'll call you later."

My next stop was at the famed Tyler Beach. It being November, most of the T-shirt shops, restaurants, motels, and hotels were closed. Some of the more pessimistic owners had nailed plywood over the windows, in the fear—which I shared—that things down south in Florida would go bad and that tropical depression would grow and start roaming this way, like some cheesy monster from a 1950s science-fiction film, looking to wreak havoc on any vacation spot that was in the way.

There were just a few cars motoring around, and with the November winds, sand was beginning to drift over the streets. Along the beach, the state had erected long, orange plastic fences along the sidewalks to keep most of the sand in place.

The Tyler police station is a bunker-like concrete building, right next to the Tyler fire department, and I parked in a visitor spot; and after a brief conversation with a dispatcher behind thick bulletproof glass, the door leading in was buzzed open and I met with Captain Kate Nickerson.

She was friendly but slightly wary, and had on a dark green Tyler police uniform with heavy-looking black boots. Her blond hair was short and she had simple gold earrings in each ear, and her office was small, its one desk being shared with two other captains who worked other shifts. But on one corner of the desk was a photo of a man I assumed was her husband, along with a young boy and girl, all three laughing and sitting on a park bench. Black filing cabinets and a bulletin board were about the only other features in the office.

I took a chair across from her, and she said "Detective Woods called a while ago, saying you'd stop by for a visit."

"Thanks for taking the time," I said.

She folded her hands in front of her. "Sorry to say, even with Diane's phone call, I don't have much to offer you. Paula Quinn came in, I talked to her, took down some information . . . and that's it."

"I know," I said. "Being an adult and leaving without telling anybody isn't a crime."

"That's right. But Paula being with the newspaper, and Mark being the town counsel, I made some phone calls, checked to see if anybody was injured at the local hospitals with no ID . . . even checked the county morgues. Nothing. And that's about that."

"How about putting an alert on his credit cards? In case they get used?"

She pursed her lips. "That needs a warrant from a judge, and what can I say to a judge to request a warrant? No sign of a crime, no threats, no ransom notes, nothing . . . and for all you and I know, he might have just decided to toss away his law career and take a Greyhound to Key West."

"Or he might be dead."

"Or he might be dead," she agreed. "And if he is . . . well, don't tell Paula this, please, but there's a good chance he'll be found in a week or two. When our citizen militia goes out on drills."

She was smiling, and I think she was teasing me. So I took the bait. "What militia?"

"Deer hunters," she said. "Bow hunters, muzzle-loaders, regular hunters. They start tramping through the woods and the meadows. That's when we find bones, that's when we find missing persons. So that's when and where I think we'll find Mark Spencer."

The town hall for Tyler is back up at the center of the town, next to the uptown fire station. It's in a white building that looks like a particularly large Cape Cod house—complete with black shutters—and even without an appointment, I got a meeting with Glen Torrance, the town manager. In most towns in New Hampshire, the government hasn't changed much in the past 375 years—an elected board of selectmen, sometimes three members, sometimes five. And those with five selectmen usually hire a town manager to run the day-to-day operations for the town, since selectmen most often have other jobs and get paid the magnificent sum of five hundred dollars a year.

But the real fun part is the makeup of the five selectmen. If you get a mix of rabid left-wingers and right-wingers, it can make the town manager's job miserable, trying to answer to five different masters, meaning you have towns that go through town managers like tires on NASCAR racing cars.

But Glen had been here for four years—nearly an eternity in small-town politics—and I was happy he'd see me on such short notice. His office was on the second floor, with a great view of the parking lot behind the town hall, and I took a chair across from his clean and ordered desk. Glen was tall, about six foot six, but with not much fat or muscle. His face was lean and angular and sort of melancholy, like he had a hard time ducking problems and low-hanging ceilings. His hair was a mix of gray-brown, and it was parted to the side. He had on a blue Oxford shirt with button collar, no necktie, and dark gray slacks.

"Hey, I'm glad to see Ray issued you the building permit for your place, Lewis."

"Thanks," I said. "Hope I can get some work done before any heavy weather gets up here."

He grimaced. "Yeah. That depression off Florida. Hope it holds."

"Or at least gets some Prozac into it," I said, making his grimace disappear. He put his long hands behind his head, leaned back into his chair. "So. What can the town of Tyler do for you today?"

"Tell me where you think your town counsel is."

The grimace returned. "Pretty strange, isn't it. I was supposed to meet with him last Friday, over some worker-compensation paperwork, but he never showed up. Called him at home, at his office, even tried his cell. Nothing."

"What did his office say?"

The sour expression on his face remained. "Why are you asking?"

"Doing a favor for a friend. Paula Quinn. There's no sign of a struggle, or a violent crime, or anything illegal, so the police aren't doing much."

"Which is true," he said. "But still . . . that's not Mark."

"How do you mean that?"

He lowered his hands, put them in his lap. "Last February. We were having a meeting over a possible lawsuit against the town because of some zoning matter. An important meeting, but nothing life-or-death, you understand? The meeting was set for two P.M., with me, Bud Tyson, the selectmen chairman, and Wanda Fogarty, from the zoning board of adjustment. A storm that was predicted to be rain changed unexpectedly into snow, heavy, wet snow. You probably remember. Mark called us from his cell phone, saying he was coming up from Boston and that he would make it."

Glen paused. "Yeah, he made it, all right. About a half hour late, covered with snow. He had been driving so fast that he dropped his car in a ditch just off the exit from I-95. He walked, ran, and hitchhiked to get to the town hall after he did that. Didn't even wait for a tow truck. That's our town counsel. It's not like him to just disappear."

"What do you think might have happened?"

"No idea," Glen said. "But town-counsel work . . . it's mostly planning-board or zoning-board disputes, a few worker-comp cases. Very dry, normal, and boring. But he also does some work for his firm. I'd start there, Lewis. If there are any questions, I think it would have to be there. Not with the Town of Tyler."

I got up, extended my hand. "Fair enough. And how are the selectmen treating you?"

Another grimace. "Like the legendary red-headed stepchild . . . but the elementary school is great, and once Tina graduates from there, it'll be time for me to tell them what I really think of them."

"You think you'll have enough time for that?"

Glen smiled. "I'll make the time."

A phone call to the law firm of Adams & Lessard was unsuccessful, as I was eventually talked to by a brisk-sounding and very competent Hannah Adams, the senior partner.

"Mister Cole, are you a member of any law-enforcement agency?"

"No, I'm not."

"And are you a private investigator?"

"No."

"Are you a relative of Mister Spencer?"

I sighed. "No, once more."

"Then have a nice day," she said, as she hung up on me in a not-very-nice way.

Twelve Rockland Ridge was off High Street, near where Paula had her own condo. It was set back from the road, and the developers had wisely kept as many trees as possible. There were two old farm stone walls set along the grounds. Hard to believe that my home state is one of the most forested in the nation, yet more than a century ago it was mostly cleared farmland. But when lands opened up out west, and the farmers here realized they could own property that wasn't peppered with granite boulders, they quickly abandoned their farms and hit the road.

The condo buildings were white with black shingles, and each unit was three stories tall, sandwiched next to its neighbor, with oval-shaped parking lots in front of the units. Before I went into Unit 4, I spent a depressing hour knocking on doors and talking to Mark's alleged neighbors. It's nice to believe in the myth of the small New Hampshire town where neighbors look out for each other, but the truth is—especially in these new condo units dumped in the local countryside—the residents are transients, staying for a year or two before going on to a bigger place, or a bigger job, or a divorce court.

Which meant that out of the fifteen doors I knocked on that afternoon, fourteen were answered, and nobody knew anything about Mark Spencer. A couple of them knew he lived in Unit 4, but seeing him leave for work in the morning and come back at night was about the extent of their interaction with their town's local lawyer. With respect to their questions as to why I was inquiring about Mark Spencer, I said "routine background check," and that seemed satisfactory.

My feet were tired and my right leg ached. I went to Unit 4, unlocked it with the key Paula had passed on, and entered a tiny foyer. To the left was an empty, clean garage, with some tools hanging properly on a pegboard. Before me was a steep set of wooden stairs, and at the top was a wooden door which opened easily enough. To the left was a small and clean kitchen; beyond the kitchen, a good-sized living room.

I just took a moment to walk through the second floor, and then went upstairs to see a bathroom, bedroom, and small office. The office had a tiny wooden desk, black office chair, but no laptop. There were bookcases lined with volumes about the law, management, and business. No history, no science, and no fiction.

Out back to the bedroom. I spent a few minutes going through the closets and drawers. Clothes clean, folded, and hung in order. Shined shoes lined up like soldiers on the floor of the largest closet. No newspapers or magazines, and no dust bunnies. I stepped out of the bedroom, gave it one last glance, managed to keep the thought of Paula up here out of my mind.

Downstairs in the living room, a slight success. About a half dozen photos of Mark with Paula, including one where they were both wearing bathing suits—he black trunks, she a well-filled-out light orange bikini on a small sandy beach with pine trees in the distance—and Mark had his arm around her shoulders, smiling. I leaned in at the photo, saw a smudge or something on his wrist, and murmured "So you can smile without fainting, Counselor. Congratulations."

The living room was tidy and, except for the photos of him and Paula, was practically sterile. I went into the kitchen. Nothing out of the ordinary here, and back to the living room, where I sat down.

Too sterile, too quiet, too empty.

Aloud, I said "What the hell does Paula see in you, anyway, pal?"

I went through the thin batch of papers Paula had given me, and looked again at something I had earlier missed.

"Especially," I added, "since you've been lying to her from the day the two of you met."

CHAPTER THREE

As my first day ended as Lewis Cole, intrepid boy investigator, I had one more appointment to fulfill, up in Wallis, a town just above Tyler and North Tyler. There are large homes along the twisting coastline that could house a prep-school dorm population, but I ended up at the Wallis Bed & Breakfast Inn, a Victorian-style building set on an outcropping of rock. Including the Bed and the Breakfast, they also had a small dining room with a spectacular menu and an equally spectacular view of the Atlantic.

As I walked into the carpeted dining room, Felix Tinios, originally from the North End of Boston and now residing in North Tyler as a security consultant—which he always manages to say with a straight face—got up from the table, extended a hand. I gave it a quick shake and sat down, and he said "Don't take this personally, Lewis, but it looks like you've been living in the back of your rental car."

"Such a keen observer you are, Felix," I said. "Next, you'll be telling me that winter's approaching."

He flipped a white napkin onto his lap, and I said "What have you been up to?"

Felix passed over a leather-clad menu. "Resolving a union dispute in the fair commonwealth to the south, between electricians and carpenters."

"Really?" I asked. "Were a lot of offers made, offers that couldn't be refused?"

"Not at all," he said. "It seems that some outside forces from New York were trying to stir up trouble between the two groups so they could swoop in and pretend to be their saviors. I've had dealings with both unions in the past, their leadership trusts me, and I did a little digging, told them what was really going on. Peace has now broken out, I'm owed a bunch of favors, and certain men from New York have gone home with their legs and arms in casts."

"Slips and falls," I said. "The hidden threat."

"You got it, friend."

We then got to work reviewing the menus, and I tried not to gulp hard at seeing the prices. Felix and I had eaten here on many occasions, back when my bank account was fat and I had a steady income stream; but now that I had neither, I felt like a Midwest farmer with a dustbowl for a field and a grim-faced mortgage-company rep knocking on the door.

Felix caught my expression, closed the black leather-clad menu. He had on a dark blue heavy knit sweater, and his usual olive-colored skin was tanned after having earlier spent a few weeks in Florida. His black hair was its usual thick and styled self, and his brown eyes were as sharp and as intelligent as always.

"Don't worry, tonight's on me."

"Only if you keep a running tally."

"Of course. And speaking of tally and such, why the hell are you still camping out in the back of your Pilot? You know I could set you up at a hotel for a bit, or you could crash on my couch."

"Maybe I'm not in the mood for receiving favors."

He raised an eyebrow. "Really?"

I put my own menu down. "No, not really . . . but look, are you in the mood for granting favors?"

"Not usually, but you've caught me in a giving place. What do you have in mind? Hotel, or my spare bedroom?"

"Neither," I said. "I'm looking for someone."

"Who's the someone?"

From my inside jacket pocket, I took out the photo of Mark Spencer, slid it over the white tablecloth. Felix picked up the photo and said "Handsome young lad. Missing?"

"Yes."

"Didn't take you for a skip tracer or missing-persons investigator."

"I'm not," I said. "Like you, I'm trading in favors. That's Mark Spencer, town counsel and soon-to-be husband of Paula Quinn."

He put the photo down. "Ah, yes, the delectable Paula Quinn. Your first—quote, romance, unquote—after you relocated to these fair shores. And you're still in the mood to do her a favor?"

"Guess I am."

"What's the story?"

I told him, and he nodded a few times and then picked up the photo again. "Odd."

"I know. Care to explain more?"

"Most guys who go missing . . . they have unrewarding lives, or excessive debt, or responsibilities that they're running away from. Some little voice inside their head tells them today is the day to strike out for the territories, and off they go."

I said, "But Mark is a lawyer, counsel for the town of Tyler, and a couple of weeks ago, he asked Paula Quinn to marry him."

"Not the sign of someone who is preparing to run."

"No," I said. "Which is why I think he's probably dead, maybe in a one-car accident on a remote road, or maybe he got swept off a break-water somewhere along the coast and drowned. Or some other death by misadventure."

He put the photo down again. "If that's what you think, then what kind of favor do you need me for?"

A young waitress dressed in tight black slacks and white top came by to take our order. She had full brunette hair, an engaging smile, and said her name was Corey. Felix placed an order for a filet mignon—medium rare—with a side of two lobster tails, risotto, and house salad, and I tried to make do with a Caesar salad and a crock of French onion soup.

Felix took the menu from my hand and said: "Corey?"

"Yes?" she said, smiling widely.

"This fine fellow across from me is . . . what you call 'special.' He's confused about his order, so forget what he just said and bring him the same as me."

"Felix. . . ."

"Please, dad, don't make a scene in front of this sweet young lady, okay?" Felix said in a soothing voice.

I kept my mouth shut and noted that Corey looked back at us twice as she walked back into the kitchen.

Correction: she looked back twice at Felix.

"Still waiting for an answer. What do you think I can do for you?" he asked.

"The way Mark left . . . sudden but not in a rush. I spent some time at his condo. Looked like the maid had just visited. Nothing out of place. Nothing to indicate that he was in one hell of a hurry to leave."

"But he's still gone."

"Yeah. Like he was terribly scared of something, something so bad that he left without telling his law firm, the town, or his fiancée."

"What did the town say? Any angry workers or lawyers after him for some legal-related matter?"

"No."

"His law firm?"

"They still believe in confidentiality. So no joy there. But they don't do much in the way of criminal work . . . but I'm thinking something about his law career got him into a spot that scared him. Or his past."

That got his attention. "What about his past? I thought he was a straight shooter, straight dresser, straight boredom."

"Me too. But I checked out the missing-persons report Paula filed with the Tyler cops. Supposedly he was born in Vermont, went to school in Massachusetts, ended up here in New Hampshire. But his Social Security number begins with the numerals five-two-zero."

That really got Felix's attention. "New England Social Security numbers don't begin with five. They begin with zero."

"That's right. They don't."

"And he spent his entire life in New England?"

"In Vermont, Massachusetts, and New Hampshire. According to his records. But a Social Security number that begins with five-two-zero means it was assigned in Wyoming."

Felix said, "His records are wrong. Or they've been messed with. Or a combination thereof. What are you thinking?"

Our salads were placed in front of us by the attentive Corey. Correction: I received about twenty percent of the attention; Felix received the other eighty percent.

"I was thinking of WITSEC," I said. "Witness protection. But that doesn't make sense. He's too young, to begin with. Most WITSEC are people who've been doing criminal things for a long time. Secondly, he's in too public a position. WITSEC likes to relocate their people to remote areas. Tyler and Tyler Beach aren't Long Beach, but you still get tens of thousands of people rolling in every summer weekend. And his job . . . a lawyer? Counsel for the town? His name and photo get in the newspaper about once a week because of his job."

Felix picked up his fork. "Isn't he the same fellow you told me a few weeks ago was planning a run for state senate?"

"True," I said. "That doesn't mean C-SPAN is going to start doing live feeds of debates from up in Concord; but if he was in WITSEC for real, there's no way his handlers would have put him here, with that job, with that exposure."

We ate in silence for a few minutes. Felix picked up Mark Spencer's photo, glanced at it, put it back. He put his fork down, gently wiped his fingers with his napkin, and from his own coat pocket withdrew a hand-held that could have been an iPhone or an Android or a Terminator, for all I knew.

"This your only photo of him?"

"Yes."

He took a few photos with his handheld, slid the photo back to me, where it went back into my coat pocket. "You really should consider joining the twenty-first century, Lewis. They have phones that take photos, little tablets that let you surf porn wherever you like, and units that can tell you your exact longitude and latitude down to a single meter."

"I like my phone just as it is. For making and receiving phone calls."

"You know it can send and receive a text, right?"

"Hypothetically, I suppose you're right. But I've never dug that deep into the instruction manual."

"You know all the cool kids laugh at you for using a phone with a flip-top."

"I don't care."

He made a point of shaking his head and said, "Something has scared your girlfriend's boy, that's for sure."

"She's not my girlfriend."

"So says you. Anyway, I'll see what I can find out. If there's a person or crew looking for this lawyer, they'll be making little ripples out there. Some of my former associates and customers might have gotten wind of something. But those who might be looking for Mark Spencer, to scare him so much that he's bailed out like this, those folks are going to be careful. Going against a lawyer and a town official, unless they do it very quietly and under cover of darkness, is eventually going to raise a lot of hell, a lot of attention."

"I'm sure."

"But a word of advice, and a word of warning. Which do you want first?"

"Advice."

"You've started poking at something that wants to remain un-poked. So prepare yourself."

"Got it. What's the warning?"

Felix picked up his fork again. "I might be able to find out who's chasing after Mark Spencer. But as to why, and to where he is . . . that's probably going to be your job. Just make sure you want to take it that far."

Paula, I thought.

"I'll make sure."

When dinner, dessert, and coffee were consumed and then paid for by Felix, and the hefty bill and bundle of twenty-dollar bills taken away by a very grateful Corey, he once again offered me a couch or spare bedroom at his place, or the choice of any hotel room within a ten-mile radius. I gently declined; but as I backed my Pilot into my spot at the Lafayette Hotel's parking lot, I was already beginning to regret my stubbornness. I felt full and warm and fuzzy from a good meal and a shared bottle of wine, and after parking my rental Pilot, I stepped out into the cold November air.

The sharp wind off the ocean cut right through me as I got out of the driver's side and went to the rear, where I opened the hatchback. The lights from the Lafayette House looked even more inviting than ever before. Before me was the clammy sleeping bag and my meager provisions. Across the street was comfort and warmth and safety.

All it would take would be a simple slide of a plastic card, and comfort would be mine tonight.

I looked once more at the lights, climbed in, and closed the hatchback behind me.

Later in the night, I woke up with a start. Something had disturbed me. I wasn't sure what it had been, but my heart was thumping and my skin was moist. A bad dream? Some indigestion?

A thump of some sort, coming from the direction of my house. It must have been loud for me to hear it. I rolled out of my sleeping bag, reached for my headlamp, and then thought better of that. Even with the newspapers covering the rear windows, lighting up the interior would just show anybody out there that I was up and about.

Instead, I rummaged around and found my 9mm Beretta and a flashlight and, after some struggling, managed to slip on a pair of boots. I reached up, disabled the rear interior lights, and opened up the rear passenger door, the one farther away from my home. I stepped outside. The stars were so hard and bright, on any other night I would have paused and admired the view.

Not tonight.

Another thump.

I skirted around the rear of my rental, ducked down so I wasn't backlit by any lights from the parking lot, and made my way down the rutted path of my driveway. With the starlight and ambient light from the hotel across the street, I had a pretty good view of the situation as I descended to where I once had lived. The wind shifted and I caught again that nasty smell of wet and burnt wood.

When I got fairly close to my house, I had my Beretta in my right hand and my flashlight in my left. Unlike what you see in the movies or television—with cops or robbers who approach the darkness bracing their wrists against each other, weapon and flashlight side-by-side up to their chests—Diane Woods had taught me a different approach. I held out my left hand high up and switched on the light. "That way," Diane had explained, "if somebody sees the light and takes a shot at it, chances are it'll miss you."

The light flared out and everything snapped into view. My rocky front yard, my crumpled home, the destroyed outbuilding, and the flapping blue tarpaulin nailed to what was left of the roof and walls.

But nobody seemed to be there.

I took my time walking around the house, flashing the light here and there, catching only rocks and the waves coming into my private little cove. I flashed the light at the door and the windows, didn't see anything ajar or burst open.

I looked up at the blue tarpaulin again.

The wind caught a side and made it flap, and the nails held fast.

Was *that* what I had heard? After the events of the past few weeks, had paranoia taken permanent residence in my mind?

"Back to bed," I said aloud, and went back up to the parking lot.

Inside the Pilot, I didn't feel like reading and lighting up the interior, so I fumbled around and finally found my shortwave radio, stuck in a little storage compartment on the left. I settled into my clammy sleeping bag, put in a set of earphones, and started crawling through the radio ether, finding WBZ-AM, the powerful radio station out of Boston. I listened to a late-night talk-show host and then the news at the top of the hour, and it took me a long, long while to fall asleep, because of two reasons.

The first being that the tropical depression off the eastern coast of Florida had become Tropical Storm Toni.

And the second being that I was positive that I had earlier placed my radio in a storage compartment on the right.

Not the left.

CHAPTER FOUR

A fter a lousy night of sleeping, I got up the next morning and drove into Tyler proper and splurged for breakfast at a small brick building called the Common Grill & Grill, set near the town common where the *Tyler Chronicle* was located. Many years ago it used to be called the Common Bar & Grill, until the owner lost his liquor license, and the new owner decided to drop the "Bar" and replace it with a spare "Grill." I had a satisfying and fortifying breakfast of scrambled eggs, sausage, and coffee, and then strolled across the street to a stretch of white clapboard office buildings that held a jewelry store, a card shop, a hardware store, and the law offices of Adams & Lessard.

Said offices were located up on the second floor, and there was a small but pleasant waiting area with three chairs and a young male sitting behind a wooden desk. The desk supported a computer terminal and keyboard, and the cliché of the IN and OUT baskets. The nameplate on the desk said KENNETH SHEEN, and he had on a white shirt and blue bow tie with little red dots, and his black hair was cut short and neatly.

"Can I help you, sir?" he asked as I entered the office. Behind him was a closed door with frosted glass and gold letters that said PRIVATE, and I said "I'd like to see either Mister Lessard or Ms. Adams."

He glanced down at a calendar on his desk. "Do you have an appointment?"

"I do not."

"Oh. Well, would you like to make an appointment? I might be able to fit you in later in the week, if you tell me what this is concerning."

"No, I would not like to make an appointment," I said, sitting down in one of the empty chairs. "I'd like to see either Mister Lessard or Ms. Adams, at their earliest convenience."

"Oh." It seemed to be his favorite word. He picked up a pen. "Your name, sir?"

"Lewis Cole."

"And this is in reference to . . ."

"Mark Spencer."

"Oh." He got up from behind his desk. "Let me see what I can do."

"Thanks."

He opened the PRIVATE door and closed it behind him, and I waited and picked up a copy of that day's *Union Leader* newspaper, which is our only statewide paper. I caught up on the latest news from Concord—the governor wanted to cut the budget, the legislature wanted to cut it even more, and it was a charming debate on who would blink first—and then Kenneth came back in.

"So sorry, Mister Cole," he said, holding a legal pad up to his chest like it was providing some form of defense. "Neither Mister Lessard or Ms. Adams is available."

"That's fine," I said, turning a page of the paper. "I don't mind waiting."

"You don't understand," he said. "They can't see you today."

I lifted up the paper. "Mister Sheen, is there another exit from this office?"

He looked confused. "No, there isn't."

I rattled the paper for emphasis. "Then unless your law firm intends to crawl out the windows, I intend to stay right here until they walk by me."

A half hour passed, and his phone rang; he answered it and disappeared behind the door once more. When he emerged, his face was flushed, like he had been chewed out or something, and he said, "I'm sorry to say, Mister

Cole, but I've been informed to tell you that unless you depart the premises, the Tyler police will have to be called."

"Unh-hunh," I said, working through that day's crossword puzzle. "Tell you what: my best friend in the world is the senior detective on the force, and I have at least a nodding acquaintance with every officer in the department. Do you?"

"Ah, no."

"Then call the police. And after you call them, I'll call my other best friend, the assistant editor of the *Chronicle*, to see why a local law firm is so insistent on tossing out a peaceable citizen who just wants to see someone. We'll see who ends up having a better day."

He started toward the PRIVATE door again, and I said, "Oh, a question before you leave?"

"I guess so."

"Do you know what's the capital of Outer Mongolia?"

"Ah, no, I'm afraid I don't."

"Pity," I said.

He walked out, closed the door, and I murmured "Ulan Bator," and scribbled it in.

He returned about ten minutes later, his face bright and smiling. "Mister Cole, I'm happy to tell you that Ms. Adams can see you now."

"Outstanding."

I carefully folded up the newspaper, put it on a coffee table in front of me, and followed young Kenneth beyond the PRIVATE door into a narrow hallway. There was an office at the end of the hallway, and two others on either side, and he led me to the near one. Attorney Hannah Adams was sitting behind a big desk, with piles of papers and folders neatly arranged across the polished top. There were framed certificates announcing that she was admitted to the bar in Maine, New Hampshire, Massachusetts, and New York, and two crowded bookcases. Before her desk were two comfortable-looking leather chairs, and I took the near one.

A large window overlooked Route 1 and the Tyler downtown, and the town common, and the Common Grill & Grill. If she had been looking out this window at the right time a while ago, she would have seen me stroll across the street to get here. Lucky for me, I guess she hadn't seen me, because she could have dropped one of those thick law volumes on my head pretty easily.

Hannah Adams seemed to be in her early sixties, professionally groomed and dressed in a light gray pantsuit, ivory blouse, and simple gold jewelry on her wrists. Her eyes were cold blue, and her hair was a light blonde, tightly coiffed.

"Let's make this quick," she said. "You're wasting my time and the firm's time. What are you looking for?"

"A polite conversation, if you don't mind."

"Can't guarantee how polite it'll be," she said. "All up to you."

"Haven't you ever heard of shared responsibility?" I asked. "I understand it's all the rage in negotiations nowadays."

Her lips pursed. "Why are you here?"

"To see you face to face," I said. "To see why you don't seem too concerned about Mark Spencer. Who hasn't been seen by friends and acquaintances in at least four days."

"And you determined that because . . . ?"

"Because of our last conversation."

"I see," she said, gently tapping an index finger on her desk. "Because I was brusque with you? Because I wouldn't answer your questions?"

"Among other things," I said. "I'm looking for answers as a favor for a friend. You know he's been gone for a few days. Do you have any idea of where he might be?"

"No."

"And you're not concerned?"

"My feelings don't matter."

"Have you contacted the police? The State Police?"

"Go ask them," she said. "As a taxpayer, you pay for their services."

I felt like I was wrestling with someone who had four arms and heavy experience in using all of them. "Was there anything Mark Spencer was involved with that concerned you? Or Mister Lessard?"

"Please."

"His employment . . . was he—"

Adams interrupted me. "He was the perfect lawyer. No problems, no issues, no drama. First one in in the morning, last one to leave in the evening."

"He was from Vermont, correct?"

"True."

"Even though his Social Security number was issued in Wyoming?"

A shrug. "Not my department, now, is it. Are we done?"

"One more thing," I said. "Why the attitude? Why the pushback? I'm just trying to find someone who works here with you. I would think you'd like to cooperate. We both want the same thing: Mark Spencer safely located."

"Gosh, I guess I really hurt your feelings," she said. "So let me go a little further. Leave now, and we're even. You keep on harassing me, hanging out in my office, making future phone calls, you can't believe the trouble I can cause you, including but not limited to seizure of assets."

I got up, gave her a friendly smile. "Do your best. You do a credit report or background check on me . . . you'll be surprised what you don't find."

I left the office and walked back across the street, ducked into the *Tyler Chronicle* to see if Paula was available, but the boy with the lip stud told me she was at a Chamber of Commerce luncheon. I then retrieved my Pilot—sniffing in distaste at the ripe smells coming from inside—and drove a short distance to the Tyler Memorial Public Library.

Inside the library, I was fortunate enough to locate an empty computer terminal, and I sat down and got to work. My own computer was melted plastic and metal back on Tyler Beach, and I was fortunate—or smart enough—to have backed up a lot of my files and photographs to that amazing Cloud out there.

First I had to go through the Town of Tyler's home page, which included meeting listings for the week and exciting news about the delivery of new trash recycle bins, and then I went to the all-knowing and all-seeing Google to get to work. I spent about an hour checking out the cyberspace records of Mark Spencer, and I was puzzled at what I found.

Which was a lot, which didn't make sense. I located a couple of old stories and photographs of Mark Spencer as a Little League player and then a debate-team member while going to schools in Trenton, Vermont. Then he was off to the New England School of Law, where he was fairly active in school activities.

So my initial theory, that a young Mark Spencer had done something deep and dark earlier in his life and was in the Witness Protection Program, had gone the way of the theory of a hollow earth.

Didn't make sense.

But what of his Social Security number?

It began with the number 520, which meant it had been assigned in Wyoming.

But I didn't see any evidence or indication that Mark Spencer had any connection with the state of Wyoming.

I got up from my cubicle, sniffed the air again—nothing seemed untoward, so I guess I could go one more day without a shower—and I went back to the *Tyler Chronicle*.

Paula took me back into the same conference room as before, except this time there wasn't any thumping of music coming from the dance studio next door. She had on a simple light blue dress that hugged her in some nice places, and her face looked better today, like she had gotten four or five hours of sleep last night.

We sat down at the tiny conference-room table, and she said "The Lafayette House still treating you all right?"

"Like a king," I said.

That got a flash of a smile and I went on. "I'm not making much progress, Paula, but I'm getting some points covered. Tell me, you ever meet Mark's boss at the law firm, Hannah Adams?"

"A few times, at a reception or function," she said, brushing a strand of hair behind one of her prominent ears. "Why do you ask?"

"I'm asking because I just had a few minutes with her, talking about Mark, and she didn't seem that concerned. If anything, she seemed more concerned about me wasting her time and getting in the way."

"That's Hannah for you," Paula said. "Her life is work, work, and more work. Mark said she has never taken a day off or a vacation since he's been there, and he joked once that if lawyers were gotten rid of, like the guy wants to do in that Shakespeare play, she'd kill herself because she wouldn't know what to do."

"So if she doesn't appear concerned about Mark being gone, that wouldn't surprise you?

She shook her head. "Mark said that she was a tough but fair boss, with ice water in her veins. From what I've seen, if she's upset about anything, it's losing billable hours."

"The firm's secretary? Guy named Kenneth?"

"Nope, nothing there."

"How about the other law partner? Lessard?"

She moved yet another strand of hair. "Carl Lessard. Gray skinny guy, wears gray suits, keeps to himself. I've seen him at the same functions with Hannah Adams. Sticks to himself, nurses one drink, and then slides out when it looks like he's put in enough time to be social. Hannah bosses him around like he's a paralegal, but he just seems to take it, poor fellow."

I said, "I visited Mark's condo unit. Nothing there appeared disturbed or out of place, except for his laptop."

"Which he still hasn't used to answer my e-mails," she said, exasperation in her voice. "What else?"

"I did a canvass of most of his neighbors. He sure likes to keep a low profile."

Paula said, "You forget his place in town. He's the town lawyer. Everywhere he goes, he's under a spotlight. The grocery store, the gas station, a local restaurant. Eyes and ears keeping view, scooping up gossip to use later. That's why we've gone out of town for most of our dates."

"Makes sense," I said. "He was born in Vermont, right?"

She looked up. "That's what I said. Why?"

"Because his Social Security number . . . it begins with the numbers 520. That means it was issued in Wyoming. He ever mention spending time in Wyoming?"

"Not at all."

"And he's never said anything about having an odd Social Security number?"

"Lewis . . . I know you've had experiences working with the federal government. What, you think they can't make mistakes here and there?"

"Fair point," I admitted.

"You go to the cops?"

"I did. I talked to Captain Nickerson. I'm sorry, there's no joy on that end. He's an adult, and—"

"—and being an adult and skipping out is not against the law. Yeah, I got the same goddamn message. Hey, he's a prominent lawyer in town, he's the lawyer for Tyler, for Christ's sake, and oh, he's even thinking of running for state senate down the road, but hey, no problem if he disappears."

"Paula. . . ."

"What?"

"What else is there? There's no sign of violence, you and his boss both say none of his work-related activities involved him in anything with a possibility of someone seeking revenge, and you said he appeared to be in a good mood recently."

She scrunched up her face, like she was trying to decide to get angry, or tearful, or both. I reached over, gently touched her hand. "Plus he just put a ring on that lovely finger. That doesn't sound like a guy looking over his shoulder, or a guy who's about to run off and end it all."

Paula's right hand started rubbing at a faint smudge on the table. "You giving up?"

"No."

"You sure? It sounds like you're giving up."

"I'm not. I'm just . . . letting you know what I've done. And I don't intend to give up."

She then decided, and the tears started to flow. "Okay. Sorry if I was snippy back there. Trying to get a newspaper out between checking police reports for car accidents, or checking in with local ER admissions folks to see if someone you love has been admitted . . . takes a lot out of a girl."

I got up from the table, went around and hugged her, and kissed the top of her head. "I'm still on it . . . and you'll call me if you think of anything, okay?"

I felt her nod under my touch, and I started for the door—and stopped when she called out my name.

"I'm sorry about the news, Lewis."

I turned. "I'm sorry: What news?"

"That Tropical Storm Toni," she said. "It's been upgraded to a hurricane and is coming up the East Coast."

Back to Porter I went, to the Porter Rehab and Extended Care Center and Room 209. Diane Woods was sitting up in bed, and next to her was her companion and fiancée, Kara Miles. The color in Diane's face was improving and her hair looked freshly washed. Kara was sitting next to her, her dark hair razored up in some sort of cutting-edge fashion, I guess, and she had on a COLBY sweatshirt and dungarees.

I kissed Diane on the cheek, and Kara asked: "Hey, you making moves on my woman while I watch?"

Diane said, "Then look away, silly girl."

Some wide smiles from that little exchange that warmed me, and I sat down in a spare chair. Both women were working on a slab of cheesecake with cream and strawberries on top, and I asked: "The dietitian here know what you're eating?"

"Nope," Diane said, and Kara said "Ditto."

"Might be against rehab rules and regulations," I said.

"Might be," Diane replied. "But in the meantime, we're destroying the evidence. Wish we had some to share."

"No worries," I said, and I sat with them as they chatted and laughed and gossiped some, and Kara looked to me and said: "Great news today. Looks like our fair princess will be going home in a few days."

"That's outstanding."

"Sure is," Diane said, licking off her fork. "Still have work to do on the PT and OT side, but I need to do some cop stuff. I can just imagine the pile of shit that's waiting for me at the station."

Kara said "Then imagine something else. Don't be in such a hurry to get back to the grind."

Diane stuck out her tongue, Kara made an extraordinarily rude comment that made Diane laugh and me blush, and in a couple of minutes Kara got up and said "Back to the salt mines, boys and girls. I'll see you later tonight."

"Deal," Diane said, and Kara gave her a quick kiss on her lips, and then came around the bed and did the same to me, which surprised me.

Diane called out, "Hey, you making moves on my woman while I watch?"

"I was just sitting here, minding my own business."

"Hah. Like you put up a fight then."

Kara giggled and left, and Diane and I were alone, and I said "Great news, about going home."

"Oh, Christ, you know it. I may bump into the furniture and the walls, but they'll be *my* furniture and walls. Even the police union promised to kick in if I needed handrails installed or a temporary chairlift to go up to the second floor. Still, I need to get back to work, to feel productive. Sitting on my ass most days, shuffling up and down the hallways, it's not my idea of living."

"Nor mine."

"Speaking of home and living," she said, "Thanksgiving's in a few days. Unless you have any plans, you're invited to spend the day at our place."

I smiled. "My calendar's clear, unless something stupid comes along."

"Great. We'll set an extra plate. But be warned . . . I don't know why, but Kara loves football on Thanksgiving. Be prepared to eat in the living room, balancing a plate on your lap."

"No problem."

She put her empty plate and fork down on an adjacent table. "So, how goes the search for Mark Spencer?"

"Going in pretty odd places. Still no word about where he is. Captain Nickerson did her best, but she was pure professional. No sign of trauma, no sign of anything criminal going on, and once again, it's not a crime to skip out and not leave a note. But I don't like it."

"Who would? Where else have you gone?"

"Your town manager doesn't seem particularly upset. And Hannah Adams from Mark's law firm, she's taking it in stride."

Diane said, "Glen Torrance wants to stay as town manager as long as possible. The longer the tenure, the more attractive he looks in being a candidate for a bigger town with a bigger salary. So if he gets even a tingle that making a fuss about Mark Spencer will blow back on him, he won't do a damn thing."

"How about Mark's boss?"

"Hannah Adams is one of those deadly lawyers who sees everything through a lawyer's prism. Oh, most lawyers do a good job for their clients and try not to gum up the works, but Hannah . . . she eats, breathes, and lives the law. If Mark is gone under unfortunate circumstances, it might cast aspersions on her and her firm."

"What about Carl Lessard, her law partner?"

Diane wiped her fingers clean with a napkin. "Carl the Gray Ghost? Poor slob had been in town for years, working alone, until somehow he got roped into an association with Hannah. He gets all the grunt cases, like appearing before the selectmen or the planning board or zoning board. Real dry stuff that would bore any sane or non-lawyer person to tears. But that work brings in a steady income and allows Hannah to let loose at Wentworth Superior Court, where she loves being in the spotlight."

"Still doesn't make sense," I said. "Seems like the only person concerned because he's gone is Paula."

She shrugged. "People who work with him, they'd be concerned. But they most likely wouldn't take the effort and trouble to try to find him. But a loved one, what do you expect?"

"You've worked with Mark. Did you ever think he'd take off like this?"

That gave her pause. "A good question. I don't know. Mark is tightly wound, well versed, smart about the law . . . but not a warm guy. Didn't ever reveal much of his personal life. Makes you wonder why Paula. . . ."

Diane's voice dribbled off. I took up the gauntlet. "Makes you wonder why Paula took up with a guy like that. Instead of me."

A nod from Diane. "But the tightly wound guys, when they cut loose, watch out. They've got years of frustrations and anxieties bubbling down there that, when they come out, they tend to spread wide and burn anyone in the way."

I got up and asked her: "Any last-minute words of advice?"

"You check in with your Mafia friend?"

"Felix? He'd dispute the Mafia insult, but yes, he's asking around."

"Doubtful he'll find out much. Most crimes in this state revolve around heroin or meth and the crimes that raise money to help fuel it. I don't think Felix moves much in those circles." She stretched out on the hospital bed, winced. "Hate to say it, but go back again. Widen the net. Do the unexpected, ask the unexpected. And be prepared if something shakes out."

I went to her to kiss her good-bye, and she surprised me by grabbing my hand and squeezing it tight. "I was thinking about you when I woke up this morning," she said, her voice serious.

"Not sure if I should be sad or glad about that."

The squeeze of her hand increased. "I woke up and realized I hadn't had a single nightmare during the night. I slept well . . . and that happened only after you told me what you did about Curt Chesak."

That brought back a quick memory from a few weeks ago. Up in the small town of Osgood, in a big house, a fresh bullet wound in my thigh, an armed and angry Curt Chesak coming my way, moments from shooting me, until an unexpected ally arrived and severed his lower spine with one quick flash of a Gurkha knife.

I kissed the top of her head. "Glad I could help."

She released my hand. "Promise me someday you'll tell me about it."

I strolled out of the room, gave her a wave and a smile.

"Sorry," I said. "That'll never happen."

CHAPTER FIVE

I needed to make a phone call, and I sat in the Pilot and retrieved my cell phone, but the smell of old clothes, old meals, and a damp sleeping bag drove me outside. I leaned against the cold fender, saw the air traffic over the nearby McIntosh Air Force Base, and went to work. I dialed a number from memory, went through the usual menu, and after about ten or so minutes—half of it on hold, listening to "The Girl from Ipanema"—I got through to the insurance agent allegedly handling my claim.

"Adrian Zimmerman," came the young man's voice. "How can I help you?"

"Hello, Adrian," I said. "It's Lewis Cole, your faithful Tyler Beach correspondent. Anything new on my claim status?"

Even though I was outside, I was pretty sure I could hear his sigh. "No, there's nothing new to report. That's what I said yesterday, last Friday, and the day before that. And like I said, I will call you the moment I hear any news."

"Gee, Adrian, what's the matter, you don't like hearing my voice? We're not friends anymore?"

"Mister Cole. . . ."

"Look, ever since my place burned down, you said that my claim for my house and car are under review, because it was arson. It's been weeks now. How much longer?"

"You're forgetting the other arson. The one for which you were arrested."

Right, I thought. The arson that charred the remains of Curt Chesak and two others.

"Come, now, Adrian, the charges were dropped."

"They were, but the charges were certainly made. That all has to be taken into consideration."

"Well, consider this," I said. "You ever watch the Weather Channel?"

His voice grew cautious. "No, not really. . . ."

"You should," I said. "There's a hurricane forming off the coast of Florida, and it's heading this way over the next several days. I can't wait anymore. I need to get my contractor in there, make temporary repairs, at least, before the storm destroys whatever's left."

"I'll make sure the hurricane is taken into consideration, Mister Cole."

"Meaning what?"

"Meaning . . . I'll make sure it's taken into consideration. Is there anything else?"

I was now standing up straight, my legs quivering, like a hunting dog eager to sink its teeth into something. "There sure is. I won't be happy if, through your feet-dragging, my property is destroyed and swept away."

He didn't say anything for a moment, making me wonder if he had quietly hung up on me, and then he spoke up. "That might be just for the best, don't you think?"

"How? How the hell can my house being destroyed be for the best?"

Adrian's voice quickened. "You recall when we first met, when I did a survey of the property? I said that I was going to recommend that the house and the garage be declared a total loss, to be completely razed. If the hurricane helps that process along, so much the better."

"But it's a historical house! More than a hundred and fifty years old!"

I swear I could sense the smile on his face as he spoke next. "Is your home listed in the National Registry of Historical Places? Is it in a designated historical zone for the town of Tyler? Does it have any certification whatsoever that it's historical?"

46

No, no, and no, I thought. But then again, a fair chunk of homes in Tyler and the surrounding towns had been built in the 1700s and 1800s, and none of them bore any historical certification, because . . . well, that's just the way things were in this part of the world. Every town had old homes. They were just part of the landscape.

"I think you already know the answer," I said.

"Then as far as we're concerned, your home isn't historical. Have a good day, now, Mister Cole."

And he hung up on me.

I drove into the Lafayette House parking lot on Tyler Beach, spotting a green-and-white Tyler police cruiser amble out. The parking lot looked pretty quiet, and I then had a warm thought: that Diane Woods had spread the word to the shift sergeants, to make sure that what was left of my house got a look-see from the regular beach patrols during the day.

I backed my Pilot into its usual space and then walked down to my house. The wind was blowing in a different direction, so there wasn't that sad smell of burnt things as I got there. There was the usual flapping noise of the blue tarpaulins echoing with the sound of the crashing waves, and, clenched hands in my coat pockets, I wandered around the house, at the rear deck, the unscorched wood, the broken windows, the collapsed roof. The air was cold and the wind was sharp.

I stood still for a moment, saw a spot where the tarpaulin had torn free, near the doorway, and I unlocked the door, again thumped my shoulder against the door to pry it open. I retrieved a handful of nails and the Craftsman hammer that had brained me the other day, and went to work. I hammered in the nails and stood back to admire my work.

Not much to admire. The blue tarp looked primed to tear again, and this was from the normal gusts of wind coming off the Atlantic. I imagined a hurricane coming up here, and even if it stayed at a Category One and missed Tyler Beach and only grazed it, there could be winds of up to seventy or eighty miles an hour. That said, this tarpaulin would fly off in an instant and end up in Newfoundland, and the interior of the house would be soaked. The high winds would probably also shift some of the timbers, causing more destruction; and if I was having a particularly bad day, a bigger-than-usual high tide would sweep up here and scour the place down to bedrock.

I turned and snapped and tossed the Craftsman hammer at a nearby rock, where it bounced up and disappeared.

What was the point?

Damn it, what was the point?

My breathing quickened and I closed my eyes, thought back through some of the happy memories of this special place, the meals, the small get-togethers, the women who had spent some sweet times here. And above all, the day-after-day healing solitude of being in a piece of warm and safe history, while all the storms out there passed me by.

I let my breath out, opened my eyes. I went over to the rocks and after a few minutes found and retrieved my hammer. It had a few new scratches on it, and I juggled it in the air a few times.

"Sorry," I said. "Not your fault."

I put the hammer back in the house, pulled a few times to close the door, locked it, and then walked back up to the parking lot.

Dinner was quick and got the job done, meaning I sat in the small dining room of the Tyler McDonald's, on Route 1 heading up to North Tyler. There have been times when I've been very hungry and traveling, and any fast-food menu was something to be savored. But now I wasn't very hungry, and I wasn't going anyplace far, and so the Le Beef Royale and Coke were serving as fuel and not much else.

With some time to kill, I went through a few newspapers and carefully read all the stories concerning Hurricane Toni. With each newspaper, there was a different prediction as to its course, but all agreed that this was probably going to be the last hurricane of the season and would drench this part of New England with heavy rains and winds on or around Thanksgiving. Happy Turkey Day.

After I was through with my disappointing dinner—though, to be truthful, to any European peasant alive from 1000 A.D. to 1500 A.D. that meal would have been considered a feast fit for any ruler alive—I made a short drive across the street to the Tyler Blue Ribbon cleaners. I gathered up all of my clothes and my sleeping bag, and trundled into the place. It was hot, steamy, with the smell of detergent, wet clothes, and disappoint-ments from the men and women mechanically doing their laundry without looking at each other.

It took a while to get everything sorted, to make change and get fist-fuls of quarters, but I got things rolling and then went to the Pilot, drove another few yards to a service station, and used up more of my quarters to buy time on a vacuum machine.

With that job done, I drove back in time to see that my loads were finished, and into the dryer they went. Outside, I opened up every door to the Pilot and the hatchback as well, retrieved my Rick Atkinson book, and went inside to wait out the dryers, sitting on a scuffed orange plastic chair.

At least four times during the drying cycle, somebody came up to me and asked me if that was my Honda out there, and was I aware everything was open. I said yes, thanks for the heads-up, explaining that I was just airing the place out.

When the dryers slowly rolled to a stop, more time was spent sorting and folding, and rolling up my sleeping bag. Out into the snap-cold November air I went, and bustled everything back into the Pilot, closed the doors and hatchback, and drove away, now seeking some entertainment.

Such was the life of the nomad, the homeless.

I didn't like it.

Some time ago, the four-screen movie theater for downtown Tyler had closed and was replaced by—surprise, surprise—yet another drug store for this crowded stretch of Route 1. With no available entertainment, I did the next best thing and drove to the Tyler Town Hall. There was plenty of parking and I checked my watch, saw it was seven P.M., and went into the selectmen's meeting room.

There was no selectmen's meeting tonight, but there was a session of the town's zoning board of adjustment, and I had noted the time and agenda when I had been at the town library earlier today. Inside the narrow room were rows of folding wooden chairs set on a light green carpet, and at the far end of the room was a long table, covered with an equally long table-cloth. On the walls were plaques and photos honoring past town officials and the history of Tyler.

At the table sat five residents of the town—three women and two men—who were serving as zoning board members. This was a volunteer position—like most of the government work in Tyler and other New Hampshire towns—and gave new meaning to the phrase "thankless job."

Basically, any new construction or renovation project in town or at the beach needed an affirmative vote from the town's planning board, to make sure zoning laws were followed and fat-rendering plants weren't built next to a kindergarten, that sort of thing. But if the planning board turned down a project, the builder or owner's last best hope before taking the town to court was to argue their case before five fellow citizens. They could plead special circumstances, or point out quirky loopholes in the regulations, or throw themselves on the mercy of the board. Sometimes the board said yes, sometimes it said no, and more often than not it ended up with lots of bruised feelings, which could make later school functions or church meetings with neighbors interesting.

Tonight the room was about a quarter full, and up at the front left row was Jason, the young studded lad from the *Tyler Chronicle*, frantically tapping away on his laptop as the meeting droned on. It was nice to see a member of the Fourth Estate keeping view on the action, but I was also pleased to see an older man, sitting just a few feet away from the zoning board members, legal pad and pen in his hands. He had on a light gray suit, the ends of the sleeves shiny with use, and a white shirt and black necktie. His face was splotched with red, like some of his blood vessels had given up the ghost years ago, and his pale eyes blinked slowly behind brown-rimmed glasses.

Carl Lessard, no doubt, of the firm of Adams & Lessard, representing the good people of Tyler this evening.

The meeting went on, went on, went on. There were eight items on the agenda, and it took nearly forty minutes to dispose of the first item, concerning a developer who wanted to build four condo units on a narrow road bordering the marshlands at the beach. The planned buildings were too close to an exclusion line prohibiting construction next to the vulnerable marshlands, and the developer and his lawyer were trying to arrange a deal where they could build a berm and swap out other land to the town so there wouldn't be a net loss of marshland.

There was a lot of give and take, a few residents in the audience expressing either support or opposition, and then the board took the vote, which went three to two against the developer.

His lawyer rolled up some blueprints of the proposed buildings and development, whispered something in the developer's ear, but whatever he said didn't take, because the man's face got very red. He stood up from the front row, pointed his finger at them, and loudly said: "You had your chance! I'll see you all in court next month . . . you jerks!"

He stomped out, face flushed, muttering curses and threats, his reading glasses bouncing off his round chest, his fists clenched.

The chairwoman of the board took it all in stride, looked down at her paperwork, and asked, "Mister Mullen, are you ready?"

"Yes, ma'am," Mullen said, stepping forward in front of the five board members.

Carl Lessard made notes. Jason *tap-tapped* on the keyboard, and I folded my arms and waited and tried to stay awake.

When the meeting adjourned at 12:34 A.M., I was the only person sitting in the audience. In ones and twos, the others had drifted out, and even the young reporter gave up at 11 P.M. When the chairwoman rapped her little brown gavel and said "And we're adjourned" and another board member whispered "Thank God," I walked up to Carl Lessard.

"Mister Lessard? Could I have a moment?"

He didn't look up, just concentrated on putting his paperwork back into folders, and then carefully putting all the folders into a soft brown leather briefcase that had one of its two handles repaired with black electrician's tape.

"Mister Lessard?"

He looked up this time, blinked, and said, "I suppose so. A moment or two."

I dragged a chair over as the five members of the zoning board packed up their own belongings, grabbed their coats and jackets, and bustled their way out the meeting-room door. They looked like prisoners finally getting a long-promised parole. The chairwoman, a plump woman with short blond hair, called out, "Carl? Will you lock up and shut off the lights?"

Lessard waved and said to me, "Would you like to make an appointment for tomorrow?"

"This won't take long, I promise," I said. "It's about Mark Spencer."

"Oh." He seemed to peer at me closer and said, "You're the guy who was in our office this morning, right? The one who camped out in our reception area?"

"That's me," I said.

"But I thought you talked to Hannah."

"I did. But I want to talk to you."

He had a deep, rattling cough, took out a handkerchief, and wiped at his lips. "Then talk away."

"Mark," I said. "He's been missing now for about five days. Aren't you concerned?"

"Concerned? About his safety? His well-being? His future with the firm?"

I leaned forward. "How about a straight answer for once? You and your partner . . . you seem happy to dance around and duel with words, and all I'm looking for are some answers. Your fellow attorney is missing. Yet nobody seems concerned about that."

"Are you a friend?"

"No," I said. "An acquaintance, doing a favor for a friend."

He carefully put his handkerchief away in his pants pocket. "Ah, that would be a female friend, correct? Paula Quinn?"

A bit of a surprise. "Yes, Paula Quinn. How did you know?"

"Please . . . I keep my eyes and ears open. Paula is a sweet girl. All right, then, I guess the reason I'm not concerned, or Hannah, is that Mark is fine."

A bigger bit of a surprise. "How do you know that?"

Some sort of emotion played across his face that I couldn't decipher. "Why, because he informed me so today, that's why."

CHAPTER SIX

The uptown fire station for Tyler is right next door to the town hall, and I was positive that if every piece of their equipment were to leave right then, sirens and horns blaring, I would not move an inch.

I stared into the pale eyes of Carl Lessard. "Say again? You talked to Mark Spencer today?"

"He informed me he was safe. Like the day before, and the day before that."

I tried to process what I was hearing, as he zipped his leather bag shut and started to get up. I stood up with him and held out my hand.

"Please, just one more moment," I said. "Where is he?"

"I don't know."

"But you know he's safe."

"I do."

"But . . . why did he leave? And why hasn't he contacted Paula, or the town manager? Why just you?"

"I'm afraid I can't answer that."

He started walking out and I stepped in front of him.

"Please . . . this is important to me. Why can't you say any more?"

His watery eyes blinked. "You want me to say more?"

"Please."

He shifted his leather bag from one hand to the other. "Mister Cole, I'm exactly one year, one month, and three days away from retiring, with a healthy retirement plan that will keep me going quite well for at least three decades. During the next one year, one month, and three days, I intend to be the perfect, quiet, and hard-working attorney, even though I work for a woman whose ancestry, I believe, could be traced to the Borgias of Renaissance Italy."

"But—"

Lessard stepped closer, and I caught the smell of mothballs and pencil shavings. He said, "I represent a town made up mostly of quiet citizens, going about their lives day in and day out, but I have to endure and work with a number of liars, fools, and grifters seeking their own gain against the interest of Tyler. So be it."

I said nothing, letting him go on, and go on he did. "I've done one favor for Mark Spencer, and seeing you suffer through tonight's zoning board meeting in order to speak to me, that encouraged me to do another favor. But the favor bank is now empty. I'm leaving now, and based on who you are and what I know about you, I know you're not going to do anything physical to prevent my departure. Excuse me, then."

He walked by me and, knowing when I was defeated, I followed him. At the exit to the building, he shut off the lights to the hall and gestured me out, and I stepped outside into the early-morning darkness of the next day. A streetlight in the nearly empty parking lot gave everything a cold, harsh illumination.

Behind me he locked the door, and we stood together on the granite steps. He said: "I'm sorry if I'm brusque, Mister Cole. It's just that in one year and three months, I intend to be on a secluded beach somewhere in the Gulf of Mexico, relaxing and never doing anything in the legal profession, ever again. And perhaps it's the late hour or my exhaustion, I intend to get drunk and get laid every day, to make up for lost time."

"Sounds like a plan."

"The way things have turned out, and it was no grand plan, I've come to this point in my life with no real friends, no family. And I intend to unplug my legal mind and enjoy what's left to come."

He walked over to his car, a salt-stained red Chrysler LeBaron, and I called out, "Can you pass a message along to Mark Spencer, then?"

Lessard paused, turned. Seemed to consider that for a moment.

"No," he said, and he got into his car, started the engine, and drove off.

About sixty seconds later, I did the same.

Sleep didn't come well to me, and I tossed and turned, even though my sleeping bag was recently washed and the inside of the Pilot smelled fairly reasonable. At some point I was awake and there was no going back to sleep, and I stretched and looked out the window.

Everything was wrong.

There was no Lafayette House parking lot, no stone wall, no breaking waves of the Atlantic Ocean.

Instead, there were some pine trees, a crowded parking lot, and the white buildings of Twelve Rockland Ridge.

Mark Spencer's home.

I climbed out of my Pilot, stretched, and then washed up in a nearby grove of woods with some bottled water. I checked myself out in a sideview mirror, guessed I was reasonably presentable, and went to work, remembering what Diane Woods had said yesterday.

Hate to say it, but go back again.

Which is what I was doing this early morning. In my previous canvass of Mark's residence, I had managed to talk to every one of his neighbors save one. I stood by the front end of the Pilot, waiting. Mark Spencer's condo was number 4, and the parking spot there was empty. The spot for number 3 was empty as well, and had been empty when I drove in here last night.

I waited. Watched as men and women, young and not so young, trundled out of their condo units, to head off to work, or to school, or some combination thereof. A handful of kids trooped out as well, to walk down to the small intersection of Rockland Ridge and High Street, and in a few minutes a bright yellow school bus came to a halt, picked up the students, and headed out for the day, leaving me alone in the parking lot.

Something hollow ached in my chest. All these couples, all these families, all having a place and a purpose to their lives and their loved ones, and here I was, standing alone, my own home shattered and—unless something drastic and unexpected happened within the next day or two—was about to get hammered by a hurricane named Toni.

I waited.

About ten minutes after the school bus had left, a light yellow Toyota Corolla with a bad muffler rumbled up the road and pulled into the empty spot next to Mark Spencer's equally empty spot. A tired-looking man got out, folded newspaper in hand, wearing black slacks, black shoes, and dark blue windbreaker. He unlocked the door to his unit, walked in, and closed the door behind him.

I waited, and then I went to join him.

I knocked on the door, and in a few seconds the man—Dave Chaplain—opened it up. With his coat off, I saw that he was wearing a blue uniform shirt with his name stitched on one side, and the name of a service station/mini-mart chain on the other. He appeared to be in his mid-forties, reddish-blond hair tied back in a small ponytail, and light green eyes. The scent of sugar and old coffee came through the open door.

And he looked exhausted. "Yeah?"

"Sorry to bother you, Mister Chaplain," I said. "My name is Lewis Cole, I'm a freelance writer, used to be a columnist for *Shoreline* magazine." I passed over my business card and pressed ahead. "I'm working on an article about the disappearance of your neighbor, Mark Spencer."

He examined both sides of the card and said "A writer?"

"Yes."

He grinned. "I'm a writer too. Come on in."

His unit was identical to Mark's, except he had more books in the living room overlooking the parking lot. Lots and lots of books. Enough books to set up a small-town library somewhere in a rural town in this state. He sat down at a small kitchen table, stretched out his legs, sighed. "I'd offer you a cup of coffee, but I don't have the strength to make it, and even if I did, I need to go to sleep."

"I'm sure."

He put his hands behind his head, stretched again. "All those hours, on your goddamn feet, and you really can't take a serious break, 'cause the whole store is under video surveillance, and if you're caught slacking off . . . that's all she wrote."

"Where do you work?"

A shrug. "Up on Lafayette Road, at the mini-mart. Eleven P.M. to seven A.M. shift, Wednesday through Sunday. Hell of a career choice, isn't it. But like I said, I'm a writer too."

I kept an engaging smile on my face, having heard this story plenty of times before in my previous job at *Shoreline*. Everybody thinks they can write, and once they find out that you make a living putting words to paper, they're eager to share their dreams, their aspirations, and their ideas with you.

Especially if you agree to hear their ideas, agree to write what they want, and split the money, "fifty-fifty."

But I was quickly and ashamedly put back to earth when Dave said, "I have an outline for a nice history of post-Revolutionary New Hampshire, if I ever get the time, and I've sold two articles over the years to *American Heritage* magazine." He pointed to the mini-mart's logo on his shirt. "See what a doctorate in history gets you?"

"Excuse me?"

"Sure, Lewis," he said. He plucked at his shirt again. "What, you think this was my career choice? Really? Nope, worked and studied and struggled to get a doctorate in American history, had a plan to get a nice college gig, write articles and then books. . . ."

"Then reality struck."

"Hah, yeah, a good way of putting it. Oh, I taught here and there, strictly as an adjunct professor, working year to year, never getting a permanent position, never getting on a tenure track. If I had been born ten or fifteen years earlier, boy, would I have had it made. . . ."

"Colleges have changed a lot, haven't they."

"Certainly have. Since medieval times, universities and colleges were designed to be a little oasis of knowledge, where students get a good grounding in education, humanities and philosophy. Now it's all career-and-employment track, setting up 'partnerships' with corporations, so our little conveyor belt of knowledge can pop out ready-made technocrats or consumers after four or six years of schooling."

"You sure don't sound bitter."

He laughed. "Good one. You'd think the so-called higher institutions of learning would help us future professors along, but nope. Those who had tenure stayed at the top of their ivory tower, after pulling the ladder up, and the college administrators . . . as long as they got their new buildings, and new layers of deans and assistant deans and junior assistant deans. . . ."

"They didn't particularly care."

"Nope," Dave said. "But hey, enough of my troubles. Mark Spencer. Missing, for real?"

"For five days. Car gone, laptop gone. No word left with his law firm, the town, or his fiancée. Have you seen him at all during the last week?"

"No, can't say that I have," he said, lowering his arms and folding them across his chest. "My work schedule doesn't really permit a lot of interaction with the neighbors . . . not to mention the fair sex. But he seemed like an okay guy. Dressed all right, kept quiet, no banging around or loud music or television. Kept pretty much to himself."

So much for starting over again, I thought.

"Anything unusual? Late-night visitors? Loud arguments with someone?"

"Nothing at all."

"Late-night phone calls you might have heard?"

"The walls here are thin, but not that thin."

"His mood seem different in any way?"

"Mood? His mood was like he couldn't wait to get out of here in the morning to get to work . . . he gave me a quick wave now and then, usual neighbor stuff. Once gave me a hand when the goddamn ravens poked holes in my trash bag, but that's about it."

"Anything else about him you can think of, that might help?"

"No, not really," Dave said, and then he smiled. "Got to say, though, that I'm envious. I mean, if he's left and nothing bad's happened to him. Don't you ever think of packing everything in and heading out? Just abandoning it all, chucking it away? Like Huck Finn lighting out for another territory?"

"Once upon a time, I did," I said, getting up from his kitchen table. "But I'm sort of a stay-at-home kind of guy."

"Good for you," he said. "Well, hope you and the cops find him."

"Not likely, since the cops aren't looking for him."

He looked surprised. "Of course they are."

"No, they're not."

"Well, you're wrong," he said. "I had a county sheriff in here yesterday, asking the same questions you're asking."

I slowly sat back down.

Dave said "He was very polite, well dressed. Showed me his deputy sheriff's badge and identification. Said he was investigating the disappearance as well."

"I see. Do you recall his name?"

"Sure. Reeve Longwood."

"And he said he was from Wentworth County?"

"Yep."

"What was he looking for?"

"Same as you. Said a town official that goes missing is a big deal, worthy of investigation. Asked me questions about his work habits, neighbors, friends. I'm afraid I told him about the same I told you. Not very much."

"What did he look like? Was he wearing a county sheriff's uniform?"

"What does a county sheriff's uniform look like?"

"Brown and tan. Campaign-style wide hat."

"Oh, cripes, no. Was wearing a nice suit. I figured deputy sheriffs don't have to be wearing their uniform all the time, now, do they?"

"No, they don't. Besides his clothing, how else did he look?"

"Physically? Maybe thirty, thirty-five years old. Wore a nice suit. Bulky guy, like he worked out a lot . . . which makes sense, if he's a cop."

"Yes," I said, growing more terrified with each word he said. "Go on."

"He had on a cloth cap, but I think he was bald. Had a funny black beard, like one of those, whaddya call 'em, Vandykes. Right. That triangular thing. Let's see, what else . . . oh, yeah, he had some tattoos."

"Really? How could you tell? Were they on his face? Hands?"

"Nope," Dave said. "I got up to make him a cup of tea—he turned down coffee—and when I was behind him, pouring it, I could see tattoos at the base of his neck. Couldn't tell what kind . . . they were black, that's all . . . oh, and he had one on his right wrist. He reached over for some sugar, sleeve rolled back, and there it was. Some kind of angry bird."

Holy crap.

"Did the deputy sheriff know that you saw his tattoos?"

"No, I'm pretty sure he didn't."

Good for you, I thought.

I got up one more time. "Did he leave you a business card or anything?"

"No, he said he had run out, that they were at the printers. But he said he had my name and number, and would follow up with me in a few days." He paused, looking closely at my face. "Hey, is everything all right?"

Everything is so not right, I don't know where to begin, which is what I thought. In this state, county sheriffs run the county prisons, help administer the superior courts, transport prisoners, and serve warrants or other court paperwork. They certainly don't do serious investigative work, especially ones involving missing persons. And they don't wear beards, Vandykes or otherwise.

I lied easily. "Everything is just fine. And I appreciate your time."

He got up and said "Cool. Like I said, I hope you or the cops find him quick. Let me show you out."

We walked to the door leading out when something struck me and I stopped suddenly, and Dave bumped into me. "Sorry," I said. "One more thing just came to me . . . when the deputy sheriff asked about friends and family, did you mention that Mark had a girlfriend?"

"Yeah, I did. I told him that he should make sure to talk to her, to get leads and shit."

"Her name," I said quickly. "Did you tell him her name?"

"Nope, I didn't, 'cause I didn't know it."

"Oh," I said, feeling relief. "Thanks."

I got through the door, started down the stairs leading outside, and Dave called out to me, "Oh, but I did tell him she was a newspaper reporter at some local paper, I do remember that."

By the time I got to the bottom of the stairs, Dave Chaplain had closed the upper door, and I had burst through the door going outside, running to the Pilot. I got in and started the engine, grabbed my cell phone, and called the *Tyler Chronicle*.

It went to voicemail.

I next called Felix Tinios.

No answer.

By now I was on High Street, heading to the center of Tyler, and about three or four minutes away from the *Tyler Chronicle*.

I called the newspaper one more time.

A woman's voice answered. "*Tyler Chronicle*, this is Melanie."

"Melanie, Paula Quinn, please."

"Oh, hold on," she said. "Let me see if she's here. . . ."

A clunk of the phone being dropped on the desk.

Up ahead there was a traffic light, flicking over to yellow. A blue Volvo with Vermont plates decided to be a good citizen and quickly braked to a halt.

I almost slammed into the Volvo's rear. I fumed, hand tight on the steering wheel, other hand on the cell phone.

A clatter of the phone being picked up.

"Sorry," Melanie said. "You just missed her."

"Do you know where she is?"

"Nope, all I know is that she left with a man who said he needed to talk to her."

Shit.

"Was this guy bulky, with a slight beard?"

"Um . . . yeah . . . who's calling, please?"

I tossed my cell phone onto the passenger's seat. Up ahead the light turned green. The road was marked with a double yellow line, indicating no passing.

I punched the accelerator and passed the Volvo anyway, causing a blare of a horn to follow me as I sped up High Street, driving awkwardly, with one hand still on the steering wheel, and the other hand scrabbling underneath my front seat, grabbing the Bianchi leather holster that contained my Beretta 9mm pistol.

CHAPTER SEVEN

In about sixty more seconds of driving, I got to the intersection of High Street and Lafayette Road, right in the center of the town of Tyler proper. Traffic was heavy for this time of the morning, and I was stuck at a red light, with the evil Volvo behind me, the young female driver waving at me with one finger extended. A quick left onto Lafayette Road and then a quick right past the Common, and I'd be at the *Chronicle*.

But she wasn't there. That's what Melanie had said.

You just missed her.

Right behind the small building containing the *Chronicle* was a set of railroad tracks, which paralleled a grove of pine trees. Would he take her there? Or would that be too risky? What kind of tale could he spin to get Paula out of the *Chronicle* and to walk across the railroad tracks?

No, he'd be cautious. He'd want her away in peace and quiet.

But it didn't mean *I'd* have to be cautious.

I swore, spun the steering wheel left, flashed my headlights and horn, and blasted my way through the oncoming traffic. There were three lanes— two heading to Lafayette Road, one of which was a turning lane to the right—and the other which was the incoming lane from Lafayette Road, full of cars heading in my direction. There was the squeal of brakes, horns blaring in my direction, a few more one-fingered salutes, and I got onto Lafayette Road. Before me were the white buildings and black shutters that, among other things, contained the law offices of Adams & Lessard, and on the right was the Common, the Common Grill & Grill, the Tyler Professional Office Building, and—

A black Chevrolet Suburban, heading out into traffic, with a bulky man driving, cloth cap on his head, a Vandyke beard on his face, with a blond-haired woman as his passenger.

I slammed the accelerator down again, the Pilot roared in response, and I cut off the Suburban just as he was edging out into traffic. He braked suddenly, his female passenger flailing forward, and I hammered my brakes as well, sliding to a stop about a foot in front of him. Other cars and trucks halted at seeing what was unfolding before them.

I threw the door open, managing to remove my Beretta from the leather holster, and I ran right up to the driver.

"Hands!" I yelled. "Show me your hands, right now!"

He hesitated just for a moment, and maybe it was my eyes or the Beretta or the way I yelled again, louder, "Hands!" but both hands came off the steering wheel.

And just like Dave Chaplain had said, there was a tattoo of a bird on his right wrist.

"Paula! Get out! Now!"

She emerged from the passenger's side door, face red, blond hair cascading in the wind, purse in hand, and boy, was she glad to see me.

"Lewis, you idiot! What the hell are you doing?"

I didn't dare remove my stare from the driver. His eyes had narrowed into two dark spots, but at least his hands were still visible. "Get into my Pilot! Now!"

"Lewis! He's a federal agent; he knows where Mark is!"

"He's an impostor! Yesterday he was a deputy sheriff! Paula, if you've ever trusted me . . . move!"

Out of the corner of my eye, I saw her hesitate, for the briefest of moments, and despair seized me, thinking: what do I do? What do I do? Try to manhandle her into my Pilot, while taking my eye and attention away from her kidnapper? From his look and appearance, I knew if this man had a brief second of opportunity, he would take it, and I'd quickly be on the cold asphalt of Lafayette Road, bleeding out.

Paula moved. She went around the front of the Suburban, cursing, and got into my Pilot. I started slowly backing away, and the man in the Suburban—Reeve Longwood, if that was his real name—managed to use an elbow to toggle a switch, and the window lowered.

His voice was slow, gravelly, like a country music star just wrapping up a four-hour gig. "Pretty bold move, bro, and I'll give you this one. But what, you think I'm just gonna sit here and watch you drive away?"

"Thanks for pointing that out," I said, and I pulled the trigger twice on my Beretta, shooting out a front and rear tire of his Suburban.

With Paula secure in the passenger's seat, I drove south on Lafayette Road. In about a mile or so, we'd get to Route 101, the state's main east-west highway, which also intersected I-95. There were options, but not too many. If I took the intersection to the Interstate, I'd hit the main Tyler tolls, which could quickly have a State Police roadblock. So instead I stayed on Lafayette Road and made a quick right onto one of the side country roads, and in a few minutes we were away from the crowded chaos of downtown Tyler and on a road that drifted through farmland, housing developments, and lots of trees.

With that bit of driving over, I spared a glance at Paula and said, "Look, are you—"

She punched me in the arm. I stammered something out, and then she burst into tears and asked "What the hell was that? What the hell was that? Stop the car . . . stop it now!"

"Nope," I said.

"Stop the car!"

"Paula, you can punch me, you can scratch me, you can pull my hair, but I'm not stopping. That man back there . . . he was about two or three minutes away from asking you some very serious questions about Mark."

"What, so you had to rescue me? Is that it? Why didn't you call the cops if you thought I was in danger?"

"Didn't have time."

"Lewis. . . ."

I turned, snapped at her. "You know Dave Chaplain? Mark's neighbor? Yesterday that big guy told him he was a deputy sheriff, investigating Mark's disappearance. Even showed him a sheriff's badge. How long have you been a newspaper reporter, Paula? Hunh? You know how the sheriff's department operates. Do they conduct any missing-persons investigations?"

Her arms were clasped tight against her light red coat, her face pale. "He . . . he told me he was with the federal government. He said Mark had uncovered some corruption involving the town and a defense-related industry that was preparing to move in over at the Tyler Industrial Park. He . . . he said Mark was in hiding, and that if I cooperated and kept it confidential, I could see him."

I came to a three-way intersection, with no street signs. There were woods and low stone walls. Just for the hell of it, I turned left. A light blue Ford pickup truck passed by and the driver waved, and I waved back. No one-finger salutes this time. I took a breath. Besides the usual smells of my home on wheels, there was also the sharp bitter tang of a pistol being recently fired.

Paula lowered her head, started crying again.

We kept on driving.

Sometime later we passed into Massachusetts, only knowing so by seeing a white post with black letters that said STATE LINE. I had no idea what town we were in, not that it mattered. It was still rural, which suited me well. About ten minutes after passing into our fair neighbor to the south, I spotted a dirt road on the left. I slowed, backed in, and backed in some more, as the road jigged to the right, until I couldn't see the nameless road we had just come from. I lowered my window and Paula's window some, to give us some fresh air.

It was suddenly quiet. Paula's head was turned, looking out at the trees.

I cleared my throat. "For what it's worth, as of last night, Mark was alive and in good health."

Her head slowly moved. Her usual pretty features were there, only hidden by her red eyes and puffy face. "How do you know that?"

"Carl Lessard told me, after the zoning board meeting let out last night . . . or early this morning."

"What did he say?"

"He said that Mark had been in contact with him, and that he was doing fine."

"Did he say where he was?"

"No."

"Did he say why he's gone?"

"No."

Her face was red with anger. "And why the hell didn't you tell me when you found this out?"

"Because like I just said, it was after midnight, that's why. I didn't want to wake you up. And I wasn't done yet, because I hadn't yet talked to Mark's neighbor, Dave Chaplain. And he told me about this guy's visit yesterday, pretending to be a deputy sheriff. Dave also said he told the guy about you, Mark's girlfriend. That's when I came racing into town."

The anger seemed to seep out, and my dear friend looked so very tired. "Damn."

"What did he say his name was?"

"Reeve Laughlin."

"He told Dave it was Reeve Longwood. He's experienced, then."

"How?"

"You use an assumed name, you take on one that's similar to your real name . . . so you can respond correctly when someone talks to you. That takes discipline and practice. Did he say what branch of the federal government he was with?"

"No."

"Did he show you some identification?"

"Yes . . . a leather wallet, with his photo and lettering and mumbo-jumbo."

"Hold on . . . you didn't see what it said?"

"No, I didn't, because he was telling me that Mark was safe and nearby . . . and if we hurried, I could see him."

I didn't say anything, and Paula said, "Damn it, he told me Mark was alive and a few minutes away. Sorry if I didn't play Paula, cynical and doubting reporter. . . ." A few more tears trickled down her cheeks. "I was Paula, worried fiancée . . . so fucking sue me."

I reached over, squeezed her hand. "Lucky for Mark he has you, no matter what you call yourself."

She twisted her wrist so her hand was in mine, and we sat like that in silence for a few minutes, two scared people, on the run.

Her voice was now quiet and determined. "What now?"

"We try to find Mark, ahead of whatever bad people are looking for him."

"And not call the cops? I mean, this is more than just a missing-persons case, isn't it?"

"It is, and if we call the cops, they won't be investigating Mark: they'll be looking into me. The evidence will show that I drove like a maniac through downtown traffic, breaking a half dozen traffic laws, and then threatening a man who wasn't posing a threat to me, and then I discharged a firearm in town limits, shooting out two car tires. If you're a cop, what do you investigate first? Unprovoked gunfire in downtown Tyler, or the claims that some tattooed guy is looking for the town counsel and uses assumed names?"

"Damn. How about Diane? Couldn't she help?"

Something let loose inside of me, and I wasn't at my best. "Sure, off on medical leave, in the middle of physical therapy and occupational therapy, learning to walk again and think again, I'm sure she'll jump right in to volunteer."

"I'm looking for my fiancé, Lewis, when nobody else wants to help!" she snapped back. "I'm sorry!"

I took a breath. "No, I'm sorry too. The priority is to find Mark. If I thought Diane could help, I'd do it. But even she'd have a hard time overlooking me firing off two rounds in downtown Tyler without better evidence."

Paula wiped at her eyes. "What now?"

"We look for better evidence."

I started up the Pilot and, back on the road, I made a left and kept on driving.

Within the hour, we were in the town of Merrimac, Massachusetts and, in a few minutes of quiet driving, found the town library. We were lucky in that in most small New England towns, the library is plopped right down in the center of things, which meant we didn't have to ask for directions.

I parked the Pilot at the rear of the building so it couldn't be spotted by any curious eyes that might be driving by. "We're going to go in, do a bit more anonymous Internet research about Mark and the guy who was asking about him. But Paula . . . I'm going to ask some tough questions, questions you might not like."

She nodded. "You're doing this for Mark, I appreciate it. Just . . . don't give up."

"I won't."

Paula swiveled, glanced back at the cluttered rear of my car. "Lewis . . . I've got to ask you. Have you been living in the rear of your car?"

"That I have."

"But you said you were staying at the Lafayette House."

"Nope, I said I was a guest of the Lafayette House. Which I was. Residing in their parking lot."

She looked again at the plastic bags, the open sleeping bag, the pile of clothes. "Oh, Lewis . . . if you need money, I could—"

"One of these days, the insurance company will come through with a big fat check."

"But you could be staying at my place!"

I smiled, opened the door. "And how much sleep would I get, knowing the temptation that was just a few yards away from me?"

That got a brief smile in reply, and I was so very pleased.

The interior of the library was a mix of the old and the new, lots of old leather books, vaulted ceilings, and six computer terminals. We were asked if we had library cards or were town residents, but Paula surprised me by pulling out her press identification—issued by the N.H. Department of Safety—and quickly explained that she was working on an important news story, and would it be all right if she and her friend did a little research?

Worked well, and in a few minutes we were in front of a terminal, me on a keyboard, she sitting next to me, and I said: "That was pretty good work, Paula. In professional circles, it's called a pretense call or conversation."

"Guess I've learned some, hanging around with you."

I wasn't sure if she was joking or not, so I got to work, under the watchful eye of one of the assistant librarians.

I typed in a search phrase on the Google home page, and Paula asked "What does that mean?"

The assistant librarian, a slim older woman, was pretending not to listen as I replied. "What it means is that we need to be quiet here. You got any questions or concerns, make note of them, all right? In the meantime . . . just let me do what I need to do."

She rummaged in her large purse, pulled out a reporter's notebook and black Bic pen. "Then do it," she said.

An hour later, we were back in the Pilot, and after we got in Paula said, sharply, "Well? Mind telling me what that was about?"

It was cold, so I started the engine and the heater. "That was finding out what I could."

"A motorcycle gang! From out west! How in hell does that have anything to do with Mark?"

I rubbed the steering wheel. "The man who called himself Reeve, he had a tattoo of a bird on his right wrist, along with tats on his neck. Mark's neighbor saw it, and so did I. A mean-looking falcon or hawk. You saw the Internet research I did, saw what results came up. The Stonecold Falcons Motorcycle Club. From Wyoming."

"But Wyoming! What does—"

"Mark's Social Security number," I said. "Numerals five-two-zero. Meaning it was issued in Wyoming. Paula, please, think hard again. Did Mark ever mention Wyoming at all?"

"No."

"No family, relatives, friends?"

"No, he said he was from Vermont. He was born in Vermont. Hell, I've even seen pictures of him playing in Little League when he was a kid!"

I thought some more, fingers still absent-mindedly moving around the smoothness of the Pilot's steering wheel. "Your trip out west. Where he proposed to you. Where did you go?"

"Colorado."

"Why Colorado?"

"Lewis, I—"

"Sorry, I meant: who suggested Colorado? You or him?"

"Him."

"How did it come about? Did he just casually say he wanted to go out west for some time off, and he picked Colorado?"

She sighed. "No, we were looking to take a mini-vacation, get out of New Hampshire for a while after what had happened at the nuke-plant protests, and he said let's do something different, instead of going to Florida or someplace like that. So I asked him what he had in mind, and he said, well, he's always been fascinated with the American West, even growing up as a kid in Vermont, and there were excursions and trains you could take, look at ghost towns and old mining sites . . . and God, we had such a good time. . . ."

Her eyes watered and she sat up straighter, like she didn't want her emotions to overwhelm her. "Colorado. We stayed in Colorado. We were never in Wyoming."

"Were you together all the time?"

"Of course."

"Think some more, Paula . . . was there any time when you were by yourself, when he left for some reason?"

She started to speak, then caught herself. "Well. . . ."

"Paula."

"There was one time. The day before he proposed to me. We were spending the night at a bed-and-breakfast, and he told me that he had to take a walk, to clear his head. It was right after we'd had an early dinner. . . ."

"How long was he gone?"

"A few hours."

"Really? Weren't you concerned?"

"Of course I was, but he came back, smiling and all apologies, and he opened up the ring case, showed me the ring he had picked out. Mark said he had been nervous, that's all. . . ."

"I see. What was the name of the town?"

"Fort Collins. Gorgeous town. Lots of micro-breweries, Colorado State University is there. So very pretty."

"Your phone. Does it have Internet capability?"

"Of course: it's an iPhone."

"Let's take a look. Show me a map of Fort Collins."

"Why don't we go back into the library? Oh, forget it. I understand."

"As few digital footprints as possible. Show me what you've got."

Which took just a few seconds. She held up the display, and I said, "Zoom it out, slowly. See what we can find."

Using two of her fingers, Paula manipulated the screen of her iPhone, as the map of northern Colorado expanded; in a second or two, the state border of Wyoming was displayed, along with the city of Cheyenne, and a blue line marking Interstate 25, which connected that city and Fort Collins.

"Oh," she whispered.

"One more thing," I said, as the Pilot's engine grumbled along while we remained in PARK. "Do a quick trip request, see how long it would take to drive from Ft. Collins to Cheyenne."

Her fingers flew across the iPhone, and I remembered what Felix had said, about the cool kids teasing me about my flip-top cell phone. Maybe when this was all over, hah, it would be time for an upgrade.

"Forty-five minutes," she said, voice dull. "Forty-five minutes to get from Fort Collins to Cheyenne."

"And you said he was gone the night he proposed to you. How long did you say that was?"

"Three . . . maybe four hours."

"Yeah."

She stared at her iPhone for a few moments, like she was trying to change the information there with just the power of her mind. And then she said, quietly, "What's going on?"

"Not sure. But he has a Wyoming connection for sure, Paula."

"But that wasn't the point of the trip! He wanted a tour of the American West, the old mines, the—"

I interrupted, "—ghost towns, historical sites, yes, all that. But I've been in his condo unit, Paula. I checked out his bookcase. I saw a lot of books about the law, business, management. I didn't see one book about history, never mind Western history. Not one."

She stayed quiet, fumbling some as she pressed the SLEEP/WAKE button on her iPhone and put it away. I pressed her. "Paula? Am I wrong? Did he have some books about the American West? Did he like to watch the

History Channel a lot? Was there any indication that he was so fascinated that he wanted to travel out there?"

"He proposed to me," she said. "You can't take that away."

"I don't want to take anything away," I said. "I just want to find Mark. And to do so, we have to both realize what the truth is. Somehow, he's connected to Wyoming, something illegal or dangerous, and there's at least one member of a Wyoming motorcycle gang, out here almost two thousand miles away from home, looking for him."

"But he's not interested in motorcycles! Or motorcycle gangs."

I shifted the Pilot into reverse. "Maybe so, but they're certainly interested in *him.*"

We got out on the street in front of the Merrimac Public Library and resumed our drive onto the back roads of Massachusetts. "What now, Lewis?"

"We call a friend of mine, see how he's making out in his little research project. We'll compare notes and then figure it out from there."

"Who's your friend? Not Diane, right?"

"No," I said. "Felix Tinios, from North Tyler."

She seemed to shiver and shrink inside her coat. "That Boston thug? I've heard a lot about him."

"Well, if you're lucky, you're about to meet him."

"Wonderful," she said, voice dry.

Again, I couldn't help myself. "Yes, very wonderful, if you want to see Mark again, alive and in one piece."

CHAPTER EIGHT

While we were on the road, I had a quick and productive phone call with Felix, and he suggested a place for us to meet, on the north shore of Massachusetts. I kept to the back roads and Paula assisted with navigation with her iPhone. It was late afternoon and we were both hungry, but neither of us talked about food.

"Go ahead," she said. "Ask me the question you've been dying to ask."

"What, why do you still type with two fingers most of the time?"

"No," she shot back. "Why I'm with Mark Spencer. Why I'm going to marry him. When he's so different from any other man I've met . . . especially you."

About a half mile passed, still going through rural roads, when I said "None of my business, Paula."

"But you'd still like to know."

"Yes, if you're offering, I'd like to know."

"All right," she said, looking out at the passing Massachusetts country-side. "Before Mark came along, the man in my life had been you. Oh, I dated here and there after we went our separate ways, but you . . . you got under my skin, friend."

I kept quiet.

"Then Mark was there, and he was . . . different. Safe. Almost dull. And after being with you, and knowing about some of the places you've gone and things you've done, and with your time in the Department of Defense that you still don't say much about . . . safe and dull was very appealing. Please don't be offended. I wanted safety, security. . . . And he's a good man, a very good man . . . I love him and I'm so very scared for him."

I still kept quiet, and I squeezed her hand.

Paula turned to me, face quiet, and then looked down at her iPhone.

"At the intersection coming up, take a left."

"A left it is."

We ended up in a city called Beverly, and we were in a part of the city that was still rural, with old trees and stone walls and high brush, and Paula said "Place looks like the back lot of Universal Studios back in the day. Half expect to see werewolves running around."

"I hope not," I said. "I left my silver bullets back at home."

The restaurant was called Anthony's, not a very original name, and it looked like it had started in an old New England saltbox house, with additions added onto it over the years. The parking lot was dirt and rutted, and there were three vehicles parked at the rear, including a blue Mercedes-Benz with New Hampshire license plates.

I pulled in next to the Mercedes and Felix stepped out, wearing dark charcoal-gray slacks, a black cardigan sweater, and a gray cloth coat that reached down to his knees. Around his neck was a tartan scarf, and as I approached him I said, "What's that, the scarf from the McCorleone clan?"

He smiled. "In our neck of the woods, it's called family, not clan." Smile getting wider, he extended his hand to Paula. "Ah, Paula Quinn of the *Chronicle*. So we meet after all this time."

Felix can charm a young nun into forgetting her vows for an hour or three, but his charm ran up against Paula's mood like the *Titanic* hitting an iceberg. She said nothing, shook his hand briefly, and stood there.

But it didn't seem to bother Felix. "You've been busy and bad, Lewis. A dangerous combination. Gunfire in downtown Tyler? Who would have guessed?"

"Just wanted to surprise people. You got anything for me?"

"Sure," he said. "But you first."

I looked to Paula, who had no apparent expression on her face, and to Felix I said: "Mark is being chased by a motorcycle gang, out from Wyoming. It's called the Stonecold Falcons Motorcycle Club. And they're not here to bug Mark about overdue payments on his club membership."

There have been very few times when I've surprised and impressed Felix, and I cherished what he said next.

"Damn you, Cole, if you knew all of that, why in hell did you bother me to do some snooping around?"

I gently slapped him on his shoulder. "Just wanted to see how good you were."

"Hah," he replied, rubbing his hands together. "It's getting cold out here. Let's get inside for something to eat while we talk things over."

The inside of the restaurant was empty, and a restaurant with dim lights and empty tables and chairs is a depressing sight indeed. But Felix ushered us into a small private dining room that was well lit, warm, and comfortable, with a solitary square table in the center covered with a thick white tablecloth. Felix first moved to take off Paula's coat, and then his own, and then he took mine. A white-haired man with dark, wrinkled skin came in, wearing a white starched shirt, black bow tie, black slacks, black shoes, and a white apron that reached his ankles and was tied around his waist.

Felix murmured something in Italian, kissed him on both cheeks, and the man walked away with the coats. Felix held the chair for Paula, and she sat down and both of us followed. A bust of Julius Caesar was on a nearby shelf, and there were oil paintings of the Forum and the Coliseum.

"But it looks like this place is closed," Paula said.

Leather-bound menus were in front of us, and Felix said, "It is closed, but the owner owes me some favors, and I told him I needed a quiet place for a fine meal and productive conversation."

"I'll bet," Paula muttered, as she opened her menu, and Felix was still in a good mood.

"Oh, it's not like that, Paula," he explained. "Sometimes in my business dealings, there's need for a neutral restaurant in a neutral location that serves great food and that's out of the way. Anthony's fits the bill."

"Who's Anthony?"

Felix opened his menu. "The owner."

"Does he know we're here?"

Felix said, "You can ask him. He was the fine gentleman who took our coats."

Felix had a veal dish with a side of pasta, while I had lobster fettuccine and Paula made do with plain penne pasta with tomato sauce. Felix ordered a bottle of Chianti for the table, and while I begged off having a glass of wine, Felix would have none of it.

"Look, a bit of wine isn't going to slow you down," he said. "In fact, it'll relax you and probably put you in a better place. And 'relaxed' is the word of the day. Let's avoid talking about Topic A until we're done eating. It'll help all our digestions."

So I did have a glass of Chianti, and so did Paula, while Felix manfully finished off the rest of the bottle. Anthony came back several times, talking Italian to Felix, with lots of laughs and two-handed handshakes; and when our dishes were finally cleared away and replaced with a small tray of Italian pastries and strong coffee, I was feeling warm, well fed, and, with Felix across from me, safe indeed.

He patted his lips with his white cloth napkin and turned to Paula. "M'dear, I'm sorry to say, the next several minutes are going to be uncomfortable for you. My apologies in advance, but it can't be helped, not if we're going to find Mark Spencer."

Mouth pursed, Paula nodded. "I understand."

"No, I don't think you do," Felix said. "But you will."

His attention came to me. "So, care to explain that shooting in downtown Tyler this morning?"

And that's how the next several minutes were used, by me explaining my canvassing of Mark Spencer's condo complex, learning of the fake deputy sheriff, and then coming across Paula and the now-fake federal official, and how he was traced back to Wyoming, along with Mark Spencer, though with Paula's reluctant agreement.

Felix nodded a few times and pulled his handheld phone out of his pants pocket. He manipulated the screen a few times, then put it on the tablecloth and slid it across so Paula and I could take a gander.

"Is that your man?"

It certainly was, though he wasn't wearing a cloth cap and the tank top T-shirt he did have on revealed a fair number of tattoos around his neck and chest. Paula brought a hand up to her mouth, just nodded.

"Either him or his handsome twin," I said.

"I see," Felix said. "This is Reeve Langley, president of the Stonecold Falcons Motorcycle Club of Wyoming."

"Damn," I said.

"What's wrong?" Paula asked.

Felix retrieved his handheld. "My guess is that Lewis is responding to Mister Langley's position in the motorcycle club."

"I'm sorry," Paula said. "I don't understand."

"He's the president, their head guy," I said. "To have him come here to the East Coast, to be the one leading the search for Mark Spencer, means it's something very, very important to him. Otherwise he'd send a minion or three to track him down. He wouldn't come here to do the job personally."

"Paula . . . what did Mark do?" Felix quietly asked.

"Nothing!"

"Paula . . . Lewis and I, we don't care what he did, where he did it, or who he did it to. We're not law enforcement, not even close. All we want to do is find Mark. Right now, a motorcycle gang from Wyoming is looking for him . . . and they've also called in some friends."

"Other gang members from here?"

"That's right," Felix said. "Word I've got is that there are two New Hampshire motorcycle gangs who've been contacted by the Stonecold Falcons."

"I didn't know we had motorcycle gangs in New Hampshire," Paula said.

"Oh, we do," Felix said. "They keep a very low profile, very low, and are involved in marijuana, heroin, or crystal meth. But they have alliances with other motorcycle clubs across the country, and they can get a lot of prestige and deposits in the ol' karma bank by helping their fellow one-percenters.

Still, having the head of a Wyoming club out here, tracking down a small-town lawyer, that's an outlier."

Felix's expression suddenly got cold, and he said to Paula: "So let it out. Like it or not, your fiancé has a bounty on his head, and if you want his head to stay untouched, tell us what he did."

Paula's face was scrunched up, and at first I thought she was trying hard not to cry, but then I realized something different: she was trying very hard not to lose her temper. She chewed on her lower lip and took a deep breath and said, "For the last goddamn time, Mark is from Vermont. He went to the New England College of Law. I've seen photos, transcripts, and information about his background. I know there's something odd with his Social Security number, but I don't know why it came from Wyoming. He's never said anything about Wyoming, not once."

"But the two of them," I told Felix, "were on a trip to Colorado a few weeks ago. They spent the night in a city less than an hour from the Wyoming border."

Felix said, "Any chance he could have slipped over and back?"

Paula took another deep breath. "Possible, but there's no evidence."

Felix took that in and held up both of his hands. "All right. We'll set aside the possibility that Mark did something illegal. But legal or illegal, or maybe mistaken identity, there's now some bloody hunters looking for him. We're doing the same thing, but we have something they don't: his fiancée."

Paula said "Gee, thanks."

"Does he have any family in the area? Or in Vermont?"

"No, he doesn't," she said. "His parents died in a car accident when he was young. There's no relatives there or in New Hampshire. In fact . . . one of the reasons he's said he's going to enjoy being my husband is becoming part of my family, as nutty as it can be. Twice we've gone out to Vermont so we could visit his parents' grave. He held my hand and told me how much he hated not having a family, and how much he was looking forward to starting a family with me . . . oh, Christ. . . ."

The tears came out and her napkin went up, and Felix and I took a few seconds to add sugar or cream to our respective coffees and examine the pastry tray. After a moment, Paula lowered the napkin and said "It's okay, I'm going to be okay."

Felix smiled, teeth white and perfect. "Of course you are. Now. No family, no real close friends except for you . . . was there a favorite place the two of you liked to go to? A hotel? Bed-and-breakfast? Vacation spot that if something were to rattle him, he'd feel comfortable grabbing a 'go bag' and driving there to hide out?"

A firm shake of her head.

"And there's been no texts, e-mails, or phone calls for nearly a week?"

A nod of her head. It seemed like she couldn't talk at the moment.

Felix went to me again. "The shootout in Tyler this morning. How did Reeve respond? Did he say anything?"

"He wasn't happy," I said.

"I can imagine. How did it come about?"

"Earlier in the morning, I had talked to a neighbor of Mark Spencer's, and he described a deputy sheriff coming by to check on Mark's disappearance."

"Knowing what deputy sheriffs do in this state, pretty dumb story."

"Agreed. But that's how they work in Wyoming. Then I called Paula to let her know what was going on, and that's when I found out that she had just left with a guy fitting the deputy sheriff's description."

Felix said to Paula, "True enough?"

"Yes," she said. "He told me he was a federal agent, that Mark was being kept nearby, and if we moved quickly, we could meet up with him. We were in his Suburban when Lewis arrived . . . and ordered me out."

Felix put his hands together. "Lucky for you he did. Otherwise Langley would have started asking you questions, assisted by a propane torch."

Paula slowly swallowed, looked like she was about to lose her meal all over the pristine white tablecloth.

"When she got over to me," I said, "Reeve said something about me doing a bold move, and then he said something about following me."

"That's when you shot out the tires."

"Not all the tires; the near ones."

"Why two?"

"Got caught up in the excitement of the moment, I guess," I said.

Felix's eyes twinkled and Paula regained some of her composure, and she asked "What now?"

"Now?" Felix asked. "I think we find someplace safe to keep you secure until—"

She shook her head. "No. A non-starter. I stick with whatever the two of you come up with . . . I might remember something or come up with a lead. So we stop talking about that. Deal?"

Felix looked to me, and I gave him a bland look in return. There was no way I was going to debate with Paula at a time like this in front of Felix. "All right, Paula. Deal. But what are you going to do about work?"

"I'll call in sick. Rollie Grandmaison is due back next Monday anyway; he can start a day or two early. But the cops . . . won't they be able to help?"

Felix said: "Absolutely. They'll be able to write up a nice report and take some great crime-scene photographs when it's over. But if you want Mark back and alive and happy to be with you . . . don't go to the cops. At this point in time, they'll just get in the way."

"Lewis?" she said, asking me about a page worth of questions in that one word.

"Felix knows what he's talking about," I said. "He might not be able to go into details of what he's done and learned along the way, but I trust him to do the right thing, and I trust him to find Mark. If there's anyone in the state who can do it, it's him."

Felix looked pleased. "Only one state?"

"Don't get cocky."

We discussed a few more things after that, and Felix said: "That Pilot of yours has to go. By now, every cop in New Hampshire and this part of Massachusetts has a description of the Pilot and its license plate. Give me a few minutes and we'll get a new set of wheels for both of us."

"Both of us?" I asked.

Felix said: "What, you think I'm going to go into harm's way with my Benz? Nope. Like I said, new wheels for both of us."

Paula said: "Excuse me, what did you just say? You're going to have new vehicles here in a few minutes? For real?"

"That's right," Felix said. "For real."

She briefly shook her head. "I feel like I'm trapped in a bad mob movie."

I said, "You still have a chance to opt out. We can find you someplace safe to stay over the next few days."

"No," she said. "I stay with you. For real."

Paula and I stayed in the dining room while Felix made a few phone calls, and he came back about five minutes later and said, "All set. About fifteen minutes, we'll be heading . . . okay, Lewis, where are we heading?"

"North. Back to Tyler."

"Why?" Felix asked. "You got some laundry to pick up?"

"No," I said. "Besides being town counsel, Mark worked for a small law firm in town, run by Hannah Adams and Carl Lessard. Carl told me last night that Mark had been in contact with him, telling him that he was safe."

"Did he say anything else?" Felix asked.

"No. I pressed him, but he wouldn't say any more."

Felix reflected on that for a few seconds. "All right, north it is. We'll see if we can find Carl at his office or court, find a quiet moment to chat, and try to convince him of the error of his ways."

"Suppose that doesn't work?" Paula asked.

Felix checked his watch. "There's other ways of convincing."

Outside in the parking lot of Anthony's, my Honda Pilot and Felix's Mercedes-Benz were missing. In their place was a dark blue Chevrolet Tahoe, engine running, bearing New Hampshire license plates.

"Not that I'm not grateful, Felix, but I had some stuff in that Pilot."

"All belongings were transferred when the Tahoe came here."

"That's nice, but the Pilot's also a rental."

"True," Felix said, "and a man about your age, identifying himself as Lewis Cole, has just called the Tyler Police Department to report that his rental vehicle had earlier been stolen."

"Where's he calling from?"

"One of the few pay phones still in existence in Tyler. He's also going to say that he will be unable to make a report in person to the Tyler police because of extenuating circumstances."

"What kind of circumstances?"

Felix slapped his hands together. "How the hell would I know? What, you think I know everything?"

Paula said "You sure give that impression."

In the Tahoe, I took the rear, while Paula and Felix sat up front. I saw that my possessions were folded and piled neatly in the back of the Tahoe, and placed in the center of the rear seat was my 9mm Beretta in its Bianchi leather holster. Next to my pistol was a box of 9mm ammunition. I removed the magazine from the Beretta, worked the action to take out the round in the chamber, and then slipped the round into the magazine. From the box of cartridges I removed two additional rounds, pushed them into the magazine with my thumb.

Fully loaded now, I slipped the magazine back into the handle of the Beretta, heard the satisfying click as it snapped in, and then worked the action, lowered the hammer, and placed the Beretta on safe.

Sliding my pistol back into the holster, I glanced up, saw that Paula had turned in her seat, had watched every motion.

"Even when you were shooting back there, in Tyler, it all seemed make-believe," Paula said. "Now . . . it's too goddamn real."

I put my holstered weapon back at my side.

"Lots to be said for make-believe," I said. Paula turned around, and soon we were on Interstate 95, heading north back to Tyler.

Along the drive north, Paula made two phone calls, both relatively quick: she called the *Chronicle* and said she wasn't coming in for the rest of the day, or tomorrow. She also called the law offices of Adams & Lessard, and said "unh-hunh, unh-hunh" a few times, and then disconnected her call.

"Must be something going around," Paula said. "Carl Lessard called in sick today as well."

"Hope it's not catching," Felix said. "Paula, you know where Attorney Lessard lives?"

"Sure," she said. "Easy enough to get to. Spent a couple of ghastly evenings there with the witch that's the partner and Mark, along with assorted friends and spouses."

Up ahead finally were the main Tyler tollbooths, which greet northbound travelers about five minutes after they cross the border into my home state. Probably not much of a welcome, but at least there's a state liquor store just before to ease the pain. Before we got to the tollbooths, Felix took the last exit, which took us into Falconer and Route 1, thereby avoiding being tracked via the tollbooth. During the drive, Felix had the Tahoe's radio set to WBZ-AM, the main news station out of Boston; and when we got on the main road leading to Tyler, there was a news-brief at the bottom of the hour, and the second news item concerned Hurricane Toni. It had been upgraded to a Category Two hurricane, and was still heading north. In a couple of days, the National Weather Service said, it was possible that all of New England would be under a hurricane watch.

Paula turned once more. "Sorry to hear that, Lewis."

"I'll be all right, thanks."

Felix said, "What's going on? Still no insurance settlement?"

"Not yet."

"Maybe your insurance agent needs some encouragement. You ever think of that?"

"One Don Quixote mission at a time," I said.

Paula muttered, "Don Quixote was an optimist."

We then stopped at the intersection of Lafayette Road and High Street, where several hours ago I had broken several traffic laws, town ordinances, and state laws to grab Paula before she got taken away by Reeve Langley. The street in front of the town common was clear. There was no Suburban with shot-out tires resting there.

"Paula, any idea what happened to the Suburban that was there this morning?"

"Jonah told me, right after I told him I was calling in sick. He said that after the shooting . . . the Suburban drove out on two flat tires, got abandoned in the woods off Meadowland Road. Police are currently investigating, so forth and so on."

The light turned green. Felix said: "Threatening a motorcycle gang leader, taking somebody away that he wanted to talk to, and disabling his ride. Hell of a full morning you had there, Lewis."

"True, and I'm hoping the rest of the day isn't as full."

"Don't count on it," Felix said, and we drove down High Street in silence.

CHAPTER NINE

ollowing Paula's directions, Felix took a series of turns off of High Street, near the famed Tyler Beach. It was starting to get dark as the sun set, and I saw an old, faded JACKSON HALE FOR PRESIDENT sign flapping in the breeze.

That campaign sign seemed to get Paula's attention, and she asked, "Hey, whatever happened to that lawyer girl you were dating, Lewis, the one who was working on Senator Hale's campaign?"

"It's been over now for almost a month."

"Oh. Sorry to hear that. What happened?"

"Politics."

"A conflict, then?"

"I suppose," I said. "She loved politics. I didn't. End of story."

Felix grunted. We were on Herbert Street, near the ocean, and then Paula said "That's the house up there, on the right. The gray ranch."

Which made sort of ironic sense, I suppose. The gray man, the gray lawyer, living in a gray house. It had gray siding, black shingles, and black shutters on the windows. The yard was small but neatly kept, with only a few fall leaves making a stand on the perfectly groomed grass. There was an attached one-car garage to the right, and Carl Lessard's vehicle, a salt-stained red Chrysler LeBaron, was parked in the driveway. There was another house to the right, and to the left—a rarity in Tyler—there was an undeveloped stretch of woods.

Felix didn't slow down as he drove past Carl's house, and Paula said, "Hey, that's the place! You're driving right by it!"

"I certainly am," Felix said. "Hold on for a sec, young lady."

He went on for about twenty yards or so, and there was a wide dirt-and-gravel space off the road to the right. Felix pulled in, dimmed the lights, kept the engine running.

"No need to advertise to the world that we're here for a visit," he said. "So Lewis and I, we'll step out, trot up to the house for a friendly visit, a friendly chit-chat, and then we'll come back here."

Paula said "No, I want to come along."

"Ah, but as you pointed out earlier, that's a non-starter. Lewis and I will do what needs to be done."

She turned in my direction, face red. "Lewis?"

I didn't hesitate. "Felix is right. Three people are one too many. And Felix and I . . . we may get insistent. It's best for you if you stay behind, so if there's any . . . complications, you won't get caught up in it."

"I can handle myself!"

"Absolutely," I said. "But suppose . . . and I know this is a wild shot in the dark . . . but suppose everything gets cleared up in a day or two. We find out the Stonecold Falcons have made a mistake, I pay for two tires, give apologies, and we find Mark safe and happy. What kind of reception will he get back at work if you were there when we talked to someone from his firm?"

She seemed primed for a fight, and then she sat back in her seat. "Damn you. That does make sense."

"Good!" Felix said. "I'll leave the keys here so you can listen to the radio. Climb over here and take the steering wheel. We shouldn't be gone long. But if something unusual happens, anything at all, drive away. Lewis and I will be able to fend for ourselves."

"What do you mean 'unusual'?"

Felix opened the door. "You'll know it when you see it."

I stepped out with Felix, carrying the leather shoulder holster that held my Beretta, and we walked a bit; and when we were out of view of Paula, I shrugged off my jacket, slipped on the holster, and put my jacket back on.

"Glad to see you're carrying," Felix murmured.

"Wish I wasn't."

"Me too," he said, as we approached the front of Carl Lessard's house.

We went up the flagstone walkway and I peered into a bay window in front, where I could see that a television was on, and not much else. Felix rang the doorbell by using the blunt end of a fountain pen. I could hear the chimes ring out, and waited, running through scenarios, points of conversation, ways of convincing Carl that he had to tell us where Mark was hiding out.

Felix pushed the doorbell again. I peered through the window. It looked like the five P.M. news program from the main television station over in Manchester. Even from here I could hear the volume.

Felix went to push the doorbell once more, hesitated. I nodded. "He's not coming to the door."

"Nope."

"Still . . . I think we need to check out what we can."

No answer from Felix; but through some alchemy he's able to do, his own 9mm pistol was in his right hand. In his left was a handkerchief, and he slowly opened the storm door. I had my own pistol in hand, pulled back the hammer. Putting the handkerchief on the doorknob, Felix slowly rotated it.

It was unlocked.

He pushed the door open and I followed him in. The living room was sparse, neat, the furniture looking like it had come in from Sears about thirty years earlier. Adjacent to the living room was a wide kitchen, and there was a hallway to the left, down which Felix disappeared. I went to the kitchen, gave it a quick glance; and then Felix came back from the hallway, his face calm and looking like it had just been carved from stone.

"They got to him," he said. "Let's go."

I moved past Felix and started down the narrow carpeted hallway, and the dull smell of copper reached me. Felix said "You don't have to look."

"Sure I do," I said.

There was a closed door to the right, an open one to the left. I was preparing myself as much as I could, and even then my mind refused to process it at first. My eyes saw what they saw, and part of my mind that wanted everything to be safe and secure said hey, what you're looking at is no big deal, it must be an overdue Halloween gag or gift. There was a clothed shape sprawled out on a double bed, ankles and wrists bound by wire. Blood had stained the yellow plaster walls. There was a set of bureaus, another low bureau with a row of books. On the bureau were a few photographs, most of them black and white. I stared at the photos, just wanting to get things together.

The photos were family portraits. I saw a man and woman at a wedding, and a couple of schoolboy shots that looked like a very young Carl Lessard. The wedding portrait was probably of his parents. A smear of rust-brown blood had dripped down the glass.

I turned around. There was a pillow over the upper torso; on the floor, an empty two-liter soda bottle. Felix grabbed my arm.

"Seen enough?"

"Yes."

"You should have listened to me."

"No," I said. "I had to see this. Let's get the hell out of here."

Outside I wanted to take a minute or five just to stand out in the cool air, take deep breaths, and feel good at being alive, but I kept on moving. Bad enough what had happened in that pleasant Seacoast ranch house, but it would be worse if some inquiring neighbors saw Felix and me enter and then leave the house and hang around the front lawn.

Felix walked with me and said: "I know you feel like running, but no running. People walking around a neighborhood like this don't draw attention. Runners do."

"Not if they're wearing sweatpants and sneakers."

"Good point."

It was now past dusk, and streetlights were starting to come on. I said, "The TV was on loud to hide their work. They went at him and went at him, and when they were done, they used a pillow to mask the sound of the gunshot."

"You see the soda bottle on the floor?"

"I did."

"Poor man's silencer," Felix explained. "Put the muzzle end through the mouth of the bottle, and aim close. Sloppy as hell; but at close range, it'll work."

"Now Reeve and his crew know where Mark is hiding out. It's going to be a rough night for him unless he's very, very lucky."

Felix stopped walking. I saw what he was looking at.

The place where he had parked the Tahoe was empty. Paula Quinn was gone.

"Looks like it's going to be a rough night all around," he said. "You got your cell phone?"

"I most certainly do. It's in the Tahoe. You?"

"In the Tahoe as well." He sighed. "Well, maybe they're in the back seat, copulating, and we'll have a tablet when this is all done."

I looked around at the deserted street. I could make out the distant sound of waves coming in.

"Felix."

"Yeah."

"Less than a day ago, I was talking with Carl Lessard. At this point, all he wanted in life was to work one more year, and then retire south to Florida, where he could have a life he's always dreamed of. You saw what they did to him . . . in the bedroom of his own home. I don't feel like joking right now. Let's start walking."

I moved away and, silently, Felix kept beside me.

Herbert Street soon regained its collection of well-lit homes as it gently swerved to meet up with Atlantic Avenue. A few cars passed us by—none of them a Tahoe—and for a moment I wished I could take one more deep breath and keep on walking all night long, and forget the bloody horror that was splattered back in that quiet New Hampshire home.

"You know," I said, "if this was for Mark Spencer, and Mark only, I'd say to hell with it."

"I like the sound of that. So it's for his fiancée, your former girlfriend. Why not say to hell with it? You've done a fair amount of work, you rescued the fair princess from certain torture and death, and you've just seen up front what they're willing to do to get the information they're looking for."

"Because it's for Paula."

"A statement, not an answer. Why?"

The answer came quick. "Remember what I was like when I first moved here?"

"Sure. Bundle of nerves, spent most of your time hiding out, reading. Quick to laugh a lot, or get angry. First time we really met was over . . . well, you remember. I gave you what I thought was a fair and respectful warning to butt out. And you came over and blasted away four tires of the Benz I was driving that year."

"I was trying to send a message."

"No, you were sending something else," Felix said, hands in his coat pockets. "That message I got loud and clear, which is why I invited you in for a beer after you de-tired my car. But what does that have to do with Paula?"

My throat ached, thinking an old memory of an old love. "Once I came here, Paula was the first woman I was with. She helped me . . . brought me part way out of my shell, brought me back to the land of the living. I owe her that."

We were approaching the intersection of Herbert Street and Atlantic Avenue. The gray waters of the Atlantic were ahead of us.

"Fair enough," Felix said. "Latest message received, loud and clear."

At the intersection we trotted across the street, which led to a sidewalk that paralleled the seawall on this stretch of the road. The sidewalk was uneven, sprinkled with beach sand and small rocks that got tossed over the seawall by storm waves. Felix said "We can start walking left, get up to North Tyler and my house."

"That's a long walk," I said. "We turn right, we'll go past the Samson Point Wildlife Preserve, and then we'll get to my house. Quicker all around."

"Don't want to rub it in," Felix said, "but your house has seen better days. Hell, better centuries."

"But I have the Lafayette House across the street. With a phone. To call Paula, find out how she's doing." My footsteps sounded loud on the sidewalk. "She's all right, don't you think?"

"She was sitting in the driver's seat with the key in the ignition, ready to bolt at anything unusual. Chances are pretty high that's exactly what happened. If Reeve and his buddies wanted Paula, they'd just take her out and leave the Tahoe behind."

"Unless they climbed in, put a gun to her head, and carjacked her."

"My, aren't we the font of happy thoughts tonight."

"I left my happy thoughts back at Carl Lessard's house."

The road curved again. Bicyclists with flashing lights fore and aft sped by us, along with the occasional car or truck, sometimes temporarily blinding us with their headlights as they hugged the curving road.

"We should call Tyler dispatch when we get to the Lafayette House," I said.

"No, we shouldn't."

"We owe it to Carl."

"To be brutal, Lewis, no, we don't. We owe it to Paula and her man. Poor Carl . . . he's dead, he'll still be dead in an hour, will still be dead tomorrow. You call from the Lafayette House, dispatch will know within seconds where the call came from, and any surveillance video will instantly put you at the hotel at the time the call was made. You looking to be arrested tonight?"

"No, I was looking to do the right thing. Like warning Carl's partner and their secretary to get the hell out of town."

Felix let out a breath. "That we can do. Give me a few minutes to figure something out."

Up ahead were the welcoming lights of the Lafayette House. I had a thought about Hurricane Toni, gathering wind, speed, and destruction, aiming right for this stretch of coastline and what remained of my house.

Felix said "Thanksgiving isn't that far away."

"Thanks for the reminder. You getting your list of what you're thankful for in place?"

"I always keep that list updated," he said. "What I'm saying is that I'm heading to Florida, away from this cold and that approaching storm, and I'm going to have Thanksgiving with my Aunt Teresa and her current boyfriend."

"Aunt Teresa . . . I thought she was north of ninety years old."

"Which is why I said *current* boyfriend. Look, come along, we'll have some laughs, I'll introduce you to some of her medical aides, and we'll have a lot of fun."

"You think we'll be done by then?"

"By God, we better."

The lights grew brighter. "Let me get back to you. I'm still thinking of my house."

"Yeah, your poor house, but someone should think of poor Lewis. You shouldn't be alone on that day. You should stuff yourself with turkey and then find some sweet Southern lass to work off your splurging, share some fun times with people."

"I'll think about it."

"Yeah, well, don't overthink it."

We got up to the Lafayette House main entrance, and as we walked up the paved driveway a vehicle quickly emerged from the rear of the hotel and then braked to a halt beside us.

It was a light blue Chevy Tahoe. The driver's-side window lowered.

Paula leaned out. "Men. So damn predictable. Hurry up and get in."

I looked at Felix, and he looked at me, and I took the passenger's seat and he climbed into the rear.

Paula made a left onto Atlantic Avenue. "What happened that made you leave?" I asked.

"Something unusual," she said. "I was sitting there, minding my own business, contemplating my sins . . . when this scraggly-looking dude walked by, built like a fireplug, carrying a metal detector. He asked me to roll down the window, he asked me if this was the road to the beach. I said yes and he wanted to talk some more, so I started up the Tahoe, got the hell out of there."

Felix asked, "What was wrong?"

"This time of the year, guys with metal detectors go out in the morning, not in the afternoon. Gets dark too quick. And any guy with a metal detector, he's up on treasure hunting. He knows where the damn ocean is."

Paula slowed down as she came up behind an Audi taking its time. "What did you find out?" she asked.

"Reeve and his friends got there first," I said. "Carl Lessard is dead."

Paula flinched, like somebody had just struck her in the ribs. "Christ. How?"

"Long and rough," I said. "They were looking for information. I hope Mark is smart enough to keep moving."

She handled the Tahoe well, but I could see that she was shaken up, and she took a hand off the steering wheel to wipe at her eyes. "Shit," she said; and, a while later, "Shit."

From the rear, Felix said, "Paula . . . my house is a mile or so up the road. Let's head there, regroup, get something to eat, figure out our options."

Paula asked, "You call the cops?"

"Not yet."

"Damn it, Carl was a good guy . . . okay, a bore, but—"

Felix again. "We'll let the Tyler cops know soon enough. But we have to do it right. We don't have time to be interrogated, asked lots of questions."

Paula handled the big SUV with ease through some of the tight curves that made up Atlantic Avenue. Off to the east I could make out the lonely lights of the Isles of Shoals.

I said "We also have to call Hannah Adams and their secretary, Kenneth Sheen. Warn them what happened."

"How are you going to do that?" Paula demanded. "Say 'hey, sorry to bother you, but your co-worker just got slaughtered over Mark's whereabouts, so you should keep your doors and windows locked'?"

"Something like that," I said.

I think Paula was going to say something sharp when Felix beat her to it.

"Up ahead, on the right," he said. "Rosemount Lane."

She slowed down the Tahoe, switched on the turn signal, and we went onto Rosemount Lane. There are six homes on Rosemount Lane, and Felix lived in the remotest one, on a slight rise that had a great view of the ocean and a closely trimmed lawn. There are no trees or bushes on Felix's property, the better to see anyone coming up to his house. It's a one-story wide ranch, and Paula stopped the Tahoe in the driveway.

"Come along," Felix said. "Let's get some things out of the way."

He led us up a stone path to the house, and he unlocked the front door and let us in. His house is clean and spare, with lots of Scandinavian-type furniture and not much in the way of home decoration, except for two large framed prints from the Metropolitan Museum of Art. Paula and I got our coats off, and Felix said "Excuse me, just for a minute," and he took a walk down a hallway off the living room. Paula looked oddly at me, and I took off my shoulder holster and Beretta and slid them under my coat.

I took one couch and Paula took the other, opposite a low coffee table that bore copies of that day's *New York Times* and *Wall Street Journal*, along with the latest copies of *Smithsonian* magazine. Both couches were light brown leather. She ran a hand through her hair and said "I don't see it."

"See what?"

"Besides all the rumors I've heard about what he's done since he's moved here, I've also gotten the impression that he's quite the lady's man, cutting a wide swath through the local lady folk."

"That's a . . . fair statement," I said.

"Last summer, I heard a story about Dolores Palmer, she owns a hotel at the beach, a mini-mart, and was the money behind a new Italian restaurant that opened up on the Exonia Road."

"Yes, I know the place. Sofia's, right?"

"The same . . . well, I know the night manager, and she told me that Felix came by one night for a meal, she came by and joined him, and by the time they got to coffee and dessert, she was ready to leave her husband and two kids to go home with Felix."

"Did she?"

"I didn't ask . . . but like I said, I don't see it."

I looked to the hallway. Still empty.

"Guess you're missing that certain gene."

"Or I've got additional resistance."

Felix whistled some as he came back, like he was giving us a heads-up that he was going to re-enter the living room. He was juggling a cell phone in his hand and plopped himself down on my couch. He still had on his shoulder holster, but it didn't seem to bother Paula. I guess it just looked natural to her.

"All right, folks, keep it quiet," he said.

He punched in three digits, held the phone up to his ear, and, speaking slowly and clearly, he said: "There's been a homicide at the Carl Lessard residence on Herbert Street, Tyler, New Hampshire."

Then he clicked the phone off. "Paula? Any chance you might have the home numbers of Hannah Adams and Kenneth Sheen?"

She dug out her iPhone, gave Felix what he was looking for, and Felix made two more phone calls. The first was pretty straightforward. "Mister Sheen? Hello. Just want to give you a heads-up . . . I'm sorry to say your boss, Carl Lessard, has been murdered. Police are responding to his house at this moment, and the murderer has not been arrested. I strongly urge you to leave your home and go to the Tyler police station."

He clicked off again. "Poor guy. He'd started wailing by the time I hung up. Okay, one more time."

This one took a bit longer. "Hannah Adams? Yes? Well, who I am doesn't matter . . . trust me, ma'am, it doesn't . . . no, I'm not trying to sell you anything . . . I'm . . . ma'am, give me thirty seconds and I'll leave you alone . . . ma'am . . . ma'am . . . your partner Carl has been murdered . . . who I am isn't important . . . ma'am . . . he's dead, the killer's still out there . . . you need to protect yourself . . . ma'am . . . this is not a joke. . . ."

Felix shook his head, clicked the phone off. "Well, that was interesting. If Reeve does catch up with her, I'm not sure who would end up victorious. Excuse me for a second."

He got up and went to the adjacent kitchen, past a granite countertop, and he dropped the phone in a metal bowl after opening it up and taking out the SIM card. He rummaged around in a drawer, came up with a crème brûlée propane torch, which he switched on. He played the flame along the SIM card and the guts of the phone, and there was an acrid stink in the air, until he turned on an overhead fan. It only took a moment or so until he was satisfied, and then he switched off the torch and came back.

"There you go," he said. "Civic duty satisfied, my outlaw nature satisfied as well. What now?"

I shifted on my couch. While Felix had been at work, I'd been running through options, choices, and what this day had brought us.

"It's been a long day," I said.

Paula leaned back on the couch. "Tell me about it."

I said, "We've been on the run, we've been playing catch-up, we're always behind."

"True," Felix said.

"I'm tired of it," I said. "Time to change tactics."

"You have an idea?" Felix asked.

"I do," I said. "Let's get back on the road."

CHAPTER TEN

An hour later, we were in Auburn, a small town outside Manchester, the state's largest city. Felix parked the Tahoe in the rutted dirt parking lot of a bar and restaurant called the Hog Heaven Fan Club. Even in November and with the bitter cold that sometimes swept in from our supposed friends in Canada, the lot was nearly full of parked motorcycles. The place had a wooden porch and flickering neon lights, and it looked like it had started its life as a two-story chicken coop. Additions had been tacked on, each with a different style and color. It was surrounded by tall pine trees, and in the rear were two overflowing Dumpsters.

Paula leaned in between us from the rear seat and said "My, you fellows sure know how to get to a young girl's heart, all the fancy places you take her to."

The past hour had been a long one, driving here from the seacoast, and it was good to hear the tone of Paula's voice. "If we're lucky," I said, opening the door, "the next place will be even better."

"Oh, you're such a smooth talker," she said.

"Still, it might make sense for you to stay in the car," I said. "In case we run into Reeve Langley, he'll spot you right away."

She got out with us. "Oh, and who was shooting at him this morning? The Invisible Man? He'll spot you as well."

Good point, and I didn't say anything else.

We walked up as a group to the front, as country-western music thumped from inside. The windows were darkened and Felix led the way, opening the door. The smell of tobacco, stale beer, and greasy food rolled out, and Paula said, raising her voice over the music, "Wait, smoking isn't allowed in restaurants anymore."

Felix said "Didn't you see the sign? This isn't a restaurant. This is a private club. We're just guests."

Which was true. There was a small foyer guarded by a heavy-set woman wearing leather pants, a black Harley-Davidson tank top, and a large, blonde bouffant hairstyle. She pointed to an open ledger on a stand, where we all had to sign in as guests and then pay her five dollars as a cover charge. She seemed friendly enough. On her left hand she had JESUS tattooed, and on the right hand, she had LOVES inked in as well. Felix leaned over to her and said, "Tell Phil that Felix and a friend are here to see him."

She nodded and got off her stool, and we followed her in, past a beaded curtain. Hanging from the ceiling were three flatscreen televisions, showing football, basketball, and hockey. To the left were three pool tables, with large rectangular lamps hanging overhead, the yellow lights hazy in the tobacco smoke. A grill was to the rear, next to a large bar, and there were booths and wooden tables and chairs, and the place was mostly packed with men and women in biker gear, with a fair sprinkling of what I would guess would be called civilians. A couple of waitresses wandered by, young women in very tight blue jeans and wearing skimpy Harley-Davidson tank tops.

A tall, gawky-looking guy came over, with jeans and a Harley-Davidson sweatshirt, wearing a scraggly beard that was made famous back in the 1960s by a man called Ho Chi Minh. There wasn't much hair on his head but he did his best, pulling it back in a thin ponytail. He went up to Felix and said something, and Felix said something back, and Felix came over to Paula and me and said "All right, meet is on. Paula?"

She rolled her eyes. "I know the drill. Hang down here while you big boys go in the secret clubhouse and have all the fun. Go right ahead. Christ, I might even get myself a beer."

I asked her "Are you going to be all right?"

Even with the loud music blaring out, I could sense her mocking tone. "Why, Lewis, I'm a proud, upstanding member of the Fourth Estate. Who would dare touch me?"

Well, I couldn't argue with that, and Ho Chi Minh's very distant cousin took us back beyond the bar and the grill, to a narrow set of stairs. He just pointed and Felix went up, and I followed, but I made it a point to make sure we were going up by ourselves, which we were. At the top of the stairs were two doors, one that was open, showing it was a bathroom. I couldn't tell much about the details of the bathroom, because a bulky man weighing about three hundred pounds, it seemed, was on his knees inside, apparently vomiting spectacularly.

The door to the left was marked with black marker, stating YEAH, ITS GODDAMN PRIVATE, but Felix just spun the doorknob and we walked in. I closed the door, stunned at how thick and soundproofed the door was, because the sounds of the man having gastric distress and the music from downstairs were instantly lessened.

A squat man stood up from behind a wooden desk, smiling. His hair and beard were a deep brown, the beard closely trimmed, a short ponytail wrapped up at the rear. He had on clean blue jeans and a blue Oxford buttoned-down shirt, the collar open. He looked friendly enough, but his eyes were sharp and suspicious. There was a bookcase, a computer on his desk, and framed posters highlighting motorcycle rallies in Sturgis and Laconia. The floor was carpeted in light green, but it wasn't one of those industrial-strength carpets built to withstand spills of beer or blood. On a coat rack in the far corner, a leather coat hung next to a denim motorcycle vest. The vest had a large patch showing a mountain peak, and lettering said CRAWFORD NOTCH BOYS MC.

He held out his hand and Felix instantly grabbed it. "Felix . . . good to see you, bro. Was glad I could be here, see what I can do to help you."

Felix said: "Phil Tasker, this is Lewis Cole, an associate of mine."

I shook his hand as well, and it was a gentle touch, but I knew there was muscle and steel tendons back there. "Nice to meet you, Lewis," he said, going back to his desk. "Guys, look, have a seat. Can I get you anything? Tonic? Beer? Mixed drink? Cheeseburger?"

The chairs were wood and leather, and quite comfortable. Felix stretched out his legs, put his folded hands across his flat stomach, and asked, "How's business, Phil?"

"Eh, can't really complain," Phil said, picking up a letter opener, spinning it with his fingers. "When the snow and ice finally get here, that's when we're gonna take a hit . . . but like anything else in life, you just plan for it and go on."

"Nice," Felix said.

Felix stayed quiet and so did I. Phil smiled but clearly looked uncomfortable, like we were from the state Department of Revenue, getting ready to do an audit covering ten years, as well as an underwear and sock inventory.

"Well," Phil said.

More time passed. I felt the vibration from the music downstairs against my feet.

Felix made a motion of sighing, rubbing his hands together. "The Stonecold Falcons."

Phil was relieved, like finally he could talk about something. "That western bastard. . . . I wish they'd never come here. Goddamn it. All they've caused me is a lot of grief, a lot of shit I don't need."

"Have you heard from them lately?"

"Nope."

"Your guys still helping them, looking for that lawyer?"

Phil's hand went back to the letter opener, making it spin again on his desk. "Felix . . . c'mon, we've done favors for each other in the past . . . I really don't want to talk about what we're doing for that creep."

"Really?" Felix asked, sounding like an altar boy asking directions to the boy's room. "Why's that, Phil?"

"Because that Reeve is a psycho."

"I see."

I kept quiet, admiring how Felix was going about his business. I wasn't sure how he was approaching this, but even sitting here next to him, as an ally and friend, I felt the tension in the air, heavy and threatening.

Felix rapped his fingers on the arm of the chair, then suddenly leaned forward. "Hey. I really like that shirt you've got on. It's an Oxford, right?"

Phil blinked his eyes, ran a finger around the collar. "I . . . I guess so."

"Even from here, I can tell it's high quality. Must be a high thread count. Tell me, Phil, is it Egyptian cotton or American cotton?"

"Hunh?"

Felix raised his voice. "Phil, c'mon, you're wasting my time. Egyptian or American cotton, what is it?"

"I . . . I'm not sure . . . I—"

"Check the damn label, Phil."

Phil's face was red and he squirmed in his seat, and Felix leaned forward, eyes hard. "Jesus, Phil, do I have to draw you a schematic? It's on the shirt label, on your neck. Get your shirt off. C'mon."

Phil looked at me, maybe hoping I could intervene on his behalf, but I kept my face as blank as possible.

"Ah. . . ."

"Phil."

His fingers fumbled some as he undid the buttons, opening up his shirt. His chest was flabby, some chest hair and faded tattoos of American flags and eagles, and there were two furrowed scars running across his belly. He tugged the shirt off, examined the collar. Both arms were covered with tattoos as well.

"American," he said, almost a whisper.

"Here, toss it over."

It looked like Phil was going to toss the shirt and then thought better of it. He stood up and handed the shirt to Felix, and then Felix said, "Hey, nice khakis. Where did you get them?"

"I don't remember."

"Then give 'em over," Felix said, patiently. "I want to see the label."

"Felix . . . please. . . ."

"Yes, please," he said. "I forgot to say please."

Phil stood there, like he was made of wood, and said something I've rarely heard men say in Felix's presence. "No."

"Phil. . . ."

He returned behind his desk, face flushed, sat down heavily. "No. That's enough, Felix. Word gets out that you made me take off my shirt, how many days would I last, running this outfit?"

"Word still could get around," Felix said, his voice in a low timbre that I'd never heard. "Unless you tell me what I want to know."

Phil nodded. "That's because the two of you know," he said slowly. "But word getting out would depend on the two of you leaving my office, am I right?"

Felix shifted in his seat and I instantly knew what was happening: he was moving around so he could get quick access to his pistol. "Phil, my friend, we've scratched each other's backs for a very long time, and it pains me to say this: but right now I'm observing both of your hands. If either one of them moves, then that nice Sturgis poster behind your head is going to get splattered with blood and brain matter."

Phil didn't reply, but I knew he was evaluating his options. "True enough, you damn wop," he said. "But then it'll be the two of you against the club downstairs."

"If they hear anything through this soundproofing," Felix pointed out. "And if they did, that's one narrow staircase coming up to your office. It'd take a minute or two to see how brave your boys would be, in looking for revenge."

With the tension and mistrust thick in the air, I felt like tiny Belgium in 1914, caught between the marauding empires of France and Germany. I spoke up. "If he's been a pain in the ass and is a psycho, why did you help him out?"

Phil looked relieved to talk to me. "Street cred, what else?"

"Go on."

He said, "We go to Laconia or Phoenix or anywhere else next summer, if we ride with the Stonecold Falcons, then it shows everybody we're together. It gives us points. Tells other clubs that we're not to be fucked with. That's why."

"Oh, there's more to that, Phil, right?" Felix asked. "Along with the street cred comes more contacts, more friends, more opportunities for your cigarette smuggling, your weed growing, and your meth manufacturing."

A slight smile. "Yeah, there is that."

"Good enough," I said. "Street cred. Go on. Why is he here, and what are you doing to help him out?"

The tension had lessened, and Phil spoke to me like I was an ignorant bystander who had to have things explained to him. And I admired his strategy. He wasn't losing face or backing down with Felix, he was merely talking to me, a nobody, and if Felix were to overhear, well, them's the breaks.

"Reeve came here a few days ago, saying he was looking for Mark Spencer, that Tyler lawyer. I lent him two of my crew, and that's it. Haven't heard or seen him since then."

I asked: "He say why he's looking for Mark?"

"Shit, no," Phil said. "Fact is, Reeve Langley made a request. He could have been looking for a nun, a shoemaker, a carpenter, I could give a shit. Why do I care?"

"Not curious?" I asked.

"Not enough curiosity in the world to ask Reeve anything more than I have to."

Felix glanced at me, I gave a slight shrug, and Felix said, "All right, then. But if you get any more information, anything at all, about where Reeve is and why he's looking for Mark Spencer, you'll let me know? Right? As a favor?"

Phil nodded, got up and started putting his shirt back on. "All right. As a favor. But . . . Felix?"

"Yes?"

"Don't ever push me like that, ever again."

Felix got up. "I'll certainly take that under consideration."

On the stairs, I said "I thought that was quite the insult, calling you a wop."

"Didn't bother me," Felix said, raising his voice some. "I'm only a half wop."

We went back downstairs into the bar, and I had a brief flash of panic looking for Paula. She wasn't sitting at the bar, and she wasn't sitting at one of the booths or tables, and I started toward the women's bathroom, but Felix gently grasped my upper arm, pointed.

Over at the pool tables, Paula was there with a pool cue, playing with two bikers, heavyset, thick beards, tattoos up and down both arms, wearing the dungaree vests of the Crawford Notch Boys. I was going to start over there, but Felix spoke into my ear. "What's the rush? Let the girl have her fun. God knows she hasn't had much fun this past week."

A good point. I led Felix over to the bar and we sat down, and we slowly sipped bottles of Sam Adams, while I watched Paula work her magic at the pool cue. Felix was right. She was enjoying herself. It was sweet to see.

And then she was done. She put her cue stick back on the rack, shook hands with both of the bikers, some money was passed over to Paula, and, still laughing, she wended her way through the crowded pub floor and came up to us, slapped our shoulders, and said, "Well, fellas, you do what had to be done?"

"We did," I said.

She looked back to the pool tables. "Roy and Henry over there just challenged me to another game, but I'd rather head out with you two, if you'll hurry up and finish your beers."

Felix asked, "How much did you take them for?"

"Enough," she said.

"Didn't know you were a pool shark," I said.

Eyes alive, she leaned in so I could hear her better. "Back in college, when I was working on the school paper in the student union building, there was a game room on the same floor with a couple of pool tables."

Paula squeezed my shoulder. "What, you think I spent all my spare time writing news stories?"

Outside, the crisp November night air was brisk as we went over to the Tahoe. I was suddenly tired, from a long, long day, and not feeling good about where we were. We didn't know much more than we had when this day started, and the day had also ended with the death of Carl Lessard—and, chances were, Reeve and his boys were closing in fast on wherever Mark Spencer was hiding.

Felix got in the front, Paula gestured for me to take the front as well, and, after the engine was started and seatbelts were fastened, we started out away from Auburn. Now the interior of the Tahoe stank with stale tobacco smoke from the Hog Heaven Fan Club, and the stench stayed with us all the way back to the seacoast.

Paula handed a twenty-dollar bill to Felix. "My share of the gas."

Felix handed it back. "You'll get an invoice when we're finished, Paula."

"Hah," she said, retrieving the money. "Were you able to get much from Phil?"

"Not much," I said.

"Really? Even after Reeve came by earlier today with two of Phil's boys with him?"

I started to say something, but Felix quietly switched on the turn indicator and slowly pulled the Tahoe over to the side of the road. He put the gearshift in PARK and positioned himself so he could look directly at Paula.

"How did you know that?" he asked.

"My pool boys," she said. "Roy and Henry. They told me Reeve came by a couple of hours ago."

I said, "They just gave it up, just like that?"

"Lewis, please, besides being what you call a pool shark, I'm a reporter first and foremost. I find things out. I work sources. And I worked Roy and Henry. We got to talking as I was kicking their asses, and in a pause in the action, Roy wanted to know what a pretty young thing like me was doing in a dump like that."

"Charming," I said. "And?"

"And I told them that you two guys were working for me, trying to find that son-of-a-bitch lawyer from Tyler who stole my widowed mom's money."

Felix said "Well played, Paula. Do go on."

"They said 'Really?' And I said yeah, really . . . and I added a few more choice obscenities after that, as well as a couple of well-placed teardrops. Then Roy said: well, don't you worry, there's a couple of other guys looking for him as well, and trust me, sis, they will find him. And when that happens, bet that fucker lawyer gets what's coming to him."

A tractor-trailer barreled past, shaking the Tahoe. "I asked them what they meant. Henry said that some guy out West had a real hard-on for this Tyler lawyer, and just a couple of hours ago, this guy and two guys from the Crawford Notch club—George and Billy—came in and went upstairs to talk to Phil."

Felix said "Well, isn't that sweet."

"Wait, it gets better," Paula said. "I said, gee, do you think they know where he is? And Roy, he said, well, I don't think so, 'cause the three of 'em came stomping out of Phil's office, with that guy from the West saying he didn't know anything much more than when he first got here."

I took that in, and so did Felix; and Paula, her voice quieter, said "Then I pressed it . . . maybe I shouldn't have . . . but I did. . . ."

"What did you do?" I asked.

She said, "I said, dear me, do you think that Tyler lawyer ripped off that guy from the West? And Roy said, no, hon, it was a family thing, an old family thing, and then he was going to say something else when Henry rapped the back of his head with his pool cue, and they both shut up, and we went back to the game."

"An old family thing," I repeated. "Mark was raised in Vermont, orphaned in Vermont, but has a Wyoming Social Security number, and a couple of weeks ago, he might have made a quick visit to Wyoming . . . and now he's got a biker after him. For something related to family."

Felix switched the turn indicator so it was blinking to let drivers know we were about to re-join traffic. "I think I know how to straighten this out," he said, tempered steel in his voice. "We go back to the club, we see Phil again, and this time he goes downstairs with me holding his pants and his shirt, my pistol to the back of his damn head . . . and I get him up on a table and he can start singing 'I'm So Pretty' from *West Side Story*."

"Don't," I said.

"What?"

"Don't. Phil thinks he outsmarted us, got us out of the club without knowing much. But now we do. We know Mark's being hunted due to a family matter."

"We go back to the Hog Heaven Fan Club, we can still find out what that's all about."

"Maybe, but that just alerts Phil as to what we know. And besides, knowing what's driving Reeve Langley, that doesn't help us get to our goal: finding Mark."

"But they're still looking!" Paula said.

I gave her a reassuring smile. "Paula, that's the best news of the night. What your pool players said to you. They said Reeve and the two local bikers, they went out, with Reeve saying he didn't know anything much more than when he first got here. That meant what they did to Carl Lessard . . . they didn't get anything useful out of him. Reeve and the others, they're still in the dark. They still don't know where Mark is."

Paula and Felix pondered that, and then Felix put the Tahoe in DRIVE, carefully checked his sideview mirror, and we went back on the road, heading east, back to the seacoast.

Felix seemed to choose his words carefully. "Paula, if they're still unsuccessful, then maybe it might be for the best for us to stop for a while. We might stir things up without knowing it, leading the bad guys right to Mark. If he's hidden well, that might be the best option."

Paula said "But there's a chance we might get to him first."

"A chance," Felix said.

"Then that's what I want to do."

"Fair enough," Felix said. "After all, you're paying the bill."

"What bill?" she said. "I just tried to give you a twenty-dollar bill."

Felix said, "Paula, please, don't confuse me with the facts."

CHAPTER ELEVEN

Back at Felix's house an hour later, we took a break, with Felix announcing we were all going to spend the night there. Earlier, we had stopped at Paula's place so she could pick up some clothes and such, and Felix and I escorted her in and out of her condo with no difficulty. There was a spare bedroom at Felix's that went to Paula, and when the time came, I was going to get a pull-out couch in the living room. Paula and I took turns in the shower—which I found refreshing, since it had been some time since I had taken a lengthy and hot shower—and with fresh clothes on, I felt closer to being human again.

Paula was dressed in gray slacks and a dark blue UNH sweatshirt, and her still-wet hair clung to her ears and to her neck. I joined her on high stools, sitting at the large granite counter in Felix's well-equipped kitchen, and he made us scrambled eggs with sweet Italian sausage on the side, along with thick white toast. Paula and I both declined coffee and made do with freshly squeezed orange juice.

Paula sliced at a sausage and said: "So, tell me, Felix, how did you ever hook up with a motorcycle gang an hour away?"

"Oh, past business dealings, you know how it is."

"No," she said crisply, "I don't."

Felix ate a piece of toast. "Are you asking me as a lovely young lady, eating in my fair house, or as a newspaper reporter, looking for a story?"

She looked over at him. "This is the finest meal I've eaten in days. Does that answer your question?"

"I guess," Felix said. "For a variety of reasons, once I moved up here from the North End, I had a bit of a reputation."

"An organized-crime reputation?"

He shook his head. "Not as organized as you would think. Which is one of the reasons I got out. You see, my dad was Greek, my mom was Sicilian. Which meant I was a half-breed. I would never, ever be completely trusted. But when I was young and full of energy and anger, I didn't care that much. The older I got, the more I realized that as a half-breed, to those running the show and their friends and allies, I was nothing more than cannon fodder, a hired gun. And if some pressure came down from the government or some other opposing force, then I'd be sacrificed, tossed aside, for the good of my supposed superiors."

Paula chewed thoughtfully and asked, "You ever kill anybody?"

I nearly choked on my orange juice. I had never, ever heard anyone directly ask Felix Tinios that question. In the years I had been friends with Felix, I had never dreamed of being so direct, even though I had seen him in bloody action more than once.

Felix's face was impassive. It was tanned, lean, with dark eyebrows and brown eyes, and blue-black stubble along his cheeks and firm chin.

Then his eyes narrowed and he leaned over the counter, keeping Paula in his steady gaze, and I felt like I was looking at a hunting bird, freezing a furry creature in place with its deadly eyes.

"Yes," Felix said. "I have killed. That I have."

Then a grin appeared and his eyes lit up. "But they were all very, very naughty men."

Paula allowed herself to smile and said "All right. But what's the deal with the Crawford Notch Boys? How did you ever work for them?"

Felix relaxed back on his stool. "Things . . . happen. Favors are exchanged. The word goes out that some hard men are needed to guard something. Other times a lesson in force has to be applied."

"Doesn't it bother you?"

Another question I was surprised was asked, and even more surprised when it was answered. He spoke slowly, reflectively. "A good question. It should, I suppose . . . but I look at my upbringing, look at who I am and what I was hard-wired to do. I don't do anything out of cruelty or spite. Before I do anything, I need to know . . . to my own satisfaction . . . that it fits some sort of purpose. Perhaps not legal, or particularly moral, but a purpose. . . ."

"Like providing protection to a motorcycle gang?"

He lifted up his glass of orange juice. "Like finding a missing attorney."

It was late at night. I was on Felix's pull-out bed, tossing and turning. The bedding was soft and comfortable, the sheets and the pillowcase freshly washed and dried, but I couldn't get comfortable. The thoughts of finding Mark Spencer were bouncing around up there in my mind, as well as the certainty that Hurricane Toni was grinding her way north, with my partially destroyed house squarely in its path.

"Hey, Lewis," came a whisper.

I sat up. "I don't think you have to whisper. What's up?"

She came over, sat down on the edge of the pull-out bed. There was a little light coming from the stove in the adjacent kitchen. She had on a long-sleeved dark green T-shirt. "Can't sleep."

"Then join the club."

"Thanks, I think I will."

Paula climbed in and I moved around, and she was on her back and so was I. Her breathing was soft and steady. "You've been good to me these past days."

"Thanks."

"You've really been there for me. Most guys probably wouldn't."

"I like to draw outside the box."

That caused a slight giggle, and she said "I just wish . . . I just wish we had something more to go on. What do we do in the morning?"

"Watch Felix make breakfast, and then get back to work. Maybe we'll check in with Hannah Adams. Or Kenneth, the admin aide. Maybe track down some of Mark's clients. The good news is . . . the bad guys still don't have a trail yet."

She sighed. "'Yet' being the operative word."

Paula squirmed in closer to me. I could feel the warmth from her body. "Speaking of bad guys, don't you ever get scared around Felix?"

"Sometimes . . . but it's usually the other fellow who gets scared."

"How in the world did the two of you ever become friends?"

I brushed her hand with mine. She didn't move. "We met years ago. I was trying to help a woman who had gotten scammed, and Felix politely told me to stop. I didn't. He told me again, a bit more insistent. Then I did a little research, tried to find out who he was and where he lived. After that happened, I went over to visit him, to have a meeting of the minds."

"How did that go?"

"Well . . . it started off with a bang. I shot out the tires on his Mercedes."

"Holy shit," she said. "Did you run off? Hide? Did he come after you later?"

"Nope," I said. "He opened the door, saw me standing there, saw his Mercedes, and then invited me in for a drink. We quickly resolved our issues, and we've been friends ever since."

"Still doesn't answer my question. Why?"

It was hard to concentrate with her next to me, the scent and closeness, the muscle memory of what it was like to be so very close to her.

"It made sense. We . . . were kind of a yin and yang, each of us supplying something that the other was missing in our lives. He supplying the cold-bloodedness that gets things done, me supplying the little brake of conscience that keeps him from going over the edge into anarchy."

"My, sounds like quite the bromance."

"You have no idea."

A few moments of silence. "You two . . . you're still going to find Mark, aren't you?"

"Without a doubt."

"Tell you a secret?"

"Absolutely."

"It's going to make me sound like a cold-hearted, mercenary bitch."

"Mercenaries always get the bad press. Go on."

"There's more to why I'm with Mark, besides the steadiness and the stability. It's the opportunity, the opportunity to get out of newspaper work and do something else."

I held her hand, squeezed it. She went on. "For as long as I can remember, I've always wanted to write, to tell stories. Newspaper work was a relatively easy way to slide into that after college. I mean, how many classified ads are there looking for an untested writer of fiction?"

"Not a hell of a lot."

"That's right. So I'm in newspaper work. There's been a lot of high points, a lot of fun, a lot of stories I wrote that made a difference, that told something important that needed to be told. But now . . . I'm tired of being a part of all the bad news, even if it's just reporting it. I want to do something else, but with my skills what else could I do? And newspapers are dying, Lewis. There may be something romantic about being the last buggy-whip maker or the last street reporter whose only tool is a notebook and pen, but I'm looking for a new start."

"What did Mark promise you?"

She squeezed my hand back. "Well put, Lewis. So here's my deep secret. Mark promised me that when we get married, and settled in, that he'd get a job at a better firm in Porter, that he'd put his state senate race on hold and give me a year . . . a golden year . . . to quit the *Tyler Chronicle*, to do anything I wanted. Make pottery. Write bad poetry or bad fiction. Or become a sexy hausfrau for him. Whatever I wanted . . . as long as it was being part of a new family with him."

I rolled over and kissed her on the lips, just a brief moment, bringing back not-so-brief memories, and then I rolled back.

She snuggled in with me. "What was that for?"

"Congratulations," I said. "For having a plan. For having a family."

We stayed still, until her breathing slowed, until I gently untangled myself.

I woke up with the rising sun in my eyes. It was quiet, just the sound of the waves, and of Paula breathing, rolled over on her side. I checked my watch. Just past six in the morning. I'm sure a lot of people were up and about this morning, but I wasn't about to join them. I settled back in, rubbed at my eyes, thought if I was lucky I could get back to sleep for another hour or so.

Luck. Paula and her missing fiancé. Both lucky to have each other, and he was lucky to have her in his corner, pushing hard to find him. I hoped he would someday appreciate it. I had spoken bravely to her a number of hours ago, but chasing down Hannah Adams and Kenneth Sheen was the proverbial grasping at straws. All other avenues had been closed, not much was out there, and I slowly slid into a doze, thinking about all those busy people out there, lots of them preparing for Turkey Day in a few days, and I had to decide if I was going to accept Diane's invitation or Felix's, but soon it was going to be the busiest traveling season of the year, all those folks going out on vacation, to a place of escape, to sunnier shores. . . .

To sunnier shores.

A place of escape.

I rolled over and pushed Paula on her shoulders. She grunted and I said "Wake up! Paula, wake up!"

She rolled over, her hair a mess, her eyes half open. "Sweet God, do you know what time it is?"

"It's six-fourteen A.M.," I said. "I need to know something. There was a photo of you and Mark at his condo. You were both in bathing suits. A vacation photo, maybe. Where was it taken?"

She yawned and rubbed at the back of her head. "At Lake Pettis. Up near North Conway. We rented a cottage there last July. Had our own private little island."

"Could Mark be there?"

Paula sat up. "No, not a chance. He hated it. He said it was too remote, too many mosquitoes, and if we needed coffee or a quart of milk we had to fire up the outboard and motor in to the town beach. Hell, I remember him telling everybody at the firm's Labor Day party about that rental, and I even got pissed at him, because it had been my idea. If there's one place he would go to hide out, it wouldn't be there."

I got out of bed, started getting dressed. "Sorry, Paula, that's the *best* place to hide out. Where no one expects you to be."

I went over to the hallway where Felix's bedroom was located and, from past experience, I loudly knocked on the door. Once before, when I had spent the night due to some unfortunate complexities involving a column I had been researching for *Shoreline*, I had opened the door without announcing myself, and was face to face with Felix sitting up in bed, aiming a shotgun at me. Later I asked him why he had a shotgun handy like that, and he had said, "Even with my skill set, I'm not sure what I could hit with a pistol if someone was coming in at me, but a shotgun at that range would never miss."

I waited a few seconds, and Felix emerged, wide awake, wearing a dark blue robe. I told him what I had discussed with Paula, and he rubbed at his chin, his fingers making a sound like they were going across sandpaper.

"Good call," he said. "I'm just impressed that Carl Lessard was able to keep that info away from Reeve and his pals, since he had talked to Mark."

"But he *hadn't* talked to Mark."

Paula was standing next to me, and I went on. "Carl told me that Mark had 'informed' him he was safe. Twice. He didn't say if Mark told him where he was, or where he was going. He was just informed. That could mean the phone ringing in a code, two rings and a hang-up, followed by another two and a hang-up. Carl would be able to keep Mark's whereabouts secret, but he still would know that he's all right."

Paula said "That . . . that makes sense."

"Yes," Felix said. "I like the sound of that."

He gently clapped his hands together. "All right, chillun, let's get dressed, have some crepes for breakfast, and head north."

"I don't think we have time for breakfast," Paula said.

"Of course we do," Felix said. "I made the crepe batter and it's been in the refrigerator all night."

By the time Paula and I were dressed and I had folded the bed back into a couch, Felix had coffee, orange juice, smoked bacon, and crepes ready for us to eat. Unlike last night, Paula and I eagerly took in the coffee, and Paula looked on as Felix worked a thin crepe pan, pouring the batter and expertly flipping them onto our plates, where he told us how to roll them up and spread maple syrup across.

Paula said: "Ask you a question?"

Felix scraped the last of the crepe batter out of the bowl with a bright red spatula. "Are you going to ask me how many times I hurt someone's feelings over the years?"

"No, it's just that you told me last night that you had a Greek father and Italian mother. We met yesterday at an Italian restaurant. You speak Italian. But crepes . . . they're not what you call a traditional Greek *or* Italian food."

Felix had a knowing smile on his face, looked to me, and I cut into a piece of bacon. "Felix is too modest to say so," I explained, "but he learned crepe-making during a previous trip to Florida, where he spent some time with two sisters from Quebec."

"Oh," Paula said. "Is that the only thing you learned from the sisters?"

"The only thing I can show in public," Felix said.

When we got outside to the Chevy Tahoe, the sun was well above the eastern horizon, and a few brave lobstermen were heading out on the cold waters to see what they could bring in. A hardy and somewhat nutty breed, if they were to fall overboard in the summer they could survive in the cold water for a reasonable amount of time, but on days like this their survival time was whittled down to mere minutes.

Yet they still went out.

Felix took out two long black duffel bags, and I knew better than to ask him what they contained. He put them in the rear of the Tahoe and came back to the driver's side. From across the Tahoe's hood, I said: "We'll be heading north, so I have a favor to ask. I want to stop for a few minutes to see Diane Woods at the rehab center."

Paula said: "Lewis, please—"

Felix interrupted. "It'll be all right. I need to top off the Tahoe's gas tank, pick up a few things, make a phone call or two."

"Really?" Paula asked. "Phone calls?"

"Sure," he said. "In order to get things done, Miss Quinn, sometimes you never know who you'll eventually have to talk to. That means we can drop off Lewis and run those errands, and then come back to pick him up." He eyed me. "That is, if he promises to be quick."

"Promise."

"All right, then."

In Room 209 at the Porter Rehab and Extended Care Center, I met up with Diane, who was sitting in a comfortable chair, out of her bed, a cup of coffee in her hand. As I walked in, I stopped, looked again, and she said "Mister Cole."

"Detective Sergeant Woods."

She said: "You halted for a moment when you were coming in. Something catch your eye?"

"I stopped because something *didn't* catch my eye," I said. "Your walker. It's not here."

She pointed to a curved metal cane leaning against a nearby radiator. "I have moved up in mobility and have graduated to the cane. Have a seat."

I sat on the edge of her bed. Just above the two of us, a television screen hung from the ceiling, showing either *Good Morning America* or the *Today* show. I couldn't tell, and I didn't think it made much of a difference.

Diane said: "Second things second, they're giving me a break this morning, thanks to my marvelous progress."

"Glad to hear that."

"Well, I don't expect you'll be glad to hear what I'm saying next, first things first," she said, the healing bruises on her face making her look that much more stern. "What the hell happened in Tyler yesterday, and did you have any part in it?"

I kept quiet, and she rolled her eyes. "For Christ's sake, if you need me to be more specific, then I will. There was a shooting near the town common yesterday. What few witnesses we have said a male driving a green Honda Pilot drove like a maniac through the near intersection, jumped out of his car, and popped off two rounds at a man driving a Chevrolet Suburban. The Pilot drove off, the Suburban drove off. The Suburban was later abandoned, two of its tires shot off. Care to know what happened to the Pilot?"

"It was reported stolen."

"Certainly," she said, "by you. Or someone claiming to be you. You haven't filed an official report at the station. What, you're planning to do it here?"

"You're still out on the disabled list, right? Then that doesn't make sense, now, does it."

Her eyes were hard and piercing. "Not too disabled to put that shooting together with what happened later last night. Poor Carl Lessard . . . tortured and then killed with two taps to the forehead. You know anything about that, Lewis? Or the fact that their law offices were torched?"

I didn't know about the arson at the law offices of Adams & Lessard, but, based on what I've seen and learned, it didn't surprise me much. It was like we were somewhat peaceful Europeans and woke one morning to find Mongols rampaging through our lands.

I kept quiet for another second or two, and then I said, "Boy, you're feisty this morning. Glad to see that."

I got off the bed and, before she could say anything or do anything, I kissed her on the forehead, then stepped back. "There are things in motion, concerning Mark Spencer. If I'm right, then it'll all be resolved by the end of the day."

"And the guy in the Suburban, and the murder of Carl?"

"Connected . . . but I don't have enough to tell you anything yet. But I'll gladly come back and tell you all, and then you can tell Captain Nickerson back at Tyler Beach that a guilt-ridden confidential informant called to confess all."

She picked up her cup of coffee, and her expression looked like she was tempted to toss it in my face. But then her internal struggle seemed to resolve itself, for she took a sip and put it down on the radiator, near her new cane.

"All right, then," she said. "My trust in you, friend, although battered and stretched, remains in place. And I do owe you my thanks for the pleasant nights' sleep I've been getting . . . so do what you plan to do. But don't embarrass me, don't embarrass the department, and for God's sake watch your head. And your ass. Are you alone?"

"No," I said. "I'm with Felix. And Paula Quinn."

"Really? Where are they now?"

"Out gassing up our transport, picking up a few items. They'll be back here in a few minutes."

"You really think so? You left Paula alone with Felix Tinios. For all you know, she's hijacked your transport and is driving to the nearest motel, begging Felix to give her riding lessons."

I smiled. "I don't think so. She seems to be resisting his charms."

"Oh. Then she hasn't switched sides, has she, and joined my winning team?"

"I don't think so."

She picked up her coffee again. "Strange days, my friend. Strange days." Then something on the television caught her eye. "Lewis, come on back here, you're going to want to see this."

I walked back and she toggled a remote that raised the volume. It showed the path of the approaching Hurricane Toni, and it looked like our stretch of New England was going to be smack-dab in its path.

"It's up to a Category Two now," she said. "They're calling it the Thanksgiving Day storm. First of its kind in a long time. How's your house?"

"With lots of holes in it."

"What are you going to do?"

"Going to find Mark Spencer today and then get the damn house fixed, even if it means selling my blood," I said.

"That's it? That's your plan?"

I turned and strolled out of her room. "Only one I got."

CHAPTER TWELVE

I t was a two-hour drive up to Lake Pettis, going on Route 16, and Felix dodged the two tollbooths in Dover and Rochester so that our progress wouldn't be recorded. For the most part it was a quiet drive, save for one time when we were going through a town called Ossipee—and it seemed like we were going through Ossipee for a long time—and we passed a restaurant that sold pizza. From behind me Paula sighed, and I said "What's up?"

"Oh, not much," she said. "But did you see that old farmhouse by the road, right past the pizza place?"

"No, I guess I missed it."

"That's the point, I suppose," she said. "A single mom was murdered there, for no good reason. Her boyfriend was in jail, she had sort of taken over his marijuana business, and one moron asked two other morons to help kill her and rob her. She was at the house, they slammed her in the head with a blunt object, tied and taped her up, and dumped her in a pond up in North Conway."

"Charming," I said.

"It gets better. No, it gets worse. Her little girl was left behind in her car seat, in the car, parked near the pond. The three idiots sent e-mails and text messages back and forth, so they were scooped up in no time. And the poor single mom . . . she didn't die from the beating. She died from drowning, after they tossed her in."

Paula looked out the rear of the Tahoe. "A simple, old, country farmhouse in the middle of quiet New Hampshire, and it was the scene of a murder that makes me queasy to even talk about."

Felix sped up the Tahoe. "No offense, Paula, but that isn't really the stirring 'let's go get the job done against all odds' kind of speech we could use right now."

"The truth is still the truth."

"Not if you ignore it."

Since it was late November, most of the gaudy orange, red, and yellow foliage had fallen from the trees, leaving bare, gray limbs from the ghost trees along the sides of the road. Route 16 was mostly two-lane, cutting right through the heart of the White Mountains. We slowed down some as we approached the outlet-mall oasis that is North Conway, and in a few minutes of skilled driving from Felix and skilled navigating from Paula, we passed through North Conway and were again in rural New Hampshire.

"Who picked Lake Pettis?" I asked. "You or him?"

"I recommended us finding a nice remote place for a vacation, and Mark took it from there. He said a client recommended it as a good vacation spot."

Felix said, "Maybe he was looking for another recommendation. To find a place he could use as a retreat if something happened. Like a Wyoming motorcycle gang going after his butt."

I knew Paula was tempted to say once again that her fiancé had nothing to do with Wyoming or a motorcycle gang, but she kept quiet as we went through downtown Pettis: a general store with two gas pumps, a town hall, a Grange Hall, and a Civil War monument.

"Quiet," I said.

"Too quiet, that was one of Mark's complaints."

A few more minutes of directions, and we were at the northern end of Lake Pettis. It seemed long and narrow, with the narrowest point being where we parked, along a stretch of road that actually had parking spaces outlined in yellow paint. We all got out and walked across the road. We were facing a sandy beach, perhaps a hundred feet wide. It was deserted.

A raft with a diving board sticking out had been pulled to shore, and a lifeguard station was on its side.

On either side of the beach, there was a rocky shoreline, which then curved out toward the lake, with cottages and small homes scattered among tall pine trees and a few leafless birch trees. There were docks that had been pulled in, and there were a few mooring floats still bobbing in the still lake water, and an orange-and-white buoy warning NO WAKE ZONE. Out in the distance were green lumps that were the lake islands.

I shaded my eyes with a hand. "Which island out there did you rent?"

"You see that big one on the left?"

"I do."

"It's on the other side. Cute place, small blue cottage, has its own private beach."

Felix kept quiet, just keeping his eyes on the empty water, the deserted road, and the quiet homes. Then he said: "Hate to raise an obvious point, but I don't see a way of getting out there. Paula? Did you two rent a boat, or did someone take you back and forth?"

"The owner of the cottage had a small Boston Whaler that came with the rental. The owner met us here at the beach when we came up for the first day."

"Is he around?" I asked.

"No, she's not," Paula said. "She said she had a rule every year, get up to the lake a month before Memorial Day, and leave for Florida a month after Labor Day. A true snowbird."

The lake looked so quiet, so empty, so lonely. I put my hands in my coat. "Folks, best I can come up with is for you two to take the left side of the lake, I'll take the right side. Start knocking on doors until we find someone who'll take us out there."

Paula said "No offense, but why don't I come with you, Lewis?"

"Because we need a boat. We don't need Felix scaring people."

Felix said "No offense taken, Paula. C'mon, you knock on the doors, and I'll be the strong silent type, hovering in the background."

From the beach I walked along the town sidewalk, until it ended just past the rocky shoreline. I walked along the side of the road for a few minutes and then came across a dirt road to the left that was unmarked, save for a tree trunk that had about a dozen brightly painted wooden signs running up its side, each sign carrying a name, like Munce or Gilligan or Troy. Down the dirt road I started, and I ignored the first two homes I came across, since they didn't directly abut the lake. The road curved to the left and the lake came back into view, with small homes and cottages lined up along the shore, one right after another. The first two cottages—one-story, stained dark, and with front porches—had planks of wood placed over the windows. Pretty clear sign that whoever resided there was gone for the winter. As I walked, I thought about what it might be like, to live on a lake. You wouldn't have the constant to and fro of the Atlantic, seeing the sun rise over the ocean and promise a new day, nor would you see the constant stream of boat traffic that reminded one that the biggest and most populous highways in the world are the oceans.

But a lake did have its advantages, once you got past the summer people who probably raised hell with big water-ski boats and JetSkis. The spring and fall when you had the place to yourself, along with the year-round residents. And the winter, when the lake froze and snow covered everything, with the only sounds being the occasional snowmobile and lake ice shifting.

Tempting, but I planned to stay with my own damaged place back at Tyler Beach.

If Hurricane Toni would let me.

The next place was a typical New England home, and nobody answered the door. The next cottage had wood over its windows, and the next home, a bright yellow Cape Cod, had an older man with dark green chinos and checked flannel shirt, raking pine needles out of his dirt front yard.

I stopped and he looked up at me, wearing a Red Sox baseball cap. His face was worn and wrinkled, but his eyes twinkled, like he found it so very amusing to be up and about and alive on this late autumn day.

"Hi," I said.

"Hey ya," he said back.

"Looks like some work you've got going on here."

He took in his tidy yard, with two birdfeeders and even a squirrel feeder. A freshly washed light red Chevrolet pickup truck with Maine license plates was parked in a dirt lot off the side of the road. "Well, it can take some doing. I rake up all these Christly pine needles to keep the place clean, and about a week later here I am, doing it again."

I nodded and said, "Sir, my name is Cole. Lewis Cole. I was hoping to take a quick spin out on the lake, but it looks like everyone's put their boats away for the winter."

He leaned on his rake. "True enough. About October the loons and such are heading out, and most people board up their homes, get them winterized, take their boats out. Why do you want to take a ride out on the lake? Can get pretty brisk out there on the water, and most of the foliage is gone."

"I came up here with a couple of friends of mine, and I live on the ocean, and I'd just like to take a boat ride out on the lake."

He scratched at his ear. "Would you leave your driver's license behind as a deposit?"

I reached for my wallet. "Gladly. I'd even pay you some money for the gas and the bother."

He leaned his rake up against a birch tree. "Ain't no bother. Just make sure you take her out, don't bang her up against any rocks, and for Christ's sake, don't drown. That'd mean me chasing down your estate to get reimbursed."

After handing over my driver's license, I followed him down a narrow dirt path that led to the side of the house that overlooked the lake. There was a second-story deck held up by metal poles, and underneath the deck some wooden furniture, a picnic table, and other odds and ends were stored. There was a stretch of canvas over a shape that he peeled off, revealing a small—and I mean small!—aluminum skiff. A couple of minutes fussing around with a small outboard motor and a gas tank, and I then helped him haul it down to the water.

"There you go," he said, pointing inside. "A life jacket you need to have, even if you're the best swimmer in the state, otherwise the Marine Patrol will write you a nasty ticket. There's also a paddle in case the motor quits on you, which it shouldn't, since it's a Mercury and I keep her in good shape."

"Thanks," I said, shaking his hand.

"The name's Pete Kimball," he said. "And where did you say you were from?"

"Tyler Beach."

"Hey, what a coincidence!" he said. "I had a guy here last week from Tyler, rented my big rowboat, same as you. Though he paid me some money 'cause he was going to keep it for a few days."

That got my attention. "He leave a name?"

Pete Kimball looked embarrassed. "No, but he left a couple of Ben Franklins, if you know what I mean."

"Sure," I said. "Tell me, was he a good-looking guy, maybe well-dressed, black hair, sort of with an expression like he just bit into a lemon?"

"That sounds pretty fair. A friend of yours?"

"Not on your life," I said, and Pete held the bow steady as I climbed in.

I switched on the motor, squeezed the fuel bulb a couple of times, and with two quick pulls of the starting rope the Mercury started right up. I flipped the control lever from NEUTRAL to REVERSE and backed my way out onto the lake, and then I flipped it into FORWARD and slowly motored my way back to the beach. The Tahoe was still there, and after I got within about fifty yards of the deserted sand, Felix and Paula emerged from the right. Paula elbowed Felix, and when I was sure the two of them were looking at me, I gave them a hearty wave. Paula waved back. Felix didn't. He's not one for waves.

When I was close to the beach, I flipped the engine back into NEUTRAL and gently bumped into the sand. Felix and Paula came down to me and Felix said, "Fleet's in, eh?"

"Sure is," I said. "And I'm here to tell you I'm off to your vacation spot. And it also looks like Mark is over there. The guy I rented this yacht from tells me a few days ago, a man from Tyler rented a boat from him as well."

"I want to come," Paula said, eyes bright with excitement and anticipation.

"I'm sure you do," I said. "But there's no room on this little tub."

"Then what's the point when you get there?" she asked. "If I can't come out there with you, then you can't possibly come back with Mark."

"I'll take his boat and tow this little tub back."

Felix said, "Paula, it's settled, and we're wasting time." He looked up and down the empty road. "Just because Mark's hunters aren't here yet, doesn't mean they won't show up in the next few minutes. Time's wasting."

Paula went to the bow of the little boat, shoved me off. "Go get my man," she said.

"I'll do my best."

I put the motor into FORWARD and, using the fixed tiller on the Mercury, I made a U-turn and *putt-putted* my way out to the main lake.

It was slow and peaceful, motoring out onto Lake Pettis. Save for a bass-fishing boat on the southern end of the lake, I pretty much had the place to myself. The water was relatively flat, although every now and then a wave would slap against the aluminum side, splashing me with cold lake water. I thought of the lobstermen I had seen earlier this morning, knowing the Atlantic was much colder, and that if I were to dump, I could probably swim to safety.

The farther out I went onto the lake, the more I made out the close peaks of the White Mountains. A perfect fall day, and there were just a few trees along the quiet shoreline where the colorful foliage was still hanging on, for whatever reason. Overhead there were some seagulls and some smaller birds I couldn't identify.

The motor was purring right along, the tiller slightly vibrating in my hand, and I turned to the left, heading to the large island Paula had pointed out. This part of the lake was shallow, and in looking down I could see huge boulders underwater, some covered with dark-colored algae, and I also spotted a couple of tree stumps, the exposed roots sticking out like some nasty and large spider.

I turned around, could make out the line marking the beach, the tiny shape of the Tahoe, and the even tinier shapes of Felix and Paula. I shifted more to the left and lost the beach from view. I slid past the large island, which had two good-sized homes with their docks pulled up, and no lights on or boats moored ashore.

The shoreline of the island petered out to a collection of above-water boulders; giving it plenty of room, I arced around in a large loop and spotted a smaller island to the rear, just like Paula had said. I went closer to the smaller island, slowing down the speed some, and at first I didn't see anything unusual, just a thick stand of trees with exposed rocks on the shoreline.

I swung around the island and a blue cottage came into view, with a short, fixed dock, and gently bobbing at the dock was an aluminum skiff twice the length of mine. There was a small sandy beach that I recognized from the photo back at Mark's condo, and I was surprised at the flash of jealousy that slipped through me.

I slid the engine into NEUTRAL for a moment, considering what was ahead of me, and then I put it into FORWARD again, heading to the island where I believed Mark Spencer was hiding out, on the run from a Wyoming motorcycle gang wanting to do him harm.

The closer I got to the dock, the more I backed down the motor, and when I was about six feet away, I put it into NEUTRAL and slid into the side of the dock, *bump-bumping* my way forward. I took a piece of rope from up forward of my rental, tied it off to a cleat, and worked my way up onto the dock.

I stood up, stretched my legs, rearranged my clothes, then checked out my 9mm, safe and secure in my shoulder holster.

I took a breath and then started walking, to find a missing person.

A person who didn't seem to want to be found.

There was a dirt path up to the blue cottage, and I took my time, not wanting to surprise or startle him. There were some low-growth blueberry bushes and ferns and saplings, and the cottage sat on a dirt lot, one story tall, with a screened-in front porch, and I walked around it. No sounds of a television or a radio.

I went back to the front porch, opened the door. On the front porch was some old wicker furniture, a card table, and a dark green throw rug on the wooden floor. The door leading to the interior of the house was closed, but it had a large window, which I peered through.

Nobody.

I knocked on the door.

Still nothing.

I tried the doorknob, and it opened easily in my hand.

I remembered the last time I had gone into a house with an unlocked door, and I was glad that I was here alone.

"Mark? It's Lewis Cole."

I went into the house.

⁊≋⁊

It was damp and dank inside. The floor was old cracked linoleum. There was a sagging couch to the right, a small kitchen area to the left. A refrigerator and stove that looked like it had been purchased when a president had once grandly announced that he was not a crook was in the far corner. There were plastic bags with recently purchased groceries on the counter. I slowly walked in, and I reached under my jacket, took out my 9mm Beretta.

"Mark?"

Two small bedrooms, beds neatly made. In one bedroom, there was a black roll-on piece of luggage, with a laptop set on top. The other bedroom was empty, as was a tiny bathroom in the rear.

I went back out through the cottage, holstered my Beretta, and stepped out onto the porch. From here I could make out the dock, my boat and the other boat, and a bit of the sandy beach. Time to tour the island.

I got off the porch, and a man emerged from behind a thick birch tree, carrying a shotgun, said shotgun's barrel poking into my chest.

I stepped back. Mark Spencer stood there, breathing hard, wearing tan chinos, a red L.L. Bean jacket, workboots. He had a four- or five-day-old growth of beard. His hair was messy and mussed, like he had just gotten up a minute or so ago.

"Cole," he said. "I'll be damned."

"Counselor Spencer, I presume," I said, holding my hands up in a reflexive move. Hard not to do with a shotgun about a foot away from my chest. "Mind pointing that somewhere else?"

His hard breathing continued. The shotgun didn't waver. "How the hell did you find me?"

"Trade secrets," I said. "Look, mind putting that shotgun down? You know I'm not the enemy."

"Really? What makes you say that?"

Enough was enough, and I took three hard and fast steps forward, got close to him, the shotgun harmlessly sliding past my ribs, and after slapping his face I grabbed and twisted the weapon away from him. I stepped back, now armed, and Mark stood there, shocked, hand up against his face.

"You didn't have to do that!"

"The hell I didn't," I said, checking the shotgun out. It was twelve-gauge, single-shot. I broke open the breech, retrieved the cartridge, snapped it shut, put the cartridge in my pocket. "I politely asked you twice to stop pointing your shotgun at me. You didn't move. I wasn't going to ask a third time."

Voice sullen, he said, "I wasn't going to shoot you."

"Of course not," I said. "But a sudden move on your part, a sneeze, a cough, or a stumble could cause you to pull the trigger, and you'd put a good-sized hole in my chest. It's not a particularly tough or muscled chest, but it works for me."

"How the hell did you find me?"

"Didn't you hear me the first time around? Trade secret. Now, not to get all pushy and such, but we've got to get you out of here."

Mark said, "Suit yourself. I'm not going anywhere."

"Oh, yes, you are," I said. "I've got Paula Quinn on the town beach, along with Felix Tinios, and—"

"What, Felix Tinios, the mob guy?"

"You can discuss his career options later," I said. "But right now, the Stonecold Falcons are hard on your trail, and if *I* could find your hidey-hole, so can they."

He swallowed and said: "I don't care. I'm . . . I'm doing something important, and I don't care if they're after me. I need to see it through."

I stepped forward, thinking about giving him another healthy slap or two. "Listen, nitwit, there's a woman back at the town beach who's been heartsick over you ever since you bailed out. And you're coming back with me, tell her you're fine, and then you can go on your death quest or whatever the hell it is you're doing. Do you understand, Mark? And what, I leave without you and you plan to hold off motorcycle gang members with a shotgun that holds and fires one round? Is that your plan? All right, you might get one shot off, but these are very hard men after you. They'll accept that one shot, and while you're trying to reload while breathing hard and your hands shaking, they'll rush you and then nail your testicles to a log . . . and then they'll really get angry. And whatever important crap you're doing, well, forget about it."

Mark's eyes flickered and he looked to the cottage, to the trees, and then to the waters of the lake. "Paula's back there? With Felix Tinios?"

"Yes," I said. "So gather up your gear, we'll head on back, and we'll drive off. Then you and Paula can have a nice reunion, you can tell her what the hell you're up to, and we can get away from the lake."

He shifted his feet, and I said, "Christ, Counselor, do I have to draw a diagram for you? I'm here to save your sorry ass . . . not because I particularly like you, but because Paula asked me. So you're leaving this island. Your choice if you leave free or tied up."

"You think you can tie me up? Really? An old man like you?"

I spun the shotgun around so it was rising up between his legs, and I managed to stop my movements before the metal barrel struck something near and dear to the town counsel of Tyler.

"Without a doubt," I said.

After I persuaded him to leave his groceries behind, we made good progress getting out of the cottage. He had his luggage and left the shotgun behind, since it belonged to the owner of the cottage. He locked the door and went around to the side of the cottage, where there was a brick foundation that had seen better days. Mark pulled a brick out and put the key inside, and replaced the brick.

"Breaking and entering, Counselor?" I asked.

"I had permission."

"Really? Permission to come here in November?"

He glared at me and started walking away. I joined him at his aluminum skiff and tied the smaller boat to the stern, so we could return both at the same time to the generous Mister Pete Kimball. I had a lot of questions to ask him, and probably a lot of information to pass along—from the death of Carl Lessard to the arson at his place of work—but he was up forward in the skiff, slumped, staring at the water and the surroundings, not at all looking like the arrogant and self-confident town counsel I had gotten to know over the past months.

Mark's rented skiff had a more powerful engine than mine, so we made good time, heading back to the town beach, and there was the Tahoe, and there was Felix.

But no Paula.

Well . . . maybe she was in the Tahoe, warming up.

Maybe.

But why was the Tahoe parked facing the other direction?

Mark lifted his head and was going to say something—

I yelled at him: "Put your head down! Now!"

Felix was on the beach, at the water's edge, something over his shoulder, and he gave me a long, sweeping wave.

Felix's not one for waving.

I turned the skiff around, the smaller boat bumping into us, and Mark asked "What's going on? What's up?"

"I don't know, but something's wrong."

When we were parallel to the beach is when it happened.

A black Honda CRV roared in from the left, braked to a halt by the beach. Three men bailed out and by now Felix was trotting up to the beach, unlimbering what he had over his shoulder, which was an H&K MP5 semi-automatic rifle. The three men were reaching under their coats and Felix was first, firing off a series of rapid three- and four-round bursts. The CRV's windshield and fender were pockmarked with Felix's outgoing rounds, and I completed the turn with the boat, slammed the throttle wide open.

We roared back out onto the open lake. I spared a glance back.

The Tahoe was gone. The CRV was still there, with the three men. Two were standing by themselves, but the third was looking out at us with binoculars.

I turned and lowered my head, but I knew it was too late.

Reeve Langley had spotted me.

CHAPTER THIRTEEN

To get out of view of the beach, I made a turn as quickly as I could, trying not to swamp our boat. Mark's face looked the color of the lake water, and he started stammering, trying to look behind me. "What . . . who . . . why was Felix shooting . . . was Paula there. . . ."

"Where's your car?"

"Hunh?"

"You didn't fly up here, Mark. You took your car. Where is it?"

He pointed. "Up there a bit. There's a house under construction, looks abandoned. I parked there and hiked over to where I rented the boat."

"All right, then." There were half-submerged boulders up ahead. I maneuvered to miss them, but didn't do a particularly good job of it. The smaller boat I was towing scraped up against a boulder with an ungodly screech.

"But what happened—"

"Out of order, Counselor," I said. "There'll be time to talk later."

Lots of questions rattling around, but I didn't want to get into a discussion of all that had gone on earlier. I wanted to get to Mark's car, get moving, get in contact with Felix, and then try to meet up . . . and find out what had prompted Felix to start firing off 9mm rounds so quickly.

I had no doubt that Felix had done the right thing. I just wanted to know why.

Mark turned and hunched his shoulders. Poor fellow. Just a week ago he'd been the lawyer for a prosperous town, had a nice little law practice, even considered a run for state senate, and was engaged to one of the finest women I knew.

Now he was a refugee of sorts, with a deadly motorcycle gang chasing him, depending for his safety on a Tyler Beach resident who didn't hold him in high esteem. Or low esteem.

"There," he said. "That's the house."

As he said, it was a home still under construction, though it looked like construction had started a couple of years ago. It was a two-story, built in the triangular Swiss chalet style. On its walls, old Tyvek siding was torn and slapping in the slight breeze, the plywood underneath dark from moisture and rot. Its shore was rocky, but there was a short, fixed dock where I maneuvered Mark's boat in close. Mark took the initiative to tie us off at the dock, and I switched off the engine.

We got off onto the dock and, carrying his luggage, Mark went up to the house. His light red Mazda 6 four-door sedan was pulled into a dirt rectangle near a couple of high rhododendron bushes, and he led the way. He unlocked the doors and I pulled out my cell phone, to find . . .

NO SERVICE.

"You know cell phones don't work around here?"

He looked surprised as he tossed his luggage into the rear seat. "Of course. That's why I didn't like it when Paula and I vacationed here. Too damn isolated."

"Then let's get somewhere so you can call Paula, tell her you're all right."

He snorted. "She can wait. I've got other things to do."

"I don't think she can wait."

"Look, I don't care how long it's been since you first met her, I know her best. All right? And I don't want to get into a big weepy conversation with her over why I left and why I haven't kept in touch. I don't have the time."

"You looking to piss her off?"

His smile wasn't pleasant to look at. "Lewis, if I told Paula to eat a shit sandwich, not only would she do so, she'd thank me for the meal. That's the kind of girl she is."

I stepped forward and punched him hard in the jaw. Mark fell back against the Mazda and slid to the ground, legs splayed wide open, his eyes wide open as well. I bent down, grabbed his shirt collar, lifted him up for a better angle, and hit him again, harder this time.

"Hey!" he gurgled. "Stop that!"

Breathing hard, I stepped back, shaking my right hand. It hurt like hell. I shook it again. It hurt even worse.

"Sorry," I said. "I shouldn't have done that."

"I guess the hell you shouldn't have!" He got up off the ground, rubbed his right hand against his face, worked his jaw once or twice. "All right . . . you snapped. I understand. Apology accepted."

I shook my hand again, trying to ease the red-hot pain coursing through it. "What apology? I said I shouldn't have done that, because I might have broken my hand against your thick skull. And I can't use a pistol with my left hand if we run into bad guys. That's the only thing I was sorry about."

He worked his jaw again, and I said "Time for some info, Mark. Why the hell did you run off like you did?"

"Because I was scared I had gotten the attention of the Stonecold Falcons."

"I guess the hell you did," I said. "And what did you do to get their attention? Run over a motorcycle while you were out west? Get in a bar fight? Send somebody a nasty letter, threatening a lawsuit over something?"

Mark rubbed his face again. "No, nothing like that. I was looking for someone from the gang. And the Stonecold Falcons found out who I was looking for and it got nasty, real quick. I didn't expect them to come out east after me."

"Who were you looking for?"

"My dad."

If Mark had told me he was the King of Belgium, I don't think I could have been more surprised.

"Wait . . . your parents are dead. Paula told me that. Your boss told me that. Google told me that. What the hell are you talking about?"

"My real dad, Lewis. From Wyoming. My parents, in Vermont . . . they were my adoptive parents."

He lowered his hand and I spotted something on his left wrist. A blotch or something I remembered from seeing the beach photo at his condo. I grabbed his wrist, pulled the shirtsleeve and jacket back so it became more visible. It was a splotch, about the size of a half dollar.

Mark pulled his arm away, lowered his shirt and jacket sleeves. I stood still, thinking, remembering, recalling what I had seen and heard.

"The Stonecold Falcons," I started out. "I've seen some of their tattoos, close-up and on the Internet. All of the members have the falcons tattooed on their wrists. 'Falcons for Life.' That's their motto."

Mark looked enraged and embarrassed at the same time. I went on. "The missing-persons report that Paula Quinn filed. It said you had no distinguishing scars or tattoos. What did you tell her that was?"

"A skin blemish, a birth defect."

"But that's not true, is it? Your father . . . pretty prominent in the Stonecold Falcons at the time, am I right? Pretty hardcore, I bet. So hardcore that when you came along, even as a young kid, he probably arranged to have a falcon tattooed on your wrist. 'Falcons for Life.' And later on, it got burned off."

He rubbed his wrist, probably self-consciously. I continued. "Your dad . . . you were probably told he was dead, right? But he was in witness protection, maybe after turning state's evidence against the gang. You were born in Wyoming, and for some reason, you kept your correct Social Security number when you came out to Vermont and became a Little League player, honor student. But as a youngster, before Vermont, you started out life as the child of a motorcycle gang member."

"Yeah, right, that's the story, best as I could figure it out," Mark said. "Look, can we get going? We're wasting time."

"And why are we wasting time . . . oh."

It seemed like the Mazda, the trees, the bushes, the half-completed home, and the angry face of Mark Spencer had all snapped into focus. "You're not on the run because the Stonecold Falcons found out you were the son of a gang member, someone who had betrayed them. You're on the run because you're looking for your dad. He's somewhere in this part of the world, and they want you to lead them to him."

"That's right," he said. "So let's go."

For some reason, I checked my phone again. Still no service. I held out my hand. "All right, so we'll go. Give me your car keys."

"Why the hell should I do that?"

I gestured back to the dock. "Those boats don't belong to us. They belong to Pete Kimball, and we're going to take them back . . . check that, *you're* going to take them back. I'll meet you at Pete's."

His face set in anger, he said, "Why don't *you* take the boats back and I'll meet *you* at Pete Kimball's?"

I went up to him, pried the keys from his hand. "Gee, because I'm afraid if I take the boats back there, you might take your car and get lost and not show up. I guess I'm just the suspicious sort. Now let's get down to the dock and I'll help you push off."

We both went to the dock, and I held the larger skiff steady as Mark got himself in. He said, "Suppose there are cops there at the beach."

"Ignore them," I said. "What, you want to volunteer that you saw something? Saw Felix open fire to protect you?"

He frowned, face red, and got the engine started. I undid the lines and he said, "I still don't know why we have to take these two boats back. It'd be just as easy to call him and tell him where they are."

I gave the prow of the skiff a healthy shove. "Because it's the right thing to do."

I stood on the end of the dock, waited until he maneuvered the boat, headed in the right direction, and then I walked up to his Mazda.

I got into his car, started the engine, winced as my sore right hand grasped the steering wheel. Yeah, I was sorry about injuring the hand I use to hold my Beretta, but that was about the only thing I was sorry for. I drove out of the space, went up a short dirt driveway, and a dirt road was in front of me. Left or right? I chose right.

The road was bumpy, not well maintained at all, and I passed three more uninhabited cottages before the road ended in a wide spot and a dirt berm.

"We chose poorly," I muttered as I backed up and turned around. I went past the three cottages again, past the chalet that was still in mid-construction phase, and then past two very large homes that looked out of place with their neighbors. The trees and brush thinned out, and then I came out onto a paved road and turned right, heading to the beach.

It only took a couple of minutes, and up ahead I saw the beach, and I saw a State Police cruiser, blocking the road, lights flashing, the state trooper standing outside of her cruiser, speaking urgently into a microphone. There was no Honda CRV in sight, so it looked like the bikers had made an escape. I slowed down, switched on the turn indicator, and then went down the dirt road I had earlier strolled on, looking for a boat.

This time I found Mark, standing in the middle of the dirt road, hands in pockets. I drove up to him, lowered the driver's side window. "Looking for a ride, sailor?"

"Hah," he said. "Very funny."

He started toward the passenger's door, and I said, "Hold on. Everything back to where it belongs?"

"The boats are tied up. Nobody's home. There was an envelope here with your name on it at the back door. Let's go."

I took the envelope, removed my driver's license, put it back in my wallet. I put the Mazda in PARK, switched off the engine, got out. "When you rented the boat, where was it? Was it at the dock?"

"No, it was underneath the guy's back deck. Covered with a tarp."

"Same with me. You saw how old he was. You think he can haul both boats up by himself?"

He turned and walked to the lake, and so did I.

About fifteen minutes later, my arms and hands sore—especially the right one—and with my pant legs sopped with lake water, and my earlier wounded right leg protesting at being overworked, we got back into the Mazda and went back up to the paved road, neither of us saying anything. At the intersection with the town road, I looked right, where the State Police cruiser had been joined by another State Police cruiser, and one from the sheriff's department.

I decided it was in everyone's interest to take a left.

I drove for a few minutes, and then took another state road, going off to the left. I had no idea where we were going, I just wanted to put distance between us and the shooting scene at the lake. In this part of New Hampshire, you can be fairly confident that anything called a "lane" or a "street" would eventually stop at a dead end. But those paved lanes called a "road" usually go on for a long while.

"Where are we going?" Mark said.

"Where the radiation is blooming," I said.

"Where the what is what?"

"Hold on."

I drove a while longer with my good hand, and with my sore hand holding my phone, and when a couple of black bars popped up, I pulled over to the side. There was nothing on either side of us save trees and brush and drainage ditches and, on the other side of the road, a crumbling stone wall.

"Time to find out where our friends are," I said.

I put the car in PARK and dialed Felix's number, and felt the sweet rush of relief when he answered after the second ring.

"Yeah."

All right, he wasn't being particularly charming or welcoming, but it was still good to hear that voice.

"It's me."

"Glad to know it. You alone?" he asked.

"Nope, the subject in question happens to be sitting right next to me."

"Breathing?"

I made it a point to look at my passenger. "Yep. Though God knows why. Is the lady in question available to take a call?"

"Alas, no," Felix said. "We're at a small gas station in . . . hell, I don't know where. Could be Maine. She's in the restroom. I think she's having a reaction to what went on, but she told me she just wanted some privacy."

"Fair enough," I said. "Will you tell her that her man is alive and sort of well?"

"Gladly. Then what?"

I took a look at Mark, his flushed face, the marks on his skin where I had struck him. If I'd had my choice or been in a grumpier mood, I would have slipped him twenty bucks, told him to find a Greyhound bus to take him home, and then stolen his car.

"Take Paula somewhere safe," I said. "I'm involved in something that should be wrapped up in a day or two."

"You really think?"

"I really hope," I said. My right hand was really hurting. "Tell me, what happened back at the beach?"

"We were waiting there, like we were supposed to," Felix said. "Then this CRV slowly rolled by. They were eyeing us and then stopped. One guy came out, and I recognized him as somebody connected with Phil Tasker's motorcycle club, and he asked me for directions to North Conway, and I told him I didn't know. He went back to the CRV and drove away. I told Paula to get into the car and I retrieved some . . . equipment."

"Then we popped into view."

"Quite. The CRV did a U-turn and came back, and after I waved you off . . . you saw what happened next."

"Thanks."

"Just part of the service, ma'am," he said. "If you don't mind my asking, now what? Is it time to get these two star-crossed lovers together tomorrow or the day after that? Don't forget, Thanksgiving is chugging down the pike."

My hand ached even more. Mark was looking out the windshield, arms crossed, keeping his own thoughts to himself. I waited. Thought of what he had just said back at the half-built cottage.

"We're going to hold off for a bit," I said. "Seems like the man in question has a quest to fulfill. I help him get that wrapped up, then we'll set a time and place for a lovely reunion."

"Your call," Felix said. "Hey, Paula's coming out of the restroom. You want her to have a few words with her best boy?"

"No," I said, and I disconnected the phone.

I shifted in the driver's seat. "All right. You're looking for your dad. I can understand that."

His voice was bleak. "Do you? I was raised by a couple that I thought were my real mom and dad. And when they died in a car crash, I cried . . . I mourned . . . and I was now an orphan, with no family."

A thunder flash of a memory, in college in Indiana, receiving a late-night phone call at a pay phone in my dormitory, getting the call about a commuter plane with my parents aboard, circling an airport, waiting to land, until unexpected ice on the wings flipped the aircraft over and drove it into a farmer's field.

"I know what it's like," I said.

"I doubt it."

I restrained my right hand once again. "Then go on. How did you find out about your real father?"

"A client of mine," Mark said. "Jack Baker. I helped him on a probate matter a couple of months ago, when his grandmother died. An odd guy . . . knows cyberspace and the dark Internet like his own basement. Even did a thorough background check on me after I started representing him, like he wanted to make sure I was really a lawyer or something. We got to talking after his case was resolved, and he started asking about my life in Wyoming. I told him he was mistaken, that I had never been there, hadn't even been born there. But he was an odd one, wouldn't let it go, no matter how many times I told him otherwise."

"Didn't you figure you had a connection with Wyoming with your Social Security number?"

A shrug. "My Vermont parents . . . my adoptive parents . . . they told me it was a foul-up with the Social Security Administration and not to bother with it. Hey, your parents tell you something like that, you just go on and put it behind you. But when I met up with Jack Baker, he kept on telling me something different. He calls himself one of the new mole people, the kind that loves to dig and root around, find obscure information, just for the hell of it."

"Why did he decide to check you out?"

"Like I said, Lewis, he's an odd guy. If he asked you if it was raining, and you said no, he'd spend ten minutes on the Web, trying to see if you were lying or not."

"What did he find out?"

"My real dad . . . his name is Will Mallory. Worked construction in and around Cheyenne, was active in the Stonecold Falcons. Nearly thirty years back, he was the vice president, got hooked up in a smuggling charge and attempted murder, and flipped on his fellow gang members."

"What else?"

"Not much. My mom . . . she divorced him about the same time, then got cancer and died, and WITSEC promised her to put me someplace safe. Which was Vermont."

"So your real dad . . . where is he?"

"Someplace close. Jack Baker promised me he'd have the info by today, maybe tomorrow at the latest. Please, can we go?"

I started up the Mazda. "You know how to get there from here?"

"I do."

"Then lead on."

CHAPTER FOURTEEN

I followed Mark's directions and we ended up in a small town called East Conway, right next to the border with Maine. It was quite rural, with lots of bare trees silhouetted against the graying sky, and I drove slow and gentle, always keeping an eye on the rearview and sideview mirrors, ensuring we weren't being followed by a shot-up CRV.

"How much longer?" I asked.

"Five minutes or so," he said.

Up ahead on the slight country road was a grassy area on the right, with a small pond in its center. I slowed and pulled over, putting the Mazda in PARK and switching off the engine.

"All right," I said. "Let's stretch our legs, have a come-to-Jesus moment."

"I don't need to stretch my legs."

"I do," I said. "And since I have the car keys and a pistol, that's what we're going to do."

Outside, the air was crisp and sharp and I had a thought of that huge hurricane, barreling its way up the East Coast, knowing just how vulnerable my damaged house was, hunkered down on Tyler Beach.

The area around us was flat farmland with mountains in the distance. Mark came around to me and said, "What do you mean, a come-to-Jesus moment?"

"What, you don't know the name of the person a good chunk of humanity believes came to Earth to be our redeemer?"

"Stop being a pain in the ass."

"I'll give it a try, as soon as you unfocus that thick head of yours."

"Hunh?"

I turned to him. "Cheyenne, Wyoming. What happened there, on your trip out west with Paula?"

"How did you know I went to Cheyenne?"

"You had the means and opportunity and a number of missing hours. Give me some credit for puzzling you out, Mark. So what did you do, go to your dad's hometown, sniff around, ask some questions?"

"That's what I did."

"What did you find out?"

He crossed his arms, stared down at the leaf-covered ground.

"Let me guess," I said. "Not so many fond memories of your dad, decades later. You got scared. You left like your butt was on fire."

"Yeah."

"Yet your info mole kept on working. Found a New England connection with your dad. So it wasn't a wasted trip. But the Stonecold Falcons probably tracked you down, didn't they, a small-town New Hampshire lawyer. You probably got word they were snooping after you, and that's when you bailed out, without telling Paula or damn near anyone else."

"Yeah."

Not very forthcoming, but I wasn't expecting much. So I changed the subject. "Carl Lessard."

"What about him?"

"He's dead."

He seemed shocked, like the soil underneath him had suddenly wavered, shifting his center of gravity.

"When?"

"Yesterday."

"Sweet God . . . what happened to him?"

Off in the distance, three black horses slowly moved around in a fenced-in field, occasionally stopping to graze. I wished I could have stayed here in this spot and done nothing but watch them for hours.

"Murdered," I said. "No doubt by the Stonecold Falcons."

"How?"

"Does it matter, Counselor?" I took my hands out of my coat pockets, breathed into them. "Before he was murdered, I met up with him, and he told me that you were safe. He didn't say he'd talked to you, he didn't say where you were, but he did say you were safe."

Mark turned away, wiped at his eyes. I said, "What was it? A phone code? A call made at a special time each day?"

"Yeah. Once at eight A.M., and again at six P.M. Two rings, and then I would hang up. If he didn't hear from me for two calls in a row, then he'd go to the cops and tell them about me and the Falcons."

"Nice setup," I said. "So Carl knew about your background, and about the Stonecold Falcons, and you set up a way to protect yourself in case somebody came knocking. Unfortunately for him, you didn't figure out a way to protect him."

He wiped at his eyes again. "What, you think I'm happy?"

"I don't know. Are you? What I do know is that the Stonecold Falcons didn't just waltz in and ask him politely, and then shoot him when he couldn't give you up. Because he didn't have anything to give up. But the Falcons were persistent. They tied him up on his bed spread-eagle, and tortured him, and tortured him, and when they were bored, or exhausted, or decided he really didn't have anything to say, they shot him."

"I don't want to hear any more." He took a couple of steps away from me.

"Ah, but you have no choice, Mark," I said, following him. "Carl told me the exact minute and day that he was going to retire from the law and live out his life in leisure down in Florida. Instead of that, he ended his life on his own bed, terrorized, being worked over by a mad biker from Wyoming."

He whipped around in my direction. "What the hell do you want me to do? Hunh? Okay, it's my fault! I'm sorry! I'm responsible for his death. That make you happy? Is that what you wanted to hear?"

I said, "Doesn't make me happy or unhappy. And it's not what I wanted to hear."

"Then tell me what you want, damn it!"

I took three steps up to him, so there was no doubt I was in his face. "I want you to think hard. Really hard. Like you were taking the bar exam hard. Is this worth it? Getting your co-worker killed, upsetting Paula and putting her in danger, is it worth it all to make peace with a father who practically abandoned you years ago?"

"You don't know if he abandoned me!"

"True enough; but I'm looking at the evidence, Mark. If he's in WITSEC, he sure as hell didn't seem to be spending a lot of time looking for you."

A nasty comment for sure, and I wished I could say it bothered me. But it didn't.

"So think that through. And one more news flash, Mark, is that your offices had a fire in them yesterday. Some coincidence, eh?"

"What about Hannah? And Kenneth?"

"From what I know, they're all right . . . for now. But I repeat myself. Is it worth it? Or does it make sense to wrap this up, go back to Tyler and the police and let it all out about what happened, and let the cops worry about it?"

He stood silent, arms crossed, one foot moving back and forth, back and forth, brushing against bright yellow and red leaves. "I have to do it."

My turn to keep my mouth shut.

Mark's voice was quiet. "My adoptive parents . . . they did their best, I guess. But they were always distant, not really . . . not really seeming like they had bonded to me. Lots of kids, their adoptive parents are a miracle, better than any biological parent. I understand that. I respect that. Maybe my circumstances were the outlier, the one percent. For me . . . they were cool and proper. Not warm and loving."

"Did you know you were adopted?"

"No . . . not until after they were killed in a car accident. Can you imagine that, Lewis, living your entire life as a lie? Not knowing, until after the man and woman you thought were your mom and dad were in the ground, that they were fakes?"

"They weren't fakes. They were your real parents."

"To me . . . they were fakes . . . and I couldn't find anything about how I had ended up in Vermont, or who my real parents were, until I got Jack Baker as a client. Do you understand? For years I thought I was alone, an orphan, a cast-off. Now . . . I'm this close"—and he made a gesture with two fingers—"to finding my real dad. In getting a second chance . . . not to be an orphan anymore. I can talk to him, learn about him and my mom, find out what he's been doing all these years. I mean, it's pretty nutso, don't you think, that all these years we've been apart, we've been in practically the same neighborhood?"

"You can still go to the cops."

"Please . . . how many hours or days would be wasted in telling them the story, convincing them what's going on? And with those hours and days, what's the chances that the Stonecold Falcons would get there before me, or the cops?"

He shook his head. "So, to finally answer your question. Yes . . . it's worth it. As cold and shallow as it sounds, it's worth it."

We stood quietly, and then he said, "But I'll tell you this. Once we meet up with my dad and get him someplace safe, then I'll go to the cops. And make it right with Paula. I promise."

I took a deep breath of cold air. We had listened to the news on the way over here. We were two days away from Thanksgiving, which coincidentally was about the same timeframe for when Hurricane Toni was going to hit New England. Time, time, time, and I didn't have much of it left.

Other thoughts battled for attention. The memories of quiet and intimate moments with Paula. Darker thoughts of being at a graveyard in rainy Indiana, two caskets, side by side, a voice echoing in my head, *you're alone, you're alone, you're alone.* Those quiet moments at my house, before it was crippled, sitting by myself on my rear deck and just yearning for more out there than casual friends or lovers.

Lots of thoughts.

"Very well, Counselor," I said. "Let's go meet your mole and find your dad."

But then a surprising delay came my way. My cell phone rang, and in flipping open the cover, I didn't recognize the caller. Any other time, I would have ignored the call, but this wasn't any other time.

"Hello?"

"Mister Lewis Cole?" came a gravelly voice.

"The same."

A soft chuckle. "So we finally meet, bro."

I'll be damned.

"At least over the phone," I said. "So how's your day going, Mister Langley?"

Another laugh, like he had all the time in the world to find things to amuse himself. "Jus' fine, jus' fine," said the head of the Stonecold Falcons. "Got a moment to spare?"

Mark looked at me wide-eyed, whispering questions to me, and I held up my hand to him. I leaned against the Mazda's right front fender. It was warm. "Absolutely, and I have to say, I'm impressed that you found out my phone number. I was led to believe by my carrier that it was unlisted."

"Then maybe you should ask for a refund," Reeve said. "Truth is, a lot of smart fellas like to ride, even tech types, and they like to do favors for other guys who ride."

"Good for you."

"Now, speakin' of favors, how about you do me one and let me know where and how I can meet up with Mark Spencer? What's between him and me is personal, and there's no reason for you to get caught in the middle, all innocent like."

"Mmm," I said, crossing my legs. "He's not the most personable man I've ever met. After spending some time with him, that's a very attractive offer."

In a panic, Mark came closer to me, and I brushed him off again with my free hand.

"Sure is, and let me sweeten the deal," Reeve went on. "You've pissed me off twice, by shooting out my tires in Tyler, and by squirreling the little bastard away right underneath my nose, with a friend of yours shooting it out with me and my buds. In my world, that calls for me to take drastic action. But I'm in a good mood, despite all this shit, so I'll leave everything alone, let bygones be bygones, the moment you turn him over to me."

"That's a good sweetener," I said. "But the other day you were in the process of kidnapping a friend of mine. I take that very seriously."

"Hell, I wasn't gonna hurt her," he said, voice shocked, like I was accusing him of undertipping a waitress. "I was jus' gonna try to talk some sense into her, find out where Mark Spencer was hiding out. That's all. She was a fine piece . . . I wasn't gonna do a thing to her. Whaddya say, do we have a deal?"

"Not sure, Reeve," I said. "I'm afraid you're pretty low in the trustworthy tank. I can't get the thought of Carl Lessard being butchered, and those law offices being torched, out of my mind."

His voice changed so quickly it was like another man was talking to me, for the voice was darker, more urgent. "Cole . . . I've been forthright, and I've been patient. But by God, you're gonna do what I tell you, and give up Mark. I hear you're an educated fella, know books and magazines and shit, but believe me this, you don't know shit. In your deepest, darkest, scariest nightmares, you can't even come close to what I will do to you if you don't give up that shithead lawyer. Other guys might talk about knives and razors and fire, but that's nothing compared to what I will do to you. You understand me now? Do you?"

"Reeve, I certainly do," I said. "Thanks for enlightening me."

I could hear him take a satisfied breath on the other end of the phone. "Good."

"I think I'm going to change my mind."

The soft chuckle from before had returned. "Good again."

"All right, here's what we're going to do. We'll meet someplace public, grab a cup of coffee, and then you tell me, man to man, face to face, how we'll settle this so I'm not in danger, nor Mark's fiancée. All right? I'm going to need some sort of guarantee before telling you where to pick up Mark."

"Sounds righteous," Reeve said.

"Glad you like it," I said. "Now, do you know where I am?"

"No."

"Good," I said, and I hung up on him. Mark was motionless, not saying a word, as I turned my phone over, removed the battery and then the SIM card. I broke the SIM card in half and then tossed everything in the pond.

"Now you owe me a new phone," I said, walking back to the Mazda.

CHAPTER FIFTEEN

We drove on for another five minutes or so, until we stopped at an unmarked dirt road that led off to the right. Old stone walls were on either side. There was no mailbox at the end of the dirt lane.

"He's down this road?" I asked.

"Yeah," Mark said, still looking pretty shook up after hearing my end of the conversation with Reeve Langley. "At the end of the road, a few hundred yards from here."

I kept the Mazda parked, engine running. I looked around. This road was very narrow, barely enough space for one car to pass another, and the woods were deep and dark.

I didn't like it.

"Hold on for a sec," I said, and I got out. I took out my Beretta, made sure there was a round in the chamber and the safety was off, and I also checked the two spare magazines I carried with my holster. From inside the Mazda, Mark had leaned over the driver's seat to see what I was doing.

I got back into the car. Mark said, "Seems like a bit over the top, don't you think? Jack Baker's about the quietest guy I know."

"You know him, but I don't," I said. "So don't be upset if I don't take your word for it. And Reeve Langley and associates knew what part of

Lake Pettis you were hiding out at. What, you think they were doing a late-foliage tour and stumbled over us by mistake?"

"I guess not."

"Plus they had gotten my unlisted phone number. Which means they're skilled in hunting. So I'm not assuming we're driving into anyplace safe." I shifted the Mazda into DRIVE, turned, and went down the dirt road. "And neither should you."

I drove for a short distance, the backs of my hands and neck warm and tingling, and I was pleased to see a spot at the side of the road where somebody had dumped a load of dirt—maybe in prep for tearing out some trees and making a foundation—but the place was big enough for what I wanted. I stopped, put the Mazda in REVERSE, and parked it there, shutting off the engine.

"Time for a walk," I said, stepping out. "Want to see your pal Jack nice and quiet. No need to announce we're coming."

Mark got out and said "Hey, you're leaving the keys in."

"You bet."

"Suppose somebody comes by and steals it?"

I gave him a look. "Please. Where's the bustling crowd of would-be car thieves out there, Mark? And suppose you and I are at Jack's house, something goes wrong, and we're hauling ass back to the car. You want to waste an extra thirty or so seconds, grabbing car keys, putting them in the ignition?"

Mark gave me a look in return. "Paula's right. You've had an interesting life."

I started walking. "You have no idea."

It was a perfect fall afternoon for a walk, but I made note of the time and where the sun was setting. Years ago I had been up in the White Mountains with Paula Quinn for what we expected to be a brief hike, but I had misjudged the length of the trail and how long it would take us to get back to the trailhead. If we had gone up in July, we would have gotten back with no problem. But hiking in October, like we had, meant a half hour of some tough trail walking with the aid of a tiny, flickering flashlight, with no overnight gear to keep us warm when the temperatures fell.

Lesson learned.

The road ended in a wide spot, a mix of dirt and thin grass. It took me a few moments to take in the home of Mark's information mole, Jack Baker. It looked like the fevered dreams of an architectural student, realizing he was one class project away from failing. There was a mobile home—or a pre-fabricated housing unit, depending on your point of view—next to a wooden yurt that looked like it had been airdropped in from Outer Mongolia. Two other small buildings, about the size of my garage before it had become rubble, were attached to the side of the yurt. A metal chimney came up through the roof, from which a tendril of gray smoke eddied up into the November air.

A mud-splattered black Jeep Wrangler was parked to the side. It had two bumper stickers: one said MY OTHER VEHICLE GOES AT WARP SPEED, and the other said I BRAKE FOR BYTES.

I tugged my jacket open, just touched the handle of my Beretta. "Does this place look okay? That his Wrangler?"

"Yeah, that's his Jeep."

I scanned the yard and surrounding woods. Some time ago, the woods had been thinned out, and it looked almost pastoral, like this tumble-down group of buildings had been placed next to a Disney nature preserve. I didn't spot any other vehicles, didn't sense anybody out there lurking to do us harm.

"This guy is supposed to be high-tech, all the tools of the trade to go romping around the Internet?"

"That's right."

"Where are the power lines?" I looked up the road and back to the yard. "I don't see any solar panels, or a fission reactor anyplace near. So where does he get his power?"

"Jack's a smart one," Mark said. "He paid to have the power lines to his house placed underground, narrow the chances of losing power in a snow storm or ice storm."

"That's pretty pricey."

"He's got the money."

"Yeah, I see him splurging on his real estate. Come on, I'll let you make the introductions."

By climbing a creaking set of splintered stairs, we went up to the nearest door, which was on the side of the not-so-mobile home. Mark knocked on the door, yelled out "Hey, Jack! It's Mark. You in there?"

It was crowded where we were, so I went back to one of the lower steps, leaving Mark between me and the door. Maybe I was just making room, or maybe I was using Mark as a shield in case someone large and mean showed up in the door.

Who knew?

As we waited, I started imagining who this Jack Baker was. I was thinking of a large, bulky guy, beard down to his waist, wearing patched jeans and a Star Trek T-shirt, with all the grooming and hygiene skills one would expect from living as a hermit in these deep woods.

The door opened up. A slim young man opened the door. He had on pressed khakis, brown penny loafers, a hand-knit blue and white turtleneck sweater, carrying a cup of tea with the tea bag still in it. He was about ten years or so younger than me, with short brown hair and bright cheery eyes behind horn-rimmed glasses. He looked like an accountant who was happy that his daily danger quotient only extended to the odd paper cut.

"Hey, Mark, come on in," he said, opening the door. "Who's your friend?"

I stepped inside the trailer, found a warm, comfortably laid-out interior, with ivory carpeting, contemporary couches and chairs, and not a single velvet painting of Elvis hanging off the wall. The Beretta at my side, beneath my coat, felt awkward, heavy, and out of place.

It was turning out to be a day of stupid assumptions on my part, and surprises on other people's parts.

Once we were inside, Mark made the introductions and I shook Jack Baker's outstretched hand. It was smooth and warm. It didn't feel like he had spent much time chopping the wood that he used to heat his home.

"Come along," he said. "Let's see what I got for you."

From the rebuilt and well-designed mobile home trailer, Jack led us into the yurt. In the center was a woodstove with a glass door, and inside were the hot orange coals of burning wood. The stove was on a round stone base, and the metal chimney ran up to the high-pitched roof of the yurt.

Curved couches hugged the walls of the yurt, save for one side, which had a curved wooden desk that looked handmade. On the desk were three large computer monitors, and before the desk was a high-tech-looking chair. There were bookshelves, comfortable chairs, and a very large television on the other side. Small porthole-type windows looked out at the surrounding scenery.

He sat down at his high-tech chair, turned it around to look out at us. Mark took one chair and I took another. A black-and-white cat emerged from behind the woodstove, came over and sniffed Mark's feet, and then rubbed up against my left leg. I rubbed its head and saw it only had one eye.

"Bailey," Jack said. "Don't disturb our guests."

The cat yawned and then trotted back to the warmth of the woodstove. "Can I get either of you gentlemen something to drink?"

I looked to Mark and shook my head, and he said, "No, we're fine. Jack, look, how close are you to getting the information about my dad?"

Jack lazily crossed his legs. "It's taking some time, Mark." He gestured to the three monitors. "Like I told you before, it's not like I'm trying to hack a department store or the local DMV. I'm diving deep into some very secure, very dark, very dangerous waters."

"I know that, but—"

Jack talked over him and went on. "The names and addresses of people in the Witness Protection Program are kept in some of the more secure computer storage systems in the world, and you can't go at it with a sledgehammer. You have to be gentle, quiet, seductive . . . and sometimes you have to hire allies, hackers from other parts of the world, to do a little nibbling from their locations so alarms don't go off. It's like seeing a series of fishing lines stretched across a corridor, and you have to step around them, through them, and underneath them without touching a single fiber."

He took a sip from his tea cup. Mark said slowly, "I appreciate that, Jack. I really do. You're the best I've ever heard of, but . . . please. I've come a long way."

"I know you have," Jack said, his voice chipper, then giving his attention to me. "Tell me, what do you think of my little rural paradise?"

"Seems rural, seems warm. Depends on your definition of paradise, I suppose."

"True enough, but it works for me." He gestured to the terminals with his tea cup. "I have this wonderful, private little homemade home. About fifty acres of land and forest that belong to me. Private well, plenty of firewood, backup generators and batteries for power. Extreme privacy, with not even the post office knowing what I do here. I'm connected to the world—and even the International Space Station, and I hope you can keep that a secret—and with cutouts and anonymous re-mailing services, only a trusted few get to know I'm here. A perfect arrangement."

With a self-satisfied smile, he took another sip. I looked to Mark. His fists were clenched and it looked like he was about to cry.

Time for an intervention.

I said "Jack, that's all delightful and such, but as Mark pointed out, he's in quite the hurry, and so am I. So where is his dad living?"

"Mister Will Mallory?"

"That's the name," I said.

With a shrug of his shoulders, Jack said: "I don't know."

CHAPTER SIXTEEN

W hat!" Mark exclaimed, leaning out of his chair. "You told me that you'd have that information today . . . that it was going to all come together."

Jack didn't look upset at all. "It is. I always keep my promises. But, Mark . . . it'll be here in a few hours, but it's going to cost more."

"You didn't say that."

"That was then, this is now." A slight, almost apologetic shrug. "As I said, this kind of work is very delicate. I needed to call in additional resources, additional allies. That means additional expenses. Sorry."

Mark's face was flushed. "You didn't tell me it was going to cost any more. You promised the information for a flat rate. That's what you promised."

"Circumstances change," Jack said. "The information is coming my way in . . ." and he checked the time on the nearest monitor ". . . two hours. Whether it goes to you or to my trash bin is up to you. And another five thousand dollars."

"Jack . . . please . . . I'm tapped out," Mark said. "I emptied my savings, did a cash advance on my Visa, and even cashed out my IRA. I don't have anything more."

Jack didn't say a word, just kept on smiling. Mark put his hands together in his lap, folded them tight. Not a word was exchanged.

Enough.

I spoke up. "He's squeezing you, Mark. He has you by the legendary short hairs and is going to strip you clean."

Mark was really choking back tears now. "Is that true?"

Jack looked quite content, like a poker player keeping a tranquil face with four aces in his hand.

"I prefer to say it's just business, that's all," Jack said. "No offense."

"Would you take something from me?" I asked.

Both Mark and Jack seemed surprised, Mark most of all. Mark said "Lewis, please, I appreciate it, but—"

I held up my left hand. Mark quieted down. Jack still looked tranquil. I reached back, took out my wallet, removed something, and passed it over to Jack. He took the rectangular piece of cardboard and examined both sides.

"*Shoreline*?" he asked. "You're a magazine columnist?"

Not really, but he didn't need to know the ins and outs of my current employment situation. But remembering my Catholic school upbringing, I was going to do my very best.

"That's what the card says, right?"

He looked at it again, like he was trying to puzzle out some sort of hidden secret. "Very cute. But anybody can go to a print shop and have business cards made up." He flipped it back at me, and I let it fall on the floor.

I passed him something else from my wallet, and I said "A bit harder to fake this, don't you think?" "This" was my official press pass from the N.H. Department of Safety, and it had my photo, stats, and my affiliation with *Shoreline*. Thankfully, the Department of Safety doesn't do an active survey of the press passes it issues, so mine was still in effect.

I said, "Looks pretty official, doesn't it? Not something a local Kinko's can put together for you in an hour or so."

That got his attention. Mark kept quiet. Bailey the cat wandered out and flopped himself on his side.

"The thing is," I went on, "as a magazine writer, I'm always looking for story ideas. And lo and behold, here we are, with you, in this unique outpost of an Internet genius that has connection to the world and is heated by a woodstove. Don't you think that'd be a great story?"

I was thankful that Mark, for once, was keeping his mouth shut. The tranquil look on Jack's face was beginning to fade. "I forbid it," he said.

"Forbid what?" I said. "Doing a story about you? Good luck with that. Or didn't you learn anything about the Constitution during all the time you were studying computers and the Internet and Java?"

"Then you'll have no access to my property for purposes of photography."

"Gee, already taken care of," I said. "Or haven't you been told that cell phones can take photos nowadays?"

My cell phone was currently in pieces and at the bottom of the pond where I'd tossed it a little while ago, but I decided not to pass on that little gem of information.

He put his teacup down on the edge of a nearby table, and it started to fall, and he lunged to keep it in place. Some of the tea slopped out onto the table. "You . . . you can't do that," he said. "My privacy . . . the way I work . . . the way I live. You can't do that!"

"Watch me," I said. "Of course, if you were to take care of Mark here without pressing him for any additional payment, then I'm sure we could reach an arrangement."

I was hoping for a civilized, give-and-take conversation, and I was severely disappointed. The previous tranquil look on his face had faded like a summer day, and an impressive series of obscenities erupted, and I sat there and let the words just wash over me. When he paused to catch his breath, I took out a pen and small notebook in my jacket—making sure my holstered 9mm Beretta made an appearance—and said, "What do you say, let's start the interview process. Jack, if you were a tree, what kind of tree would you be?"

He said, "You have no idea who you're messing with."

"Perhaps," I said. "Why don't you enlighten me?"

Jack took a deep breath. "I will crush you. I'll go through the 'Net and destroy your credit, steal all your passwords, hack everything and anything you have, and drain your bank accounts and anything else. For starters."

He stopped and gave me a hard gaze. I looked right back at him. The silence was thick and still.

"Oh," I said. "My turn? Is that how this goes?"

"Whatever."

"All right, Jack," I said. "Take a gander at this. I'm currently living in my car. My bank account is fast approaching negative territory. My credit rating is somewhat better than Greece's. Whatever weapons you possess will have no impact on me. None. Zilch. Zero."

I displayed my notebook. "This is what I have. Who do you think will win?"

Oh, his face was very much the opposite of tranquil. "I know people," he said. "I know people who can hurt you bad."

"I know people too," I said. "Mister Beretta. Mister Smith. Mister Wesson. Do you really want to go there?"

More silence. He slowly leaned back in his very expensive, and actually quite silly-looking, chair. "Do go on."

"Oh, I will, but won't be long. Here's the set. When will you get the information that Mark was looking for?"

He took another look at the near monitor. "Two hours."

"Outstanding," I said. I got up, and Mark slowly joined me. "We'll be back in two hours and five minutes, and we'll be here to pick up Will Mallory's address. In exchange, well, you get nothing more from Mark. And as for me, you'll get no attention. Nothing. You can keep on playing in your little camp in the woods, and your secrets will be safe from the readers of *Shoreline* magazine. How does that sound for a deal?"

"It sounds fine," Jack said. "I guess."

"Glad to hear that. Mark? Feel like killing some time?"

"You know it."

Outside Jack's home, we strolled up the dirt driveway, and Mark said "Thanks for what you did back there."

"You're welcome."

"I know what you think of me . . . so why did you do it?"

I stopped walking for a moment. "You don't know enough about me to ask that."

"Hunh?"

"I did it because it'll help you get finished with your befuddled quest, which means I can get you back to Tyler, and will—though I don't know why—make Paula Quinn a happier woman. Are we done for now?"

"Yes."

"Good."

We drove to North Conway, a fair-sized town in the White Mountains that, through some curious mix of geography and commercialism, is a hotbed of discount stores from Macy's to L.L. Bean to American Eagle, and a host of other stores, including a super Wal-Mart, where I spent a few minutes picking up a cheap replacement cell phone. North Conway also has a number of smaller shops devoted to skiing, mountain climbing, and other outdoor activities; and as we slowly motored our way through the center of its crowded downtown, Mark said "I want to pick up something for my dad."

"Like what? Some flowers? Bottle of wine? Crystal meth?"

"No," he said. "He's a biker . . . from what I gathered, a biker all his life. Maybe I can get him some gear or something."

"If you think so," I said, and I found an empty spot for the Mazda right in the center of North Conway. Out on the sidewalk we walked to the south, past a couple of shops and a white-steepled church, and came upon a shoe and leather-goods store called The Beggar's Pouch that seemed to fit Mark's bill.

"You go in," I said. "I've got a couple of calls to make."

He went up a set of brick steps and into the store. It was late afternoon. I was hungry, tired, and I didn't like the look of the sky. Even at this distance from the Atlantic, the funny light in the sky seemed to warn of an approaching storm.

My first call went to Duncan Gross, the contractor who had been getting ready to start work on my house. The phone rang a half dozen times before his wife Sue answered, and I didn't feel a whole lot of warmth coming my way when she said "He'll be here in a sec. Hold on."

When he got to the phone and I announced myself, he said, "Jeez, Lewis, I thought this might be you. Look, I've bent over backwards to help you out. We got that old lumber in place, I've done some prep work, but I'm already in pretty deep with you. And not to belabor the point, but I don't know when I'm gonna get paid."

"I know that, and I appreciate that, Duncan, but last I heard, Hurricane Toni is heading right for New England."

"Sure is, and day after tomorrow is Thanksgiving, so please . . . what can I do?" He lowered his voice. "I want to help, honest to God I do, but the missus, she's my business manager. She watches every penny that comes in and out, and I can't do any more. I'm sorry. Without that insurance settlement . . . I'm stuck."

"You and me both, Duncan. Thanks anyway."

A short sigh. "Look, I might be able to slip away for an hour or so before we hit the road for turkey day. I'll try to stop by your place, see if I can nail up some additional tarp. Won't be much, but if the storm veers away, well, maybe you'll get lucky, the damage will be minimal."

After wishing him the best and not meaning it that much, I made another phone call, while two women of a certain age emerged from the store, with bulging shopping bags in their hands. Their accents said New York and lots of money, and I tried to tune them out while the phone rang and rang on the other end, and then it went to a menu, and I punched in an extension that I hoped someday to forget.

For some reason, I wasn't placed on hold, and the phone was briskly answered. "Adrian Zimmerman, how can I help you?"

"Adrian, Lewis Cole . . . was that a trick question?"

"What do you mean?"

"You said 'how can I help you?' Did you really mean that, or is that some sort of automatic reply they teach you at insurance adjuster school?"

There was no sound and I thought he had hung up on me. But he finally went on and said, "Mister Cole, there's nothing new to report. Nothing. The investigation is continuing, and that's all I can say."

"And the fact that within a couple of days, a hurricane will be hitting New England and just might destroy a historical home, that's no concern of yours?"

"My concern and that of my company is to make sure legitimate claims are promptly settled. There's still questions about the legitimacy of your claim. Plus . . . we received word that your Honda Pilot was stolen. In Tyler. True?"

"Yes," I said, which was technically true. I didn't have possession of it anymore and I didn't know where it was.

"But you haven't made an official report to the Tyler police, have you?"

"I've been . . . busy."

"Or perhaps you're concerned about what might happen if you were to show up at the Tyler police station?"

"Adrian, I'd like to point out that I'm still out here, breathing free and not under arrest," I said.

"That still doesn't answer the questions about the arsons and your stolen vehicle."

"Adrian, I need—"

"Mister Cole, I'm sorry. I appreciate your desire to get this resolved, but there are procedures to be followed, and at this moment I'm leaving the office for the upcoming holiday."

"Goody for you, Adrian," I said. "I'm sure you're going to have a nice holiday, in a nice home. Think about me while you're dining safe and warm."

"Mister Cole—"

Now it was my turn to interrupt. "Ever hear of karma, Adrian? She can be a bitch. And I guarantee you this: some time in the future, next day or next year, you're going to be in my position. And I hope you get the same level of consideration and attention you've shown to me."

By then I was talking to myself.

I turned around and was going to enter the store to check up on Mark, when one of the women standing near me said something about an "ugly biker thug" and I stopped moving.

"Excuse me, ma'am," I said, my voice polite and filled with concern. "I'm sorry, I accidentally heard you say something about a 'biker thug.' Did someone just threaten you?"

The near woman's hair was black, thick and luxurious, no doubt having come from a bottle and skilled hands. Her companion was blond, and their clothes and coats and high-heeled boots and jewelry all said they were from away. She giggled nervously and said, "Oh my, it was nothing like that. It was just that Doris and I were in this cute little shop behind us, and there was one mean-looking thug walking around. Looked like one of those biker gang members you see on television."

"Why did you think he was a biker?"

She fluttered a hand. "Oh, my word, the leather jacket he was wearing, funny beard and moustache, and my God, the tattoos; now, I'm not prejudiced and even my granddaughter, bless her, has a tattoo, but this thug . . . oh, he was scary, Doris, wasn't he."

Doris nodded hard. "Very scary."

"Is he still in the store?"

"I don't know . . . is there a problem?"

I offered up a lie and said, "My sister . . . her ex-boyfriend has been following her around, even though she has a restraining order. And the description you just gave me . . . it sounds just like him."

She brought her hand up to her mouth. "Oh, dear. That's horrible."

I walked toward the store. "You're absolutely right."

The store was well lit, with displays of shoes, belts, purses, and other leather gear, and the calming scent of leather. I didn't see Mark, and I didn't see anyone looking like Reeve Langley. At the rear of the store, two women and a man were engaged in a deep conversation. The man was tall, with round-rimmed glasses, and with a long white beard that looked like it would be in season in another month, just in time for Christmas. He was standing behind a glass display case with a shorter woman I took to be his wife, who had her hair pulled back in a simple ponytail and had an engaging smile and bright eyes behind her own set of glasses. The other woman had a bright smile as well, short blond hair, wearing black slacks and a colorful T-shirt with a coiled dragon on the rear. The three of them were discussing a Florida trip in the spring for some sort of tai chi conference, which seemed like a fantastic idea at the moment, and I was tempted to go over to see if I could join them.

Instead, I noted a set of stairs leading up to the second floor of the store, and I took them quietly, keeping to the wall, so the steps wouldn't creak, and I had my right hand under my jacket, grasping the Beretta. I had a thought of Reeve up there, with Mark, a knife at his throat or a gun to his head.

But the second floor had Mark and no one else, and plenty of displays and racks with leather gear designed for motorcyclists. Mark was examining a plain black leather vest when he saw me emerging from the stairwell.

"Hey, Lewis," he said, holding the vest up. "What do you think?"

"I think it looks nice but it's not worth buying," I said. "You don't know how tall he is, or how big his waist is."

"Yeah, you're right," he said, frowning, putting it back on the rack. "I just have this desire to show up with something as a present."

I gave the room a quick look, double-checked to make sure no one was there. "How about a gift certificate?"

"Oh, come on, I'm not sure where he's living, and whether this store is close enough."

"Then *you* can be his present, alive and breathing in one piece," I said, taking a step back down the stairs. "A couple of customers saw a mean-looking man in the store just a little while ago, somebody who looked like Reeve Langley. He's still pissed at you, and after our little chat he's extremely pissed at me. So unless you've got something you want to purchase right now, we've got to get the hell out of here."

Mark jostled a rack of motorcycle jackets on his way toward the stairs. The rack leaned one way, and then another, and remained standing.

Driving out of North Conway, Mark said, "What else?"

"What else is more than enough," I said. "Your Wyoming friend is obviously still in the area."

"Not my friend."

"Point noted. I just don't like the idea of us barely missing running into Reeve Langley at that leather-and-shoe shop."

"Maybe he was looking for a gift too."

"Really," I said. "So tell me, how many times did it take for you to pass the New Hampshire bar exam?"

"Just once," he said. "Why do you ask?"

"Could have fooled me."

Back at Jack Baker's house, I didn't bother parking away from the house or skulking around. I drove Mark's Mazda right into the yard and then spun it around so it was facing down the long driveway. The Jeep Wrangler was still there, and lights were on inside as well. Still, when I went up to the door, I had my Beretta out and in my right hand.

"You knock on the door," I said. "I'm sort of preoccupied right now."

"Why did you take out your gun?"

"It's called a pistol," I said. "And I have it out because we were almost surprised back at North Conway. I only like surprises on my birthday, and today ain't it."

But Jack was alone, save for his black-and-white friend, and if there was any reminder of our earlier business negotiations with Jack, he kept it under wraps. In the living room he passed over a slip of paper.

"Your dad is over in Maine, up the coast, nearly a seven-hour drive," he said. "Small town called North Point Harbor. There's the address. He's living there with a new name. Stan Pinkerton."

I looked down at Jack's neat handwriting, saw an address of 4 Blake's Cove Road. Mark folded up the paper, gave it a hearty squeeze like it was some sort of religious artifact that he had been hunting for years.

"Thanks," he said, voice choking up. "You have no idea what this means to me. . . ."

Jack nodded, looked down at the floor before looking up again. "You might want to hold off on thanking me, Mark."

"Why?" His voice was no longer choked.

"I was able to get other information, about his length of residency, what he's been up to, what kinds of things he's been buying," Jack said. "Among his weekly expenses is something up there called Restful Days VNA."

"VNA," I said. "Visiting Nurse Association?"

"The same," Jack said, now directing his voice to Mark. "It's a hospice outfit."

He paused.

"I'm sorry, Mark, but your dad is dying."

CHAPTER SEVENTEEN

Just over an hour later, we were having a quiet dinner at a 99 Restaurant just outside Portland, Maine's largest city. Mark had some sort of steak-tip dinner, while I paid homage to where we were located by having fish and chips. We ate mostly in silence, and Mark lost it only once, when he crumpled a napkin in his hand and said "All this time, all these years, to come this close and find him dead."

"Not dead, according to Jack," I pointed out. "Dying, I'm sorry to say, but we're only a few hours away."

"Six," he said. "And I want to know why we can't go up now."

"We're not going up now because I'm exhausted," I said. "And we're not going up now because it doesn't make any sense. We leave now and we might get up to that small town about three or four in the morning. What, you want to knock on the door of a dying man and announce yourself? Does that make any sense?"

Mark was slumped, spinning a cold French fry around on his plate. "No, no sense at all."

He looked up and said, "You know, you did good back there with Jack Baker. Especially when you showed him you were carrying. Despite the law and rules and regulations, that's what really counts, isn't it? Being armed."

"On occasion," I said.

The waitress came over, dropped off the bill, and I started calculating the tip off the bill and tried to remember how much money I had remaining in my wallet. Mark reached for his wallet as well—good man!—and I said, "We'll pay up and then go find someplace to spend the night. Someplace reasonably priced. And then we head up to North Point Harbor after the sun rises, and then you make nice with your dad. All right?"

A glum nod.

"And you remember your promise, right? About contacting the cops after you've done that? Reveal all?"

He spun the French fry around one more time.

"I said I'd do it," Mark said. "So I'll do it."

After paying our bill, I stopped at a Walgreen's to pick up a few essentials, including fresh underwear, socks, toothpaste and toothbrush. After some prodding on my part, Mark did the same, and I said "Just like Jack Reacher. We'll travel light with only the essentials."

"Jack who?"

"Mark, there are more books out there than just law and business."

We approached the counter. "Maybe so, but they don't pay the bills."

"No, but they feed the soul."

"My soul will be fine on its own," he said. "It's my bank account that needs to be fed."

After a few minutes of delicate negotiations in Mark's Mazda concerning our relative cashworthiness and credit standing, we drove around the water-front until we came upon a motel that looked like it had seen better days back when the first Arab oil embargo had struck. The place was called Ocean View Terrace, but the view was of a smelly cove that was some distance from the ocean. It seemed to be a forward-looking, liberal establishment, since it offered hourly, daily, and weekly rates.

Mark sighed as I drove his Mazda into the potholed parking lot. "Last year at this time, I was on a junket in Florida. Stayed at a resort town on the Gulf of Mexico. It was a free conference for lawyers who represent small towns. Not a big city but not small either. Right on the beach. Four days. Didn't have to pay for a single thing, just agree to attend a couple of seminars."

I found an empty spot near the office. It was one story, stretching out with two wings. "Sounds like legalized bribery to me."

"I agree."

"So why did you go?"

"Because there wasn't a chance in the world that the organizers could do anything to bribe me," he said. "It was some conservative PAC, dedicated to rolling back state income taxes to what they thought were more reasonable levels."

"New Hampshire doesn't have a state income tax."

"Right, but whoever organized this little shindig didn't know that. So why not take a vaca? I checked with the town manager, and so I went . . . and I nodded at all the right places and ate great food, stayed in a great room . . . now look where I am."

"Correction, Counselor. Look where *we* are."

"Yeah."

"Just a reminder, you're not alone on this little quest."

We got out and into the night, and the air smelled of fuel oil, saltwater, and dead fish. At the office we had to ring a buzzer before a woman wearing black sweat pants and a Portland Sea Dogs sweatshirt came out. On the counter was a sign: KATHI HAWKINS, MANAGER. After some talk, she said, "Fellas, only rooms I have left have queen beds in 'em. So I can rent you one room and you'll share, or I can give you each a separate room."

Kathi looked at us and our faces, and said "Separate rooms it is. Sign here."

We both got room keys with numbers etched on heavy, red diamond-shaped plastic; and as we went back outside and retrieved our respective kits, Mark asked "What time do you want to start tomorrow?"

"As soon as I wake up."

"When will that be?"

"When my body lets me know."

The room was spare and neat, and that's when I ran out of positive adjectives. One queen-sized bed, sagging in the center like it had been used in a previous life to support boulders. The carpet was green and beaten down, and there was a small television on a stand in the corner, with an impressive-looking stain on the carpeting before it. I closed the drapes and gingerly checked the bathroom, and then walked out, thinking a shower could definitely wait, though I could probably get away with washing my face and hands without contracting anything. I took off my jacket and holster and stretched out on the bed. That was going to be it for any disrobing tonight.

I took my new phone out and dialed a number from memory, and a brisk man answered, "Porter Rehab and Extended Care Center."

"Room 209, please."

"One moment."

The phone was answered on the first ring, and then it was dropped, and there was a clatter and fumble, and some giggles, and it was picked up and a woman said, "Chaos central, Major Disorder here, how can I help you?"

That brought a smile. It was Kara Miles, Diane Woods's partner.

"Hey, Kara, it's Lewis. Is Diane handy?"

"In the kitchen? No. In the bedroom . . . well, I'll let you tell her."

Some whispers and more laughter, and then Diane answered, her voice as strong as I'd heard it these past few weeks. "Hello, friend. Where the hell are you?"

"In Portland, in one of its fine lodging establishments."

"Oh, and which one is that? The Sheraton Shorefront? The Hyatt?"

"Not quite . . . it's a place where they change the sheets and towels once a week, whether they need it or not."

"Christ . . . you okay?"

"I hope to be. And you?"

Even over the radio waves, I could sense her smile. "Son, at this very moment, my sweetie here and I are packing up my belongings, including a pound or so of greeting cards, and once daylight comes into this room, I am gone. I am departing, I am leaving, and I'm going to happier shores."

"Damn, I wish I was there to help."

"Don't need a man's help, or have you forgotten our little talk when we first met?"

"Not hardly," I said. "But I wish I was there anyway."

"Unh-hunh," she said. "And the big day is Thursday. Are you coming by?"

Damn.

"I wish I was, Diane. I really . . . I really wish I was. Any chance for leftovers?"

"Hah. The way Kara eats, I doubt it." A muffled voice and Diane said, "Well, it's true, you can pack it away, though God knows it never shows up on your ass."

More muffled sounds and giggles and Diane lowered her voice. "All right, pal, what's going on? How's the hunt for Mark Spencer?"

"The hunt . . . is completed. He's safe."

"Sweet Jesus. Why are you in Portland, then?"

"It's complicated."

"Of course it is. Just don't tell me any more . . . but you're going to see it straight through, make it right. Correct?"

"Going to do my best."

"I'm sure . . . but Lewis, that hurricane is coming up here, landfall set for sometime Thursday."

"You and Kara going to be safe?"

"Oh, Christ, yes. The family who built these condos way back when, they were oddballs. They went above and beyond the building-code requirements, and I'm sure we're going to ride it out just fine. But what about your house?"

"It's . . . also complicated."

"Oh, Lewis. . . ."

"My contractor promised he'd get over there, put up some more tarps, but. . . ."

I just couldn't say any more.

Diane said, "You being in Maine. Pretty important stuff."

"Not to me, but to—"

"No more words necessary. Christ. What we do, eh? For those who are our families, and those we love or have friendships with. You're the truest man I know."

"Thanks," I said. "Right now, I'm the smelliest man."

She laughed and said "All right. Leftovers. I'll do my best. You want a turkey leg?"

"Nope, just some white meat, gravy, and stuffing. I'll make do."

"I'm sure you will. Be safe, come home quick . . . and thanks for sticking by me. A little bird told me that you had a job lined up at *Shoreline*, as the goddamn editor, and that you lost the job because it meant moving out of Tyler. True?"

"Well-informed bird you have there."

"So. Was it because you didn't want to leave Tyler, or didn't want to leave me?"

"Good night, Diane. Happy trails."

With that phone call put away, I made a run into the bathroom, washed my hands, wiped them on my pants, and went back and made another call.

Felix Tinios answered on the first ring and, when he heard my voice, said, "Ah, the most unpopular man in New Hampshire has decided to give me a call."

"I'm in Maine," I said.

"Fine, then. The most unpopular man in northern New England. What's up with the new phone number?"

"Had an earlier conversation with Reeve Langley. Somehow he got my number, decided to negotiate. I decided to dump my phone when the call was over."

"What was he looking for?"

"Mark Spencer, up on a silver platter."

"Bet you were tempted," Felix said.

"I was, but I couldn't do it, not to Paula."

"Speaking of Paula, she's made a number of calls to your old phone number. Maybe you should listen to them."

"I doubt it," I said. "I don't want to get discouraged so late at night."

Felix said, "Well, I was next to her when she made most of them. It's been a while since I've heard such language come from such a sweet-looking young lady. If I thought she had a sense of humor, I would have suggested another line of work involving 1-800 numbers, but I didn't want to go there."

"So where did you go?"

"From where we departed, up north. Small town called Milan. Very remote, very empty."

"Christ," I said. "Where did you put her? At some no-tell motel?"

"No, some friends of mine. They have a remote and very secure compound."

"'Compound'? Felix, who the hell are your friends? Aryan Nation? Klan?"

"Lewis . . . please." His voice was chilly. "That's quite the insult, even coming from you. You know my methods, know my associates."

I rubbed at my eyes. "Sorry. You're right. Speaking of no-tell motels, that's where I currently am, dreading to go to sleep in a few minutes because I'm not sure what's going to crawl out and greet me when the lights go off. What's in Milan, then?"

"Up here in Milan is a guy who used to work for the Federal Reserve in Boston. Did some . . . after-work details for him. Anyway, he told me he once saw some paperwork he shouldn't have, about future financial trends and such. I have a head for numbers, but even I had a hard time figuring out what he was saying."

"Is he a doomsday prepper?" I asked.

"You got it," he said. "He's convinced that some day, the strands and ties that bind this global economy are going to cut loose in a bad way that's going to make the Great Depression look like a Black Friday sale. So he sold all his upper-class goodies, and he and a few friends and neighbors, they hightailed it up north, bought a few hundred acres, and are waiting for doomsday."

"How long have they been waiting?"

"Three years. But we're still friends. So I brought Paula in, told them that it would be a considerable favor to me if she was a guest for a couple of days." Felix paused. "It will only be a couple of days, right?"

"It had better be."

"Good. I've avoided a lot of things over the years, and I don't want to add attempted kidnapping to the mix. So there she is. She put up one hell of a fight, even when I was trying to tell her to calm down and make her realize this was all being done for her own safety. Lucky for me, they have a number of puppies and horses here, which managed to distract her. Paula's cooled down some, but I wouldn't push it."

"Thanks."

"So what's on your agenda? What's the quest you're on?"

"Seems like Mark Spencer is a man with a mysterious past."

"Lewis, all men have mysterious pasts. That's why women put up with us."

"It seems his Vermont parents were his adoptive parents. His birth mom is dead, and his birth dad is alive and up here in Maine, under the Witness Protection Program. The old guy is dying, and Mark wants to see him before that happens."

"The old man from Wyoming?"

"Yes."

"The old man once a member of the Stonecold Falcons Motorcycle Club?"

"The vice president. Before he flipped and sent a number of them to prison."

"Oh, my," Felix said. "Which explains why the club's president is hot on Mark's trail. Revenge may be a dish best served cold, but when you do something like that, go against the club and put men that consider you their brother in jail . . . there's no time limit on that. Revenge will be a dish served freeze-dried, if you know what I mean."

"Unfortunately, I do. So the agenda is for the two of us to go up the coast of Maine, do a meet and greet, maybe some sobs and reconciliation, and then get the hell out and go to the police, tell them what happened back in Tyler and who's behind it."

"Sounds like a busy agenda."

"Yeah."

"Got any room on your agenda for day after tomorrow?"

"Felix. . . ."

"Don't argue. Doesn't Thanksgiving with Aunt Teresa, her current boyfriend, and lady caregivers sound like fun?"

"You really expect to fly south in this weather?"

"No, I don't, which is why they're up here, in a nice hotel in western Massachusetts. Might get some rain, but that's it. Private suite, dinner with all the trimmings. . . ."

"Felix, I can't leave until I'm done . . . and even when I'm done, there's my house."

"Oh. Your house. Anything new?"

"No, but I think there'll be a lot new after the storm comes through. A nice cellar hole where it used to be."

Felix stayed quiet, like he was embarrassed to bring up the matter, and I said: "About those doomsday preppers. Do they have a space for you when the markets collapse, or when the long-promised zombie apocalypse hits?"

"Nope."

"And why not? It sounds like something you'd want to be prepared for."

Finally a laugh from Felix. "When and if doomsday comes, it's going to be scared of me. Not the other way around. Talk to you later."

It took a while for sleep to come. I turned on the light in the bathroom and closed the door mostly shut, so there was some illumination coming into the room. It was noisy with a nearby road, horns from boats in the harbor, and some drunken shouts and yells from a bar just a ways down the street. I slept on top of the bed in my clothes, tossed and turned, and thought about what would happen in the morning. I'd sleep in as much as possible, get up and wash up, and then grab Mark and head northeast up the coast of Maine. Once we got to North Point Harbor, track down Mark's dad, do a quick reunion, and suggest—even with his illness—that dad go somewhere else on the off chance the Stonecold Falcons made it up there.

That was the plan I made during the night.

And it fell apart about ten minutes after I woke up.

CHAPTER EIGHTEEN

It was just after seven A.M. when I rolled out of bed, and I spent a handful of minutes washing up and brushing my teeth, and changing out some of my clothes from my recent Walgreen's purchase. Putting on my holstered pistol and jacket, and with my hands pretty much empty, I stepped outside, where a light rain was falling, the first gentle and deadly kisses from Hurricane Toni.

I went down one unit and banged on the door. "Mark! It's Lewis! Let's get going."

No answer. I shivered. My coat wasn't really heavy enough for the colder weather and approaching rain. A tractor-trailer rumbled by, and seagulls were trotting along the cracked pavement of the sidewalk, picking up whatever scraps that appeared to be food.

I hammered again.

"Mark!"

Then I turned and looked at the parking lot again.

His Mazda was gone.

The little bell on the office door chimed when I came in, and the same woman from last night, Kathi Hawkins, came out of the rear office. This morning her Portland Sea Dogs sweatshirt had been replaced by one from the New England Patriots.

"Hi," I said. "Sorry to bother you . . . but my friend: did you see him drive off in a Mazda, one with New Hampshire license plates?"

"Yep, about fifteen minutes ago. He rolled right in here, dropped off his key, said 'are we fine?' and I said 'yep, we're fine,' and off he went."

"Did he say he was coming back? I mean, did he say he was just going out for coffee or anything?"

"Nope."

"Did he say where he was going?" Like I needed to ask. But I was covering all the bases, as disappointing as they were.

Kathi shook her head. "Sorry, mister, nothing like that. Just dropped the key and left . . . but I can tell you this. He took a right when he got out of the parking lot. That'll lead him right back to an off-ramp. Could be heading down to Boston, up to Augusta, or up the coast. Plenty of places to go to."

I nodded, put my own key on the counter, and walked back outside.

I huddled underneath an overhang from the motel's office. The rain was coming down heavier, and puddles were forming in the parking lot. A few seagulls were still wandering about, two of them tussling over the soggy remains of a cruller. The wind was starting to come off the water, and I stamped my feet some.

What to do?

In normal times, I could catch a cab to the airport, rent a car, and start hot on Mark's trail. I knew exactly where he was going, up to North Point Harbor. Mark had a lead on me but not a wide one, though time would certainly be lost by going to the airport and renting a car.

I checked my wallet. Six dollars. Some change in my pocket. Not enough for a cab ride.

I didn't bother with my credit cards. They were already maxed out, and I had used cash to pay for last night's unforgettable stay. If I tried to rent a car, the best that could happen would be a refusal, the worst could be a refusal plus having my cards destroyed right in front of me.

What to do?

I took out my cell phone. I could just give it all up. A phone call to Felix and he'd come pick me up, and I could go someplace where I'd have a real meal, a clean shower and clean clothes, and I could call Paula and hear the anger in her voice, but tell her what had happened. That her Mark was alive but was driving up to Maine to meet his long-lost biker convict Dad, and that she would be smart and safe to stay in Milan until he contacted her.

Then I would share turkey day with Felix and his aunt and the assorted friends, and laugh and eat and laugh some more, and try to forget Paula and her slug of a fiancé, and also try not to dwell on a hurricane that was about to sweep what was left of my house out to the unforgiving and unforgetting Atlantic.

What to do?

I stared more at my cell phone. Back when I'd been at the Department of Defense, working in an obscure intelligence-analysis section, I'd often met with men and women who were active duty, going into places that I only knew from news reports and highly classified briefings. There were times when they were asked to do something impossible, or highly dangerous, or highly boring and routine, and when arguments ensued, they sometimes ended with one telling the other, "Embrace the suck."

Embrace the suck.

Wind came up harder, driving rain into my face.

I put my cell phone away, turned, and walked back into the office.

Back into the motel office, and Kathi was still there, behind the counter. "Ma'am, if I may, my name is Lewis Cole."

"Nice to meet you, Lewis," she said, tidying up a pile of receipts.

I took out my business card and my New Hampshire press pass, slid them over the counter. She looked down at them and, a bit concerned, asked: "You're a magazine writer? Really? Are you doing a story?"

"Kathi, I'm a writer," I said, leaving both the business card and my press pass on the counter. "But I'm not working on a story. In fact, I don't even work at that magazine anymore. My boss fired me a couple of weeks ago. Right now I'm trying to help a friend of mine."

"The man who left you behind?"

"No, his girlfriend."

"Oh. She your sister, then? Or daughter?"

"No, just a friend. And she asked me to watch out for him. He's . . . he's in serious trouble. I promised her that I would be at his side, all the time, and now he's gone."

"What kind of trouble?"

Good question. How to answer? What could I say?

"He's driving up the coast, looking to meet up with his dad. He hasn't seen his dad in years. The dad's dying . . . but he's also done some time in prison. And he helped put some nasty men in prison . . . and those men, they're after him and his dad."

Eyes wide, Kathi said: "Shouldn't you call the police?"

"I should. In fact, I should have done that days ago. But we don't have much time. Those nasty men are out there, and we're not too sure how much longer his dad has. I'm afraid if I called the cops, it would take too long to explain everything, without having to answer all their questions."

A pudgy finger nudged my press pass. "You don't have to tell me about cops. Christ, all depends on who's working what shift when it comes to how much help I can get when the shit hits the fan. Sometimes I get a smart cop, other times I get one who doesn't want to be bothered. I get a guy whaling on his girlfriend in one of my rooms, it might take some time before they show up, and they don't want to make an arrest or make a report. Just sweep it under the rug."

I took my wallet out, removed my fortune, placed it next to my business card and press pass.

"I'm embarrassed to say this, but this is all I have. I'm concerned he's going to get hurt without me being around. If you know of someone that I could rent a vehicle from, I'll leave my driver's license behind, I'll sign a promissory note, I'll do whatever I can, for fair compensation."

She eyed me and the pathetic display on her counter. "That man must mean a lot to you."

I shook my head. "Truth is, I could never see him again and that'd make me very happy."

"Then why put yourself out? Oh. For her. Your friend who's with him."

"That's right."

Kathi pushed my cash back, reached under the counter, took out a twenty-dollar bill, slipped that across as well. She said: "Out back, by the Dumpster, there's a black Toyota pickup truck. Can't miss it. You can borrow it, but by God, you bring it back tomorrow or I'll call the cops. With your business card here, wouldn't be that hard to track you down, now, would it."

"No. And I'll pay you back."

"Of course you will," Kathi said. "And where are you going again?"

"North Point Harbor. Way up on the coast."

A knowing nod. "Stick to Route 1, the coast road. Usually I-295 is quicker, but they're trying to wrap up so much construction before winter sets in, it'll slow you down."

"But your truck . . . aren't you going to need it?"

"Nope. It belongs to my son. You can borrow it."

"Won't your son miss it?"

"I wish he would, but he's not here. He's in the 10th Mountain Division, outside of Kabul." Her eyes welled up. "He's doing fine, will be home safe in a few weeks, but I think he'd let you borrow it, just like me."

From underneath the counter again, she took out a set of keys, and I took them from her warm hand. "You bring that truck back now, all right?"

"Guaranteed."

"Now get going. You're wasting time."

I turned; but before I got to the door, Kathi said, "Hey, mind answering a question?"

"Go right ahead."

"This woman," she said. "Why is she with him and not you?"

"A very good question," I replied, and went outside into the driving rain.

I slopped my way around the side of the motel, found the Dumpster and the Toyota pickup truck in question. It had a couple of Army decals on the rear window and the bumper. It was smelly outside and there was wet trash on the ground, but I unlocked the front door and got in. It smelled of stale cigarette smoke but was reasonably clean. It started up on the first turn of the ignition key, and the gas gauge read FULL.

Kathi Hawkins had taken good care of her son's truck, and I was going to do my best to return the favor.

From the motel I took I-295 north, away from Portland, and the rain was a steady downpour from Hurricane Toni, still grinding her way up the Atlantic Coast. As I drove, I switched music station to music station, with an emphasis on whatever passed as oldies nowadays, since I didn't want to hear any news updates about what Toni was doing.

I called Felix and left him a message, and then focused on my driving. The little pickup truck did okay but vibrated some if I went above sixty, and I forced myself to avoid doing just that. I wasn't that far behind Mark, and if some luck came my way—him being slow and cautious, or getting lost, or stopping somewhere for lunch—I just might catch up with him. Especially if he had taken the normal route of I-295.

Might.

And then what?

Have him do his business with his father, and then drag his sorry carcass back to New Hampshire and let him have whatever kind of reunion Paula was planning for him.

I hoped it was going to involve a lot of sharp tongue and cold shoulder.

From I-295—and before the construction work appeared—I got onto Route 1, Maine's coastal route, doing my best to avoid the center of capitalism and commerce that's Freeport, and in a while I passed through Brunswick, which had once hosted a Naval Air Station, which was now closed. After Brunswick, there came Bath, famed for its Bath Iron Works, maker of fine naval warships, and which is always in danger of being closed. And following Bath, I drove through Wiscasset, which had once hosted a nuclear power plant, which was now closed.

Lots of powerful things were being closed or being threatened. It must have been nice to live in a time when powerful things were being built and opened.

Eventually the driving settled down to the two lanes of Route 1, which dipped and curved as it traveled along the coast of Maine, which was

a) rugged, b) rural, c) charming, or d) poverty-stricken, or make up your own mind. Some time ago, the legislators up in Augusta were considering putting a lobster on the state license plates, as a symbol of Maine. Considering that a lot more goes on in Maine besides lobsters, I was surprised when it actually happened, although some Maine critics said that if they really wanted to describe the current state of Maine and its poverty rate, a more appropriate symbol would be a box of Kraft instant macaroni and cheese.

Outside Newcastle, the rain slowed and finally stopped, and I was able to switch off the windshield wipers.

But the sky was gray and just looked odd and out of place, like some unexpected vision of what type of chaos was waiting ahead.

Outside Bar Harbor, centuries-old playground of the rich and famous, I stopped at a McDonald's. There was a line at the drive-up, so I parked my borrowed truck and ducked in, quickly emerging with two plain quarter-pounders with cheese (or a Royale with cheese, depending on your point of view) and a large Coke. Meat, bread, cheese, and caffeine. I was depending on these four major food groups to see me through.

When I was finished eating while driving, I tried Felix once more.

No service.

No joy.

When I got to North Point Harbor, I slowed down and took my time. The town was off Route 1, and I took a minor state road to get there. It was a lobster port, built around a high and rocky cove, and the buildings were mostly white with black shutters and looked old and worn from having been near the harsh saltwaters of the ocean. Most homes had pickup trucks, and a fair amount had large stacks of lobster traps piled up in their yards, storing them for the winter, along with a number of lobster boats that had been hauled out and wrapped tight with white plastic.

I drove up to a general store that had two gas pumps up front, and pulled in and just rested for a moment. A long drive, almost there, and I suppose I should be thinking grand thoughts of strategy and tactics, but all I wanted to do was get the job done.

I got out and went to the store's entrance. There was a low creaking porch, with snow shovels, rakes, and bags of ice melt out front. A handwritten sign on a sheet of paper was taped to the door. CLOSED TOMORROW FOR THANKSGIVING. I went inside and it was warm and comfortable, and I heard some *ding-ding-dings* coming from the left, behind a low dark wooden counter. At the end of the counter was a case with some doughnuts and pies, and a cold grill and four barstools. Before the counter were tiny racks for candy bars and bags of chips, and opposite the counter were wooden shelves holding everything from canned goods to cereal boxes to laundry detergent and fishing gear. A young woman was behind the counter, saying "shhh" to someone I couldn't see.

She was in her late twenties, early thirties, and had blond hair braided to one side and was wearing black-rimmed glasses. She was wearing a white turtleneck, blue jeans, and a dark blue grocer's apron in front of her. As I went up to her, she turned and looked down and said, "Heidi! Taylor! Please be quiet!"

When I got to the counter, I glanced over and saw the source of all the noise. Two girls, who looked to be twins four or five years old, were playing on the floor, which was made of wide wooden planks. There was a kaleidoscope of toys over the floor, from dolls to little cars to Fisher-Price playthings. At the end of the counter, a wooden fence was stretched across to pen in the little ones.

I smiled. "They look like a handful."

She gave me a tired smile in return. "Oh, mister, you have no idea."

"Being a mom and running a store . . . two tough jobs at once."

Her smile still remained. "Do what you have to do. What can I help you with?"

"I'm looking for directions," I said. "Do you know where Blake's Cove Road might be?"

"Sure do," she said. "Let me write 'em down."

With a pencil stub and the back of a grocery receipt, she scribbled something down and then passed it over to me. "There you go. Anything else?"

I was going to say no, but there was now something haunting in her eyes. "Sure," I said, "I do need to pick up a few supplies."

I made a quick pass through the store, grabbed a can of motor oil, a bag of Utz potato chips, and a two-liter bottle of Coke. Back at the register,

I went through the twenty-dollar bill that Kathi Hawkins had lent me earlier in the day.

After ringing up my order and giving me a bag and change, she said "Hope you have a nice day, then."

"You too," I said, and then, "Oh. Has anybody else been by today, asking for directions to Blake's Cove Road?"

She yawned. "Mister, I've been here since six A.M., and I'll be here at closing, at seven P.M., and so far you're the first to ask me any directions."

I dumped the groceries in the front seat and started up the truck. Following the clearly written directions, I left the grocery store, went out on the narrow and quiet street that was the downtown of North Point Harbor. A small white building that was the town hall, and an even smaller building that was the Post Office, with posted hours that said it was open every day from 11:00 A.M. to 2:00 P.M., made up the downtown, save for private homes. Nobody was out walking around. I could hardly blame them, on this sharp, cold, and breezy November day.

The road curved up the large cove, allowing a great view of the harbor and, in the distance, pine tree-covered islands. The water was gray-blue, choppy, and then the road moved into rocks and trees, and I lost view of the ocean once more. About two more minutes of driving later, past a burnt-out barn that was marked in my directions, I made a right on a wide, rutted dirt road.

The road dropped quickly, went to the left. The first residence I saw was a mobile home, empty, with smashed windows and an old blue Volvo in the front yard, sagging on flat tires. Then an A-frame chalet-type house, with two cars and a truck parked in the yard, wood smoke coming up from a chimney. And then, finally, number 4. The home of Mark Spencer's convict dad, his dad who had remained hidden for years.

It was on a knoll of land, with a view of the ocean. It was a Cape Cod-style home, with an attached porch built on pilings set in exposed rocks. There was a car parked in the yard.

It wasn't a Mazda.

It was a small Dodge Omni, with Maine license plates.

I couldn't help myself. I smiled.

It looked like I had beaten Mark and had gotten here first.

I drove down the road, backed up into the yard of his father—Will Mallory or Stan Pinkerton, take your pick—and parked the truck next to the Omni. I switched off the engine, took the keys out, and stepped outside. A sharp tang of salt air greeted me, and I had a hard melancholy flashback, thinking of how familiar that smell was, back home, back at Tyler Beach, back where nothing was probably going to remain after tomorrow save for a stone foundation.

Embrace the suck, I thought.

I slid my hand under my jacket, checked the position of my shoulder holster and Beretta, and went up to the front door, where a bright yellow sign said no smoking was allowed inside because an oxygen tank was being used.

Seemed this was the right place after all.

CHAPTER NINETEEN

I hammered on the door with my left fist—my right hand still fairly sore after punching Mark yesterday—and after another round of hammering, the door opened up to an older woman wearing sensible white sneakers, white slacks, and a flowered top. Her gray-white hair was tied up in a bun, and she said "Yes?"

"Sorry to bother you, but I was hoping I could see Stan Pinkerton."

"Oh," she said. "Well. He doesn't get many visitors. He's quite ill, you know."

"Yes, I do know," I said. "I was hoping . . . well, at least to pay my respects before his time."

"Are you friends?"

"No, ma'am," I said. "More of a friend of a friend." I handed over my business card, and she took a quick look and handed it back.

"Tyler Beach," she said. "You're far from home."

"I sure am."

"'Course, I hear on the news that Tyler Beach and the north shore of Massachusetts, they're getting a wicked pounding from that storm. Most of the roads in and out of there have been closed."

"I guess I got out in time."

She opened the door wider, inviting me in. "Hah. Well, you drive under another hour, you'd run into the coast of Canada, that's how far away you are."

I stepped in, and she said: "Maureen Lein."

"Nice to meet you, Maureen," I said. "Have you been here long?"

"A month, when Stan started failing," she said. "There are other girls who come in and take care of him. It's a pity, he's all alone up here, no family. Just a few friends from church and the American Legion Post."

The air was warm but thick with the smells of medicine, ointments, and cleaners. We went through a spotless kitchen, then to an adjacent living room with a small television—turned on to the Weather Channel with the sound off, the footage showing roiling, pounding waves somewhere, blasting over a seawall—and two couches and a coffee table. The floor was shiny hardwood. Another room, maybe a dining room, had a wooden table with chairs piled up on top. I turned my gaze away from the television.

"This way," Maureen said, and led me out to the enclosed porch I had noted earlier.

The porch was as warm as the rest of the house, which I found impressive, considering how old the place seemed. Heavy storm windows kept out the cold and wind, and there was a great view of the small cove, just yards away. In the middle of the outside wall holding the windows was a door leading outside. Heavy waves stirred up by Hurricane Toni were so close that an occasional wave hit a storm window with a burst of spray and foam. Pine trees and exposed rocks went off to either side. In the porch were three old white wicker chairs with faded cushions, a battered wooden bureau, and a hospital bed.

A dying man was in the bed. He looked ageless, preserved, with white hair combed over a large bald spot, sunken cheeks, and a closely trimmed white beard. His eyes were closed and his mouth was slightly agape; and an oxygen tube was wrapped around his ears, with two plugs in his nostrils.

A side table with medicines and lotions was at the side of the hospital bed, along with a large plastic cup of water with a bendable straw, and a bag a quarter filled with urine was dangling under the bed. There was the sound of his raspy breathing, the slight hiss of the oxygen tank, and the waves crashing before his home. He had on light red pajama tops, and his wrinkled and faded hands were on top of the bed.

I just stood there and watched him.

Everything then quickly changed for me. He wasn't my father, he wasn't my friend, and he wasn't my relative, but I now felt a sense of responsibility for this man. Forces were in motion against him, were now traveling this way, and, like it or not, I was now part of it.

"Maureen . . . how much longer does he have?"

She stood on the other side of the bed, gently brushed his forehead, checked the reading on the oxygen tank. "Not sure. A couple of days. A couple of weeks. Maybe a month. He's a tough old bird he is."

"Is he always like this?"

"What, out of it? No, he's sleeping, which is a blessing. And when he wakes up, he's still a pretty sharp tack, no matter that he's practically skin and bones."

"What happened to him?"

She brushed his forehead again. "His insides are just riddled through with cancer. Maybe it was all his years smoking, or working at the ship-yard, breathing things in he shouldn't. Who knows. And right now, what difference does it make?"

I looked at her and the setup and asked: "Maureen, if I may, who's paying for all this? The medical supplies, the twenty-four-hour nursing care. Considering the state of the economy and most medical plans available, it seems . . . forgive me, it seems gold-plated."

"Sure does, doesn't it," she said. "Truth is, the hospice service is being paid by some government-funded foundation. I can't remember the name of it, but I'm sure our office manager knows. Why do you want to know?"

A government-funded foundation. Sure. Another way of setting up a shell operation, funded by the Department of Justice, to take care of those dying of old age and disease who were in the Witness Protection Program.

"Maureen, please, one more question, all right?"

She was no longer paying attention to her patient. She was paying a lot of attention to me. "Go on."

"Is there a phone number, a contact person, or anyone else listed who you can call if there's an emergency?"

"You mean, when he finally passes on?"

"No, I mean if you or anyone else thinks he might be threatened."

Maureen stepped back from the hospital bed. "I . . . you know, when we first started with the care, yes, Claire, our office manager, she told us to call her if anything happened like that. Like somebody coming by who scared us, or who threatened Mister Pinkerton."

I moved around so I could look out the far porch window. It had a good view of the dirt driveway, my borrowed truck, and her Omni.

"There are bad men coming here, to do him harm. Can we move him?"

"What do you mean, bad men?"

"Men who want to kill him, that's what I mean." I checked the bed, looked out the near door leading from the porch. Possible? If she backed her Omni down here, and we both got underneath his arms, could we do it?

She shook her head. "No. Can't be done. He's so frail, he'd probably die between here and my car."

Which just might be a blessing, considering what Reeve had done to Carl Lessard back in Tyler.

"Is there a phone in the house?"

"No. And there's no cell service here. I have to drive up to Godin Hill to get coverage."

"Yeah, I already figured that out." The man's breathing grew more raspy. "Maureen, get out of here, now. I'll stay behind. Call that contact number, and call the police."

"We don't have a police department here: we're too small. We have to rely on the State Police or the county sheriff. It'll take a while."

"Do it. I'll stay here."

Maureen's lip trembled. "It's my job. I'll stay. You go."

I went over to her, gently squeezed her hand. "Your job is to take care of him. You and the others have done a great service these past months. But, please, trust me. We're wasting time. Get going, make those phone calls. I'll stay with him."

"But . . . you don't even know him. You said so yourself!"

I squeezed her hand again, gently propelled her to the living room. "If the cops get here in time, I'll get to know him pretty well. Maureen. Go!"

I could sense the fight going on inside of her, of a dedicated caregiver who didn't want to abandon her post. But she then kissed him on his forehead and said "I'll be as quick as I can."

"I know you will."

A moment later, the outside door slammed, and Maureen ran up to her Omni, got in, and it started up and roared up the dirt road.

I checked my watch. Maybe five or so minutes to get to a location to where her cell phone worked. A few more minutes making the necessary phone calls. Then . . . the wait. Response time? Depended on a lot of things. How many troopers and deputy sheriffs were there out on the road at this moment. And if they were out there, which end of the county might they be currently patrolling. Or maybe one is in court. Maybe another one is getting his or her cruiser gassed up. Or is at the scene of a fatal car accident.

Response time?

Who the hell knew.

I took out my Beretta and moved one of the wicker chairs on the porch, so I had a good view of the dirt road and my parked and still-borrowed pickup truck.

I sat in the chair, Beretta in hand, and I waited.

A loud cough startled me, almost making me drop my pistol.

He was awake.

As cadaverous as he looked, Will Mallory or Stan Pinkerton was alert and staring right at me. He blinked his eyes twice and said, "Need a drink of water."

"Coming right up."

I holstered my pistol and went to the stand next to his hospital bed, picked up the water glass, and he eagerly sucked the straw a few times, his Adam's apple bobbing up and down in time, and then he removed his mouth and sighed in satisfaction, lowering his head back down on the pillow. He coughed once and said "My lips are pretty goddamn dry."

"Hold on."

I looked over the various lotions and supplies on the counter, picked up a tube of Carmex. I squeezed a dollop onto a finger and gently rubbed it into his cracked and dry lips. He nodded in appreciation.

"Thanks," he said. "Where the hell is Maureen?"

"Off."

"What for?"

I only hesitated for a split second. He was dying, but by God this was his life and his home, and I wasn't going to sugarcoat it. "Some men are coming here. I think they're going to kill you."

He stared up at me and grinned. He looked like a Hollywood special effect, a grinning skull with dry skin stretched across. "The fuck you say. Is this a joke?"

"No, it's not, Will Mallory," I said. "No, it's not."

"Who the fuck is Will Mallory?" he demanded, voice hoarse. "My name is Stan Pinkerton."

I found a tissue, wiped my fingers dry. "You're Will Mallory." I grasped a thin wrist, turned it over, and he put up no resistance. A faded patch of scar tissue. "A long time ago, you had a falcon tattooed there. 'Stonecold Falcon for life.' Right? At this moment, Reeve Langley of the Stonecold Falcons is coming up here to kill you."

I didn't think it was possible, but his face and demeanor looked worse.

"Shit. . . ."

"Maureen's gone to call the cops. And the Department of Justice, if I'm right. You've been in WITSEC, all these years. Correct?"

"Are . . . are you from the U.S. Marshals Service?"

"No," I said. "At the moment, I'm an unemployed magazine writer, doing a favor for someone."

"Who's that?"

"The woman set to marry your son," I said. "Mark. Mark Spencer. He's been looking for you, and that motorcycle gang has been looking too. And right now, it's a race as to who's going to get here first. Him or them."

He turned his head away and said: "Mister . . . you better get the hell out of here. Reeve Langley . . . I knew his dad . . . and if he's one-tenth the sociopath that his father was, then you're in a world of hurt."

"Did you help put his father in jail?"

Another raspy cough. "I did . . . and I'd do it again. . . ."

One more cough.

"Leave, mister . . . leave. . . ."

I pulled the chair up closer to his bed, but in a spot that still allowed me a view of the road.

"Why?" I said. "I just got here."

We sat quiet for a couple of minutes, until he said, "What's your name?"

"Lewis Cole."

"What's my son's name again?"

"Mark Spencer."

He coughed. "A good name. A strong name. What does he do?"

"He's a lawyer. Also works as the counsel for Tyler, down in New Hampshire."

His dry lips stretched into something resembling a smile. "A lawyer . . . loser like me, who'd ever think I'd bring a new lawyer into this world. Where did he end up?"

"A couple in Vermont adopted him."

"That's what I heard, second-hand from some marshals, years back. Quiet little town, away from me, away from any danger."

"How did you lose track of him?"

"My wife at the time . . . Melissa . . . filed for divorce, soon after I become a witness. Couldn't really blame her. Married the girl when she was just sixteen . . . all she knew was me and the gang. Later heard that she died in a bike accident, her grandparents put the boy up for adoption . . . I guess I could have fought that, but what for? By then I was a laborer, over at Bath Iron Works. What could I give to a kid like that. . . ."

As his real father? A lot, I thought, if you'd only known, but I kept my mouth shut and my eyes focused on the dirt road leading to the house. I wondered where Mark was, if he was closing in. I wondered where Maureen was, if she was making phone calls.

I tried not to wonder where Reeve Langley was.

"You know why I'm out here, on the porch?"

"No, I don't."

"Nearly got my scrawny ass kicked out of high school. Got caught up in some stupid juvenile shit and the judge, and my dad, told me to join the service. I never seen the ocean so I signed up. . . . What a goddamn stretch of water that was. . . . Did time on cruisers and destroyers, kept relatively squared away, could have been a twenty-year man if I stuck to it . . . but I was dating a girl back then, she convinced me to come back to Wyoming. . . ."

Part of me wished he would stay quiet, because I didn't want him deep asleep when Mark arrived. These stories he was telling were important, but they didn't belong to me: they belonged to Mark.

Will had a deep, rattling cough and, when he caught his breath, went on. "That girl dumped me, of course. . . . She had found somebody else . . . and I needed someplace to belong to, and that was the Stonecold Falcons."

"Good for you," I said.

The dirt road was still empty.

He said "I don't like the tone of your voice. . . ."

"I'll see if I can change it when your son arrives."

"You judging me, eh?" He coughed again. "Is that what you're doing, judging me?"

"Not at all."

"You are . . . and you know what, I don't care . . . in a while I'm gonna meet my maker, whoever He or She is, and I'll have to atone . . . and yeah, I rode with the Falcons, had the best times, made some good cash . . . some wild times. . . ."

I thought I heard the sound of an approaching engine.

"But everything good ends sometime, right?" I said.

Another hefty cough. "Sure. . . . I rode hard with the Falcons . . . but things changed . . . we got into the crystal meth business, and that shit ate men's brains, it did . . . and I was getting older . . . and had my boy . . . and Bruno Langley, he took charge . . . liked to humiliate guys . . . make 'em do impossible things . . . just 'cause he could get away with it. . . ."

Yes. The sound of the engine was getting louder and closer. I shifted in my seat, slid the Beretta back out again.

"Like tattooing your son?"

He was quiet, allowing me more time to gauge the closeness of the approaching vehicle.

"How did you know that?"

"I saw his arm, where it had been burned off. It happened when he was very young, so young he had no clear memory of it. I can't imagine a set of parents, no matter how drugged or doped up, allowing their child to get a tat on his wrist like that."

I looked over at Will and his eyes had welled up, and he turned his head. "What a bad dad . . . to let a slug like Bruno Langley do that . . . 'Falcons for Life' and all that bullshit. But that was just the last straw . . . he did things . . . up in Canada and elsewhere . . . stuff I still get nightmares about. . . ."

"So why not drop out? Why did you turn witness?"

"Pah," he said. "Revenge . . . I wanted to get back at him, for what he did to my boy . . . what he did to me and others . . . the Marshals, they set me up at B.I.W. . . . . did okay there . . . had a good life, hunting and fishing and shooting, but I always thought about Mark . . . what he was like . . . what I could say to him."

A Mazda with New Hampshire plates appeared on the road, coming down to the house. Mark Spencer was driving. He was alone.

I stood up.

"Lucky you," I said. "You can do that in about sixty seconds."

CHAPTER TWENTY

I left the porch and went into the living room, and to the kitchen, where I spotted Mark parking next to my borrowed truck. He stepped out and then started walking briskly to the house.

Something wasn't right.

Not right at all.

And like giant pieces of a jigsaw puzzle slamming together on their own and grandly announcing *here we are*, I knew just how wrong I had been.

I opened the door and stepped out on the stone steps. "Afternoon, Mark."

He stopped so suddenly, I thought his feet were going to slide out from underneath him. "Lewis . . . how . . . I mean, when. . . ."

I took another step down the hard stone. "A bit late, don't you think?"

His face was the color of the granite I was standing on. "I stopped a couple of times, you know, for gas . . . something to eat . . . and there was road construction. . . ."

I looked at the Mazda, which was empty. "Wrong answer, Counselor. First things first: why did you leave me behind in Portland?"

"Because," he said, defiance in his voice, "this was something I had to do on my own."

"On your own? Really?"

"You got it."

I stepped out onto the nearly bare lawn. It was overcast, and a light drizzle was starting to fall. "If you're so set on coming up here and meeting your dad before he dies, meeting your dad all alone, then why did you keep on helping Reeve Langley?"

No answer.

I said, "In other words, you're helping Reeve find your dad, to kill him. That's what you've been doing, right?"

That got his attention, and I pressed my advantage. "Everything started after you went to Wyoming. Was that a trip to find your father, or a trip to see if there was anyone around who wanted to hurt him for what he had done to his gang years ago?"

I took a step forward. Mark took a step back, holding up his hands in a gesture of frustration or surrender.

"You've got to be crazy! What the hell are you talking about?"

"Talking about you angry about being abandoned by your father. Maybe looking for revenge, and not a happy reunion. Revenge from the son of the man that your dad put in prison." I took a deep breath. "Look at the facts, Counselor. Reeve had a pretty good and quick idea of where Paula lived and worked, and he knew he could squeeze her to get to you. Then when I track you down to that island, who shows up at the same time? Reeve Langley and friends."

"A coincidence, that's all!"

"Sure. One hell of a coincidence, unless you told him you might be there. And we have time to kill while your info guru gets the information on your dad's address, and we go to North Conway, where there's dozens and dozens of shops in a one-block area alone. You choose a leather-and-shoe store. Same store that Reeve Langley had been in earlier. We had just missed him. Was that a back-up meeting point? A place to get together if something went wrong at the island meet?"

I stepped forward two more times, determined to keep him off balance. I said "This morning, you bailed out on me."

"Like I said, because I wanted to do this alone!"

"Alone, really? Or did you want the opportunity to meet up with Reeve, help lead him here to your dad? What was it? String along Reeve, maybe he's paying you off, all for the two of you to get your revenge. Him for abandoning you, Reeve for putting his dad in jail. Look, Counselor, you had at least an hour advantage over me on getting up here. If you were really in a hurry to meet your dad after all these years, I would have rolled in here and I would have found you sharing a cup of coffee out in the porch."

"You're fucked in the head."

"Probably, but you and I are going in there, and we're going to do our best to get your dad out of here before Reeve shows up."

Mark looked past me at the house. "Why the hell do we have to do that?"

"Maybe I'm just overreacting. What's your excuse?"

Mark lowered his arms. "How sick is he?"

"Pretty damn sick," I said. "His nurse said if he's moved, it might kill him."

"Then why the hell do you want to move him?"

"Because I think he'd rather die trying to be saved, than by being betrayed by his son. Let's go."

I led him into the house, quickly through the kitchen and living room, and out to the porch. I heard a sudden intake of breath from Mark, and then he went around me to look at the old man in the bed.

Will was sleeping, head turned, a line of drool running down a cheek. The oxygen tubes were still in place, and his hands were still above the bedcovers. Mark stepped forward.

"Dad?"

A wheezing sound from Will. I said, "His nurse said sometimes he falls into a deep sleep, but when he wakes up, he's one sharp guy. He and I had a good talk just before you showed up."

Mark didn't seem to be listening to me. He leaned over, gently shook Will's left shoulder. "Dad? Dad?" His voice choked up. "Sweet Jesus, Dad . . . so many, many years. Why did you leave me alone? Why didn't you try to get in touch?"

I said "He thought about it. He was a laborer at Bath Iron Works. He didn't feel like he could have offered you a good life. He was happy to hear about you growing up in Vermont."

Another gentle nudge from Mark's hand on Will's shoulder, and I looked out the porch windows. Just the Mazda and my truck. "Mark, we don't have time."

He looked at me. "Shut up."

"Mark, enough is enough. Bring your Mazda over here, we'll do our best to gently load him in the car. We drive off. The woman who was nursing him . . . she said she was going to call the cops. It'll take time, but they'll get here. Let's go."

"No."

"Mark, what the hell are you talking about?"

He reached under his jacket, pulled out a stainless-steel Ruger .357 revolver. A nice, handy, and easy-to-use revolver.

I'd had one just like it back at home before the fire destroyed it. I guess he was serious about the importance of being armed.

"We're not going anywhere until I've said my piece."

"Mark. . . ."

"I want this . . . scum to wake up and look me right in the eye, and tell me why he did what he did to me."

"For Christ's sake, Mark, either we get going now, or Reeve Langley is going to show up and things are going to get real ugly, real quick."

Mark shook his head no.

I said, "Did you hear what I just said?"

Another man's voice behind me. "Maybe he didn't, but I sure as hell did."

I turned, and a smiling and very confident-looking Reeve Langley was standing there.

It was like the porch had tilted up on its side and was threatening to tumble me over on the floor. Reeve wasn't alone: there was another bulky man standing behind him. Reeve stepped forward, smiling widely from a leathery, creased face from a long time on the back of a motorcycle. He looked calm, comfortable, freshly washed and dressed and at peace with the world. He had on khaki slacks, flannel shirt, and a Navy blue wool pea coat, opened up. The leather of his own shoulder holster was visible. On his bald head was a cloth cap with a bill, and his Vandyke was neatly trimmed.

The only jarring part of his clothing ensemble was a pair of leather boots that were oil-stained and broken in.

Reeve was well dressed, but he looked like a grizzly bear at a circus, dressed ridiculously in people clothes that weren't his.

His eyes were the color of old slate, and they terrified me. He had the merry look of a man who never doubted his own choices and decisions, no matter how bloody and obscene they were. I had seen such looks before, including a time back when I was at the Pentagon and had observed the interview of a Serbian paramilitary leader whose specialty was long-range sniping that blew off the heads of young boys and girls at play in Muslim enclaves. During the interview he was laughing, joking, and, with pen and paper at hand, delighted in mapping out his best shots.

"So, Lewis Cole," Reeve said, his voice calm and mellow. "Just yesterday we were on the phone, with you ignoring my gracious offer. And it's only been a couple of days since you shot out my tires back at . . . back at . . . Billy, what was the name of that town again?"

"Tyler," Billy said, voice uneasy. Billy was making do with his own fashion sense of soiled blue jeans, Red Sox hoodie, and dungaree jacket. He was younger than Reeve, face pockmarked, barely-there beard, and a long black ponytail. He had a Glock semi-automatic pistol in his hand.

"Ah, Tyler," Reeve said. "I'm told you're a magazine writer, right?"

"Not at the moment," I said. "Had a disagreement with my editor. On my own now."

He stepped closer to me. Mark started speaking, and Reeve raised an arm; Mark instantly shut up. His Ruger revolver was no longer in sight. I imagined he had slipped it back underneath his coat when he saw Reeve come into the porch. My Beretta was less than two feet away from my right hand, under my jacket, but reaching for it would have been suicidal. The man called Billy was covering me, and Reeve looked like he was one big coiled collection of muscles, ready to tear off my head or chase a cheetah across an African plain.

I braced myself for what was no doubt coming my way, and my terrified meter pegged off the scale at what happened next.

I was expecting shouting, a punch to the face, a kick to the groin; but instead, Reeve reached out and gently stroked my left cheek with a rough hand. "A magazine writer. A couple of years ago, a magazine writer begged me and begged me to ride along with us for a few weeks. Wanted to be the next Hunter Thompson, whoever the hell he was. I was feeling generous, and the clown showed up in a rice-burner. He tried to keep up with us for a while, and one night, at a rally, he just bored me. All these questions. Yap yap yap."

Another soft stroke to my cheek. "Last year they found his shiny stripped bones, in a grassy stretch of prairie outside Laramie. Guess his death is still being investigated. You ever been to Wyoming?"

"No, but I hope to get there one of these days."

That brought forth a smile, and his teeth were firm, clean, and very white. "Sorry, I'm afraid that's not going to happen. But later, I'll tell you all about Wyoming . . . face to face, not over the phone, and I'm going to enjoy every long delicious second."

I tried to make sure my legs weren't shaking. "I look forward to listening."

His hand came up once more and *tap-tapped* my cheek. "Remember saying that, Lewis. Remember that well. In a number of hours, you'll be begging me for a shot to the forehead, and that's when I'm going to whisper in your remaining ear that I've just begun. Billy!"

"Yeah." Billy stepped forward.

Reeve deftly reached over to me, under my jacket, and disarmed me. "First, take care of this. Second . . . this porch is getting a bit crowded. I want Mister Cole here to have a front-row seat. So go in the house, find a chair or something, and rope or duct tape. The brave magazine writer is going to get the story of his lifetime, what's left of it."

Reeve gently walked by me and said, "Oh, please don't try to make a move, all right? It'll quickly turn loud and messy. And I'm saving you for dessert."

He went to the end of Will's bed and stood there, hands clasped in front of him, and sighed loudly in satisfaction. "So very, very long . . . I've waited for this day for a very, very long time." He leaned over the end of the bed. "Hey! Hey, Will, you old bastard! Wake up!"

Will's face remained the same, eyes closed, gently rasping. Mark said, "He slides in and out of consciousness. He was talking just a while ago."

Reeve turned and, still smiling, said "Mark, young man, I don't fucking think I asked you a goddamn thing, now, did I?"

Mark seemed to lose a foot in height. "Okay."

"Ah, don't worry about it," Reeve said, sounding like a Roman emperor, allowing a bit of mercy before a gladiator match was about to start. "Even though you tried to fuck me over at the very last minute, after I was ready to pay you lots of cash to find this old piece of shit. Let's see what I can do."

From inside the house came a loud, clattering noise, and Reeve turned and yelled, "Jesus, Billy, what the hell are you doing out there? Building the goddamn thing from scratch?"

"Sorry," came the meek voice. "Found some chairs piled on top of a table . . . a couple fell to the floor . . . I'll be right there. . . ."

In a minute he was, holding a wooden dining-room chair in one hand, a length of rope in the other. He put the chair down near the door leading outside, and Reeve motioned me to have a seat. I took my time, as much as I could, hoping that Maureen had made the necessary phone calls by now, and whatever passed for the U.S. Cavalry in this part of rural Maine was riding or driving to the rescue.

I sat down and Billy came forward, and Reeve said, "Wait. Hold on, genius."

"Hunh?" Billy said.

Reeve shook his head and gave me a whaddya-gonna-do look. "Moron. You don't tie someone up with one long length of rope like that. That gives 'em too much slack. Cut the rope into four sections, and tie him off at the ankles and wrists. I don't want him floppin' around like a fish when I start playing with him later."

Billy's face reddened and, with a sharp knife, he did as he was told. He looked at me and I took a quiet, deep breath, tensed my legs and arms, twisted them some, and Billy went to work. Reeve turned his attention back to the old dying man.

"Hey! Wake up, you old bastard!"

More rasping. Reeve tugged up the bedding at the edge of the bed, said "Billy, your knife, if you please."

Mark said "Hey, what are you going to do?"

Reeve said "The fuck do you care? Considering who brought me here, just watch and keep your mouth shut."

Reeve grabbed a pasty white foot, splotched with bruises and broken blood vessels, and quickly shoved the pointed end of the knife into the sole of Will's foot. Mark gasped and I wanted to look away, but I kept still, and then Will slowly opened his eyes, coughed, and said, "Jesus Christ, what the hell was that?"

Reeve tossed the knife back at Billy, who tried to catch it and failed, the knife clattering to the porch floor. He picked it up, and Reeve said "Will, Will, Will . . . it's been a long goddamn time, hasn't it."

Will coughed. "Sure has . . . hey, is that you, Reeve? For real?"

Reeve went around to the side of the bed. "The same. In the flesh."

Will said, "Jesus . . . last time I saw you, you was crying and sniffling, shitting and pissing into your diapers . . . what, you were about thirteen then, right?"

For the briefest of moments, Reeve flinched, like something had bored its way into his armor, and then he relaxed and patted Will on a thin shoulder.

"Still got it, you old bastard."

Will moved his head and shoulders a bit. "Speaking of old bastards . . . how's your dad Bruno? Still in the SuperMax . . . eh?"

Reeve's eyes seemed to change color, became darker, more dangerous. "Don't you dare mention my dad. You got that? Don't you dare mention his name."

The old man's eyes fluttered. "Crazy old Bruno . . . just before I left Wyoming, a deputy marshal told me that his back was giving him lots of problems . . . degenerative disk disease, something like that . . . by the time he'd be sentenced, he'd be in a wheelchair . . . is that what happened to your daddy?" Will coughed. "He in a wheelchair in prison? I bet every day, lots of guys line up so he can suck them off—"

Reeve was quick. It seemed like from one breath to the next, his large right hand was squeezing Will's throat. The pale face turned pink and then red. Reeve lowered his head to Will and said "Don't. Mention. My. Dad. Again."

Then he stepped back, released his hand, and Will started breathing, hoarse and loud, and Reeve started talking again, satisfaction in his voice. "Nearly thirty damn years, but here I am, you old bastard. You broke the code. You turned on your brothers. And for that, you're going to pay a pretty hefty bill."

Will rallied some, his voice stronger. "Do your worst, you punk . . . you'll be doing me a favor . . . I'll be going out a man, instead of some weakling, pissing and shitting in his bed. . . ."

"Damn," Reeve said, "that is one hell of a nice invitation."

He put his hand underneath his pea coat, and I think all of us in the porch were surprised at what happened next.

Mark said "Step away. And leave my dad alone."

And he had his Ruger .357 revolver pointed right at Reeve.

I relaxed the best I could. By tensing up my arms and legs earlier, as I was being tied up, I had made myself a bulky target for Billy's rope-work. With me now relaxing, there was slack. Not much, but it was there. I started to do what I could while Reeve and Billy were focused on Mark's demand.

Reeve just stared, and then burst out laughing. "Oh, come on, Mark, what the hell do you think you're doing?"

His voice wavered. "I'm changing our deal. I want you to drop whatever weapon you have, and Billy, too. You're not going to hurt my dad."

Reeve laughed again. "Mark . . . what, Mister Lawyer-Man, you think this is the time to revise a contract? Do you? We had an agreement. You lead me to your scummy dad, and I give you a healthy chunk of cash."

Mark said "You broke the deal when you went after Paula."

If Reeve was concerned about having a .357 Ruger pointed at his mid-section, he was doing a good job of hiding it. He said, "Hey, I was just looking for a little . . . insurance. That's right. An insurance policy, to make sure you didn't get cold feet when the time came. Even burned down your offices to make sure you got the message after that old man didn't give you up. Can you blame me?"

Working, working on the ropes. I could feel the one binding my right wrist start to loosen, and it also seemed the old chair itself was starting to come apart. I could feel the right arm of the chair start to give way.

"Step away, get rid of your weapons. You and Billy both. Nobody's going to hurt my dad. I've changed my mind."

"Hey, hold on there," Reeve said. "You tell us where he lives, you say you're gonna wait for us there, and now you don't want to get it on?"

"That . . . that's right," Mark said, defiance in his voice.

Reeve nodded and said "All right, sport, looks like you've got the upper hand."

And damn, he moved so fast, almost as fast as Felix when he's in the zone, and Reeve slapped Mark's hand, the revolver fell to the floor, and Reeve grabbed Mark's coat and punched him hard in the right eye. Mark cried out, fell against the near wall, collapsed, sobbing.

Will coughed. "Leave . . . leave him alone. . . ."

Reeve picked up the Ruger, slipped it into his coat pocket. The air in the porch was changed, was crackling with tension and fear and the certain knowledge of approaching violence. I kept my breathing as relaxed as possible. Continued working my hands. The chair arm was definitely loose.

"Sorry, Will, old man." He turned to Mark, who was on the floor, back up against the wall, hand held up to his eye. Reeve kicked at Mark's feet, and he yelped again. "Hey, Lawyer-Man, you tried to change the scope of our contract, right? Right?"

Another kick, a low moan. Billy was standing next to me and was staring straight at the bloody scene unfolding before us.

"Now it's my turn." Reeve's head swiveled. "Billy!"

Billy was startled. "Sure, Reeve. What?"

"The car. Go to it. In the rear, black leather zippered bag. About three feet long, one foot wide. Bring it in. Now."

Billy started to go out, and Reeve said, "Oh, for Christ's sake, take the porch door. Do you think I've got all day to stick around?"

Billy brushed past me, had a moment of difficulty opening the door—it seemed stuck—and then he got it opened after a few curses, went out, and started walking away. The storm door took its time closing.

Reeve came to me, gently brushed my cheek again—I snapped my head away—and went over to Will. He patted Will's bare feet and said, "Great original plan I had with your loving son over there. He told me where you lived, we both show up at the same time. He'd get his revenge on daddy who abandoned him all these years, and I'd get revenge for what you did to my dad, you old piece of shit."

Will whispered something I couldn't hear. Reeve laughed again. "Nope, not gonna happen. But I will tell you what's gonna happen. Hey, Mark . . . get your ass up!"

Mark slowly got up. His left eye was nearly swollen shut, and blood was trickling down the side of his face.

"Jesus, why is everybody moving so goddamn slow today?" Reeve asked. He stepped over, grabbed Mark, tugged him over so they were standing next to each other at the end of Will's bed.

Holding Mark by the scruff of his neck, Reeve shook him back and forth like he was a rag doll. "See your boy, Will? Eh? See your boy? Answer me. . . ." Reeve went into his coat pocket, brought out Mark's revolver, held it against his temple. "Answer me, or I'll blow his head off into the ocean."

More coughs. "Yeah . . . I see him . . . let my boy be . . . let 'im be. . . ."

Reeve laughed again. It was the laugh of a man seeing an infant playing with a kitten, and also the laugh of a man seeing an enemy of his fall into a woodchipper.

"Let him be? Oh dear me, that's so not going to happen. You put my dad and his friends in jail. You betrayed them all. And me . . . I came all the way here from Wyoming to put a bullet between your eyes, for what you did to my dad. But like Mister Lawyer-Man here, I'm changing the terms of the contract."

Reeve shook Mark again, went on. "You're a sick, sick guy. You're gonna die tomorrow, or next week, or next month, but I'm gonna leave you with something to remember me by. You know Billy, you know what he's getting for me?"

I kept on working working working, thankful Reeve's entire attention was being directed to the dying man in front of him. My fingers hurt, a couple of fingernails had been torn. Reeve said, "First time I get sent up, part of my parole, I worked in a butcher shop. Lousy work, but so long as it kept me out of the joint for a while, I sucked it up and stayed there. That means I know my way around saws and blades . . . and I always keep a set of my old butchering tools with me."

One more shake of Mark, who groaned, arms hanging limply at his sides. "So think about this," Reeve said, slowly and carefully. "Billy's gonna come back here in a minute or two. Then he and I, we're gonna tie up your boy here, and right in front of you"—and by now his chest was heaving with anger, or excitement, or both—"I'm gonna cut off his head, and then I'm gonna take his head, put it between your legs, and then leave you be."

Mark started a low wail, like an old Irish woman learning that her youngest had been lost at sea, and Reeve pushed him to the floor, kicked him, and then took off his Navy pea coat. Will started to say something, nothing I could make out; and with his coat off, Reeve took off his shoulder holster, lowered it to his feet. He then started unbuttoning his flannel shirt.

When he'd gotten his shirt unbuttoned and tugged part way off his tattooed arms, that's when I raised myself and the chair off the floor and slammed into his back.

CHAPTER TWENTY-ONE

My mouth slammed shut hard with the force of the impact, feeling like my chin was broken, but I managed to get Reeve on the floor, with his arms tangled in the sleeves of his flannel shirt. The chair cracked and I got a hand free, pulled it out of the ropes, and got a length of a chair leg and strut, and slammed it against the back of Reeve's head.

"Move!" I yelled to Mark, and I slammed one more time and Reeve was bellowing, moving underneath me, and I got up, pulled the rest of the ropes and chair off of myself, and shouldered my way outside the porch. I could have stayed behind, I could have gotten in a wrestling match with Reeve, and I would have lost. He was an expert in hand-to-hand combat, in brutal bar fights that started and finished within seconds, and I had to get out.

Quick look to the right. Billy was coming across the lawn, carrying the leather case with Reeve's butchering tools. Billy stopped, mouth agape, and he dropped the case and started fumbling under his dungaree coat.

His Glock was coming out shortly. To the left were trees and low brush. To the front, and much closer, was a jumble of rocks and boulders and foaming water from the incoming waves. I didn't hesitate in my running: I made my way straight to the rocks.

The water was iceberg cold. I shuddered and slipped and fell, banging my ribs. Shouts were coming out of the house. I looked back.

Mark was out of the porch but was still hidden from the approaching Billy, who was still fumbling under his coat. Still had some time.

And Mark turned, and his .357 Ruger was in his right hand.

Good man! He had managed to retrieve it in all the confusion.

"Mark!" I yelled. "Over here!"

My quick thought was that he could join me by the rocks, and we could make a stand with his Ruger until the cops arrived.

Mark saw me, looked right at me, and turned and started running.

To the safety of the trees.

By now Billy had his Glock out. Reeve was at the open door of the porch, shirt off, tattoos decorating his massive chest and upper arms.

"Where are they?" he bellowed.

"The writer guy," Billy yelled back. "He's over here, by the rocks. I don't know where the other guy went!"

"Kill him!" Reeve shouted. "Kill him now!"

I kept my head down, started moving away up the cove, best I could. Reeve ducked back into the house. I moved. The rocks and boulders were cold, slimy, the foamy waves breaking over me, chilling me, choking me.

I slipped and fell, over my head. Quick thought of drowning instead of being shot. What a damn choice.

Got up, spurting water, moved some and looked up.

Billy was staring down at me.

Glock in his hand.

Staring and staring. I couldn't understand why he was waiting, or what he was thinking.

I froze still. Not moving. In the far, far distance, it looked like Reeve was out of the house again, heading to where the Mazda and pickup truck were parked, but I wasn't paying that much attention. He could have been Jimmy Hoffa for all I cared at the moment.

The Glock started to rise up.

I took a breath, thought of what to say, doubted anything was going to work.

A gunshot, part of Billy's head blew open in a spray of blood and hair, and he collapsed in front of me.

Out in front of the house, a vision from the Old Testament, a bearded and angry prophet in a robe, stumbling out of the house, a revolver in both of his shaking hands.

"Get . . . away . . . from . . . my . . . boy!" Will shouted. He moved in Reeve's direction, and another shot was fired. Reeve rolled and ducked behind the Mazda, then rose up with the speed and suddenness of a jack-in-the-box, and fired off three quick rounds, all of which hammered into Will's chest. He fell flat on his back, bare legs tangled together.

I got up from the rocks, went to Billy's body, looking for his Glock, not seeing it, not seeing it. Reeve moved around from the Mazda, spotted me, yelled out "Still got plans for you, Cole!"

No Glock.

I ducked behind Billy's body, pushed at the heavy weight, got his jacket flopped open, dove around his belt—

Got my Beretta.

Raised it up, clicked off the safety, didn't bother taking time to aim.

No time. Best to get off a quick shot, to surprise or scare the target.

I fired.

Reeve was definitely surprised, ducking down, but I doubted I had scared him.

He raised up his pistol and I shot again.

He whirled, cursed, grabbed at his side, and bounced behind the Mazda again, fired once at me, and I sent three more shots downrange at him.

I ducked behind the rocks, breathing hard, accidentally dropping the Beretta into the ocean and grabbing it with my left hand.

I moved some, raised up my head.

No movement. No motion. I stared at the Mazda. I was fortunate to be in a spot where I could see through the undercarriage.

Didn't see Reeve.

Looked to the corner of the house.

No Reeve.

I sloshed through the ocean, looked again.

Nothing.

I got to a point where a large pine tree was near the rocks, and I got out, banging both knees in the process, and spent a couple of minutes behind the wide tree trunk.

Still nothing. I moved from tree to tree until I got a good view of the far side of both the Mazda and the pickup truck, and the rear of Will's house.

Empty.

I walked over to the Mazda, pockmarked with bullet holes. On the stretch of lawn by the driver's side of the car, there was a smear of blood. My heart was pounding right along and it was hard to catch my breath, but I was pleased to see that my hands holding the Beretta were rock-solid. I made my way around the edge of the house, saw another splatter of blood.

So there you go.

Out in the distance, a siren.

Weapon still in firm hands, I went over to Will.

His eyes flickered open.

Still alive.

I knelt down. His chest was a bloody mess.

His voice wavered but still had strength behind it. "My boy. . . ."

I lowered my head to his as he said it again. "My boy. . . ."

I reached out, grabbed his hand, squeezed it hard. "He's just fine. You saved him. You saved him, Will."

I think he tried to smile, but I'm not sure. Bright pink blood foam was on his lips, a contrast to the white foam washing up on his land. I squeezed his hand again, and his eyes flickered once and remained open.

His chest was no longer moving. But there was a lot more blood lower down.

Didn't make sense. It still looked like all of Reeve's shots had struck him right in the chest. I looked more closely at his hospital gown, didn't see any tears or rips, and then it made sense.

To get out of his hospital bed, to reach his weapon, to save his boy, Will had had to tear the urinary catheter out of his body.

I squeezed his hand again. "Damn, Maureen was right. You were a tough old bird."

I got up as a white cruiser from the Washington County Sheriff's Department roared down the road and along the dirt driveway. I placed my Beretta on the ground and walked back and stood still, arms and hands extended. A young deputy sheriff in a dark blue uniform shirt and trousers stepped out, pistol extended.

I raised my hands before he could say a word. I yelled out, "There's a man in the woods, armed! He's dangerous!"

He spoke into a handheld microphone at his shoulder, head moving about, other hand holding his weapon. Then he got around the cruiser—smart move, putting it between himself and the woods—and he came to me. "You don't move, you keep your hands up, you keep still!"

"Yes, sir," I said, doing exactly what I was told. He looked at the bodies of Will and Billy and said, "Sweet fuck, what the hell happened here?"

"A shootout."

"Christ, I can see that. What the hell happened?"

I was going to point with my right hand but quickly remembered my orders. "The old man by the house . . . he shot and killed the man by the rocks. The old man was shot by a third man, the one who's in the woods."

"Why's he in the woods?" the deputy sheriff asked.

Fair question. "Because I shot him," I said.

He slowly moved around, weapon aimed right at me. "Kneel down, ankles crossed, hands behind your head."

I stood still. "Deputy, any other day of the week, I'd love to. But you've got an armed biker gang leader out in the woods, and even wounded, he's tough and quick enough to put a bullet through your head with no hesitation."

"I'm ordering you, on the ground, now!"

I refused to move. "Deputy, I have the utmost respect for law enforcement, but your best bet now is to let me pick up my pistol and for us to wait for reinforcements. I have a carry permit for here and New Hampshire."

His young face was bright red. "On the ground, now, or I'm gonna put you in a world of hurt."

Sirens.

Sirens were approaching.

I lowered myself to the ground, as ordered.

I may be dense sometimes, but I can learn on occasion.

The first down the short driveway was a gray Maine State Police cruiser, followed by another sheriff's cruiser, followed by a police cruiser from a neighboring town. I was quickly and efficiently handcuffed, someone threw a blanket over me, and then a lengthy argument proceeded over who was going to take control of me, the bodies, and the crime scene.

I just waited, standing still, legs shaking from the cold, the deputy sheriff holding on to one of my arms, a State Police trooper holding on to the other, and the local cop trying to decide which side to join. The debate sometimes got fierce and personal, and I kept my mouth shut, until I saw two black Chevrolet Impalas with blue and red flashing lights in their grilles slowly approach the parked cruisers, like they had all the time in the world.

"Sorry, fellas," I said. "I think you all just got trumped."

The next twelve hours went by in a combination of furious activity, followed by hours of me staring at blank concrete walls. I was taken away from the enthusiastic local constabulary and put in the back of one of the Impalas, which took me and a silent woman and a silent man—both well dressed and well armed, of course—to Machias, where the county jail was located. I heard a few voices being raised in protest, but I was ushered into a plain and cold cell, and waited.

Twice I was brought out to an interrogation room, and I suppose the old Lewis Cole—the one with a cushy job at *Shoreline* magazine, a fat bank account, and a warm and intact historical home—would have cracked wise and made jokes and asked for an attorney.

Instead, I told them everything, jotted down names and dates and places, and even made a sketch of Will's home and what had happened and how it had happened.

Then night came and I was given a cheese-and-baloney sandwich on white bread—at least with mustard and not mayo—and a bag of Maine's famed Humpty Dumpty potato chips, along with a container of lemonade. I didn't bother asking questions or making demands and just kept my mouth shut, and with a hard foam mattress, equally hard pillow, and two gray wool blankets that smelled heavily of disinfectant, I fell asleep in my solitary cell, a guest of both Washington County and a number of polite men and women in business suits.

Breakfast was a container of orange juice, a cup of black coffee, and a plain doughnut. I ate and drank it all and then washed my face and hands from the cold water in the stainless-steel sink.

And I waited.

And I waited.

Then they came for me.

This interview room was a bit larger, a bit more comfortable, with chairs that looked like they had been purchased recently and a polished conference-room table that didn't have cigarette burns or coffee stains or a heavy ring in the center to chain a suspect. I had been brought in sans handcuffs, which I found encouraging.

A woman was in the other chair, looking to be in her mid-thirties or so. She had on a black two-piece skirt-and-jacket ensemble, with a plain beige blouse. About her neck was a gold chain. Her hair was thick and black, professionally styled, and she had on a minimum of makeup, although her nails were a bright red. Her teeth flashed pure white at me as she smiled when I sat down, but her eyes were hard and the color of platinum.

"Mister Cole," she said.

"Ma'am," I said. There was no notebook, no legal pad, no folder, no laptop or tablet. Just the two of us.

It was silent, and I said: "Excuse me, I didn't catch your name."

The same white smile. "Don't worry about that."

"All right."

"You've been extraordinarily cooperative, and you have my personal thanks for that."

"Glad to be of help."

"Now," she said, folding her perfectly manicured hands together, leaning forward just a bit, "I have a proposition for you. Take your time thinking it through, because it's a one-time deal, available only at this point in time. Do you understand what I'm saying?"

"I certainly do," I said. "And I'm eager to learn more."

"I'm sure you are," she said. "So here it is. You leave and keep quiet about what you know and what happened at the home in North Point Harbor, then that's it. There'll be no publicity, no formal inquiry, no examination of potentially illegal activities on your part. You can go back to whatever you were doing before you were entangled in this . . . situation."

"Interesting proposal," I said. "I would guess my silence would be very helpful for those in the Department of Justice who might be embarrassed or hauled before Congress to discuss a multiple shooting involving a person in WITSEC."

"That," she said, "is a fascinating hypothesis that I'm not in a position to comment on."

"All right," I said. "Speaking of multiple shootings, have you or your associates located Reeve Langley?"

"No," she said, "although the hunt continues. We located a stolen Jeep Cherokee nearby that we believe he and the other man used."

"The other man was named Billy," I said. "What about him?"

"I believe the investigation into his death will show that he was shot by Stan Pinkerton, while attempting to rob his home."

"Will Mallory," I said.

"What?"

"The man's name was Will Mallory."

Her smile grew just a bit wider. "Like I said, the investigation will show that Billy Conklin, of a motorcycle gang from New Hampshire, shot and killed Stan Pinkerton during an attempted robbery, and that in the ensuing gunfight Mister Conklin also perished."

"Interesting theory, considering Billy Conklin was shot in the back of the head."

"As you and I both know from experience, gunfights can be very confusing. Anything else?"

"Mark Spencer."

"Found wandering in the woods about a half hour after you came with us back to this building."

"Came with us" was a pretty mellow way of saying "taken into custody," but I let it slide. "Good to hear, I guess."

"Anything else?" she asked.

"Would it be possible to connect this agreement with the lack of investigative vigor into a shooting incident in Tyler a couple of days back? Just so there's no . . . confusion."

"I don't see why not. Is that it?"

I thought for a moment and said, "Two more things."

"Don't push it."

"No worries, I won't," I said. "First, I'd like to make sure I get my Beretta back."

"Why?"

"Sentimental reasons."

"It's not here, but I promise, I can make it happen. And the second matter?"

"Gas money."

While the smile remained, there was a hint of confusion there. "Go on?"

"If you're letting me go, I'm going to need gas money to drive back to Portland," I said. "I borrowed that pickup truck, and I'm broke."

She laughed—a sound that was inviting—and reached into the dark brown leather bag hanging off the back of her chair. She pulled out a wallet, slipped out five twenty-dollar bills, and I nodded in thanks when I took them out of her hand.

"Do you want me to sign a receipt?" I asked.

"Not at all," she said.

"And about the other issues . . . do you want me to sign some form of a non-disclosure agreement?"

She folded her fine hands together. "That means a document has to be prepared. Which means other people involved, a computer record being created, other records being created as well . . . which can be subpoenaed and reviewed and investigated. Which means no. It's just between us. Agreed?"

I folded the money up and slipped it into my pants pocket. "Agreed."

"Fine." She stood up and said "We'll have you back to your borrowed pickup truck in just a while. And about the money I just lent you . . . it was a personal favor."

"Thank you," I said, standing up as well.

"You're welcome," she said, and with an impish tone to her voice, she said: "Next time you're in Manhattan, you can take me out to dinner to repay it."

"Sounds delightful," I said. "But you haven't told me your name. How will I find you?"

She slung her leather bag over her shoulder. "If you're ever in Manhattan, I'll know how and where to find you, Mister Cole. Good day."

True to her word, I was back in North Point Harbor and back at the home of Will Mallory. My borrowed pickup truck was there, and after I was dropped off from a black Chevrolet Impala driven by a silent man built like a rugby player, I went over to the truck.

A man emerged from the other side of the house.

Mark Spencer.

Well.

He looked to me, anguish in his voice, and said, "They took my Mazda. Seized it for evidence. There were bullet holes in it."

I went to the truck, unlocked the driver's side door. Everything seemed to be in order. Mark came around to my side. "Please," he said. "I don't know anybody around here, my cell phone has no service, I need a ride back to Portland."

"Then why don't you take your revolver, hijack somebody?"

Mark said "They seized that too."

"Good. How and where did you get it?"

"Before I left Portland. Gave up my watch to some guy at a pawnshop. That watch was a graduation gift."

"Tough world, ain't it," I said.

I got into the truck and he was now across from me, looking tired, beat down, whipped, fine hair and complexion all messed up.

Paula, I thought. What in the world do you see in him?

"Get in," I said. "And not one word south. Understand? Not one word, or I'll dump you on the side of the road."

He nodded in relief, trotted around the front of the truck, and climbed in.

I started up the engine, and the both of us left North Point Harbor.

CHAPTER TWENTY-TWO

As we drove on Route 1 back to Portland, I took command of the radio station and ensured that we both listened to classic rock on our long journey south. I had no desire to listen to any news stations, to hear what lies they might say about the shootings in that little coastal Maine town, or to hear what truths might be said about Hurricane Toni and what had happened to the part of the New England shoreline where she had hit.

When I got cell-phone service, I made a call to Felix and made some arrangements. After I got off the phone, I said to my sulking passenger "We've got service now. If you want to, you could get ahold of Paula."

"Later," he said. "Later."

"Whatever works," I said.

Outside the charming town of Camden—where the movie *Peyton Place* from the 1960s had been filmed—Mark cleared his throat.

"Lewis, I'm hungry. And thirsty."

That was definitely in violation of our earlier agreement, but by now a heavy rain was falling, the leading edge of Hurricane Toni no doubt, and perhaps I was feeling gracious or just tired, but I slowed the truck, reached down, and retrieved the plastic bag I had gotten yesterday at the general store in North Point Harbor. I pulled out the warm two-liter bottle of Coke and the bag of Utz potato chips and pushed them over at him.

"Have at it," I said, and then, remembering what day it was, added: "Happy Thanksgiving."

When we neared Portland, I gassed up the pickup truck at an Irving Station and got back in. Mark was huddled up against the passenger's-side door and said "Are we going back to the motel?"

"That we are," I said. "I promised the nice lady who owns it that I'd bring this truck back."

"Then what are we . . . I mean, what's going to happen next?"

"Felix Tinios will be there, ready to take you to Milan to meet up with Paula Quinn. I'll make my own arrangements to get back to Tyler."

I started up the truck, checked the time. About ten minutes. Mark said "My dad . . . one of the Feds said he was shot, trying to defend me. Is that true?"

"Yes, that's true."

"Oh."

I drove on and said: "You might want to think about that. An old man, practically dying alone . . . and when he meets his biological son for the first time in decades, he finds out his son has betrayed him for cash to an old enemy. And despite all that . . . despite his weakness and what will happen to him, he tries to save your sorry ass."

Mark wiped at his eyes. "I . . . I changed my mind, didn't I? I changed my mind. I thought he had abandoned me, had dumped me . . . I was angry and I wanted revenge. I admit it."

"Your mind . . . it should have been more open, Counselor. You were assuming facts not placed in evidence."

Up ahead were the lights of the Ocean View Terrace.

"One more thing," I said.

"What's that?"

"I want you to do right by Paula," I said.

"What the hell do you mean by that?"

"You're an educated man," I said. "You'll figure it out. Or else."

I turned into the motel's parking lot. Standing next to a Chevrolet Tahoe was Felix Tinios. He waved, and I waved back, and then I got out and went into the motel's office.

The owner and manager, Kathi Hawkins, came out to see me, this time wearing a Red Sox World Series Champion sweatshirt—and even now, I feel like looking twice to make sure it's not a hoax—and I gave her back the keys to her son's truck.

"Everything go okay?" she asked.

"Just fine," I said.

"Where to now?"

"Back to Tyler," I said, and she frowned, looked up at a television hanging from the ceiling. The sound was down low, but I didn't need sound to see what I was seeing. It was somewhere on Atlantic Avenue near Tyler Beach, and a front-end loader was evacuating residents, people huddling together in the machine's bucket.

"Oh, those poor people," Kathi said.

"Yes," I said. "Those poor people."

Underneath the overhang, I held up a hand to Felix and tried to call Diane Woods. It went straight to voicemail, which wasn't a surprise. If Tyler and vicinity were in a hurricane-induced blackout, the cell towers were probably out of service as well.

I put my cell phone away and Felix came to me, from out of the rain. He had on a heavy black windbreaker and a black Navy wool cap on his head. "Miserable day, eh?"

"Sure is."

"You got things squared away up there?"

"In a manner of speaking," I said.

"Did Mark locate his long-lost dad?"

"He did."

"Where's long-lost dad now?"

"In a funeral home somewhere up in northeast Maine," I said. "Reeve Langley put him there."

"And where's Reeve Langley?"

"If we and the world are lucky, he's bled out somewhere in the woods. He got shot as well."

"Christ," Felix said. "Who shot him? Mark's dad?"

I thought of my agreement with the lovely and nameless woman up there, earlier in the day. "There was a crossfire. Lots of shooting."

Felix eyed me, and then gently tapped me on the shoulder. "Well, damn glad to see you standing up. I'm getting ready to take Mark over to Milan. Want to hitch a ride?"

"No," I said. "I was planning to take a bus south. Should get into Tyler before the end of the day."

Felix shook his head. "Nobody's getting into Tyler today, Lewis. National Guard and State Police are manning roadblocks. The hurricane came ashore around Cape Ann, but still made a hell of a mess on the seacoast. The place is sealed off."

My house, I thought. My poor house.

Another touch to the shoulder. "Come to Milan. If you're lucky, you'll get some leftovers, and then you can head back to Tyler tomorrow. Things should be straightened out by then."

I moved my feet, suddenly just bone-deep tired from all that had gone on during the past few days.

"Can I sit in the front?"

"Of course."

"You sure?"

Felix tugged at my elbow, took me over to the Tahoe.

"I'll even tie the son-of-a-bitch to the roof if that would make you happy."

"Let me think about it."

It took nearly three hours to get to Milan, a small town just north of the famed mill city that was Berlin, N.H. I dozed most of the way as Felix took us up I-95, and then west through very rural Maine and New Hampshire. Mark sat in the back, quiet once again, and Felix played Italian opera, volume set to low. I had no idea who was doing the singing or why, and I guess it didn't make any difference. I woke up as we passed through Berlin, a city based on wood and paper processing; and through a series of back roads surrounded by mountain peaks, we reached our destination.

It was a simple graded dirt road, off to the right, with a wooden sign nailed to a tree that said HARBOR. Felix turned left and we went up the dirt road, and I was wide awake, paying attention. The dirt road was fairly narrow, and then it widened as we approached a simple wood-and-stone bridge. A fast-moving stream went under the bridge, and I spotted something curious: three concrete Jersey barriers, set side by side, on the other side. Felix drove over the bridge and a number of buildings came into view, including two barns, a large farmhouse, and smaller cottages scattered across what looked to be acres of pastureland. Some of the land was fenced in, and there were horses, cows, goats, and a number of chickens. A couple of Irish wolfhounds trotted out to greet us as Felix pulled the Tahoe to a stop.

"Mark," Felix said. "You first."

"What?" he said. "What do you mean?"

"There's somebody waiting for you here," I said. "Don't make her wait."

He got out and went across a wide dirt parking area. Three pickup trucks, a white GMC van, and a mud-splattered red Chevrolet Suburban were parked to one side. There was also a small green-and-yellow John Deere tractor with a backhoe, parked to one side, a chain and metal hook dangling from the front bucket. Now I understood the Jersey barriers I had spotted by the bridge. In just a few seconds, by using the tractor's backhoe the road leading into the compound could be blocked.

A man and a woman came out of the large farmhouse, and Mark spoke to them, and the woman went back into the house. Just seconds passed before Paula Quinn flew out, running up to Mark.

She came to a halt in front of him. Her face was red, twisted in anger or frustration, and she held up a hand. She was wearing jeans and a blue sweatshirt, and that was all. She stepped closer to Mark, and I could hear her voice—though not make out the words—as she kept on yelling at Mark.

Then, like a switch had been thrown, Paula lowered her head and rushed into Mark's arms, and they hugged and hugged. Long seconds went by, and then Paula took his hand and took him inside.

Felix said "Ain't love grand."

"So I've been told."

We both exited the Tahoe.

⌒

It was a crowded and busy night, and I forgot the name of every man and woman introduced to me, as well as the names of the dogs—which seemed as big as ponies—and the children who ran and giggled underfoot. They didn't fit the popular media stereotype of doomsday preppers: I didn't see one firearm in public, nor a *Guns & Ammo* magazine, nor a Confederate flag imprinted with the motto THE SOUTH WILL RISE AGAIN. Just . . . men and women, old and young, and a mass of kids that I found impossible to count. In one brief moment, Paula cornered me in the wide and open kitchen—where I was trying to secure a plate of leftover turkey and stuffing—and kissed me on the cheek, and whispered "Later."

"Absolutely," I said.

After I ate, the friend of Felix who had set up the place—and whose name I forgot once more—took me upstairs to the corner of a small attic loft. It was cozy, with a triangular ceiling that bumped your head when you walked in. There was a futon, pillow, and light green down comforter on the floor, and a table lamp also on the floor. A window about the size of a porthole looked out. My host bent over and switched on the lamp and, with a rueful smile, said, "Sorry, that's the best we can do." He was in his early sixties, wearing blue jeans and a gray turtleneck with a green wool shirt buttoned over it. "We weren't expecting company. Your friend there, Mark, at least he can share a room with his fiancée."

"That's all right," I said, not bothering to correct him on my status with Mark Spencer. "I appreciate the hospitality."

He started to leave the room, and I asked him: "Tell me, do you really believe all this? That civilization is going to end?"

My host smiled, revealing dimples. "All civilizations end, Mister Cole. It's one of the hard rules of history. Why should this one be any different? Oh, we have superior technology and knowledge, but that just makes us even more vulnerable, whether it's a computer virus or a flu virus. And viruses like that . . . once they're set loose, it's just a matter of the odds and time before they won't be stopped." He shrugged. "I don't think big cities are going to be particularly safe places in the future. If I'm wrong . . . well, my kids and their kids and some friends and relatives, we all grew up in a pretty part of the world and learned some important skills. And if I'm right . . . I'm giving them the chance to live. That's what dads do, when you get right down to it. Give their offspring the best chance to live, do what they can to protect their families."

We exchanged our good-nights and he closed the small door behind him, and I stripped and crawled into the futon, shivered until my body heat warmed things up, and then I switched off the light. I craned my head for a moment, to see if I could make out anything through the tiny window.

Nothing.

The futon was now warm and comfortable, but I had a hard time falling asleep. I puzzled over that and realized what was bothering me, and it was one of the Seven Deadly Sins: envy. Lust would probably have been more fun at the moment, but it was envy that was keeping me awake, and, sur-prise of surprises, it wasn't the thought of Mark cuddling up with Paula.

It was the thought of all those people down there, and the nice man who had just put me up, and something they all had that I didn't have.

Family.

I woke up at some early time and decided it was time to find my way south. I got dressed and slowly went downstairs, and there was Felix, standing before the double sink, washing pots and pans. He had on gray slacks, a buttoned-down striped Oxford shirt, and a large apron that said KISS THE COOK. There were two long wooden tables that were covered with dishes, pots, pans, glasses, knives, and forks. In a corner was a woodstove, churning out a lot of heat. Before the woodstove were two large dog beds, and the Irish wolfhounds were curled up with each other on the beds.

But they weren't alone. The blond hair of a young girl was visible just above their torsos, said girl wearing pajamas and maybe being six or seven. She gently snored.

I went over to Felix, found a reasonably dry dish towel, and started drying some of the pots and pans. "Sorry to take you away from friends and family."

"Oh, not a problem. Truth is, it was . . . confining. My Aunt Teresa yapping at her boyfriend, her boyfriend yapping back."

"And the medical aides?"

"Replaced at the last minute with two fine strapping young fellows. Quite skilled and experienced, but not what I was looking for."

He snapped the towel out of my hand, nudged me. "C'mon, what's your plans for the day? Not doing dishes with me, I hope."

I was disappointed he had taken the towel away. It had been good, mindless work, and now I was forced to think.

"Head south," I said. "Maybe grab a bus in Berlin, get over to Tyler Beach and see what's left."

Felix smiled, and I wondered how he always looked so damn good. "This way, friend." He led me to the mud room, where I secured my jacket from a pile of coats, scarves, and hats, and went out into the cold morning. A vehicle had been added to the census since we had arrived.

My rental Honda Pilot.

"Felix . . . if I may, that's been reported stolen."

"And it's been reported unstolen." He gave me the keys. "Go on and get out of here."

I took the keys and he added, "Unless you want some company. I could follow you south until you get back to Tyler Beach. . . ."

I knew what he was saying, what he was offering. He didn't want me to be alone when I saw the storm-swept cellar hole that had once been my home.

I raised the keys in salute. "Thanks, but I'm going to lone-wolf it. Maybe catch some of the Black Friday sales on my way down. And you?"

A smile and a walk back to the house. "Christ, do you have to ask? Didn't you see the piles of dishes back there?"

I got into the Pilot, which had been washed and vacuumed. In the rear were some of my belongings, including my sleeping bag and pillow, which I would be using probably in another twelve hours or so. I said, "So, we ride again, *muchachos*," and I was nearly jolted out of my seat by a loud *bang!*

I turned and Paula Quinn was there, having just pounded the hood of my Pilot. I got out and she was in a long yellow nightgown, feet in muddy Wellington boots and wearing a blue down vest. She was shivering and she passed over a mug of coffee. "Black, with two sugars. I remembered."

"So you did." I took the coffee mug from her hands, put it on the center console of the Honda, turned back to her. "You're freezing. Get back inside."

She nodded, smiled, rubbed at her bare arms. "You found him. You brought him back. Thanks so very, very much, Lewis."

"I was glad to do it," I said, and right then and there, despite what I had seen, who had died, and what was waiting for me at the end of my drive home, I meant it.

She kissed me briefly on the lips, stepped back. "He . . . he's all right, but he's not saying much."

"I'm sure he will."

"But . . . I need to know. How was he? I mean, I knew the two of you were in danger, there was some gunfire . . . did he help you? Did he have your back?"

I looked at her solemn face, her inquiring eyes, the way her slim legs trembled. I kissed her again. "He was the man I always knew he was," I said. "Now, go back inside."

She gave a wide smile, trotted back toward the house, and by the time I was in the Pilot and had started her up, she was gone.

The coffee tasted good, and I got two healthy sips in as I drove out of the compound. I switched on the heater for the seat, turned on the interior heat, and just let my mind drift. I went over the compound's bridge, down the fine dirt road, and, when I came to a stop, took a left, heading back toward what passed for the center of Milan. From there, get on Route 16 and take the long, long drive south to the seacoast. I should get there in just over three hours.

This part of the road was straight and narrow, and I took another sip of coffee and glanced up behind me to see a Range Rover speeding toward me, with New Hampshire plates. I lowered my coffee cup and the Range Rover sped up, started to pass me.

"Go right ahead," I murmured; "I'm in no goddamn hurry."

But the Range Rover didn't pass me. It fell back, accelerated again—fast—and, with its right front bumper, struck my left rear bumper.

I quickly went into a spin, the coffee splashed over my lap and hands, and the Pilot skidded and skidded, nearly turning over, until it slammed into a drainage ditch at the side of the road. The seatbelt and harness held firm as I snapped forward and, when I was able to take a deep breath and open my eyes, looked up at the rearview mirror.

The Range Rover had stopped. A man got out.

Even with mirror twisted, it was easy to see who it was.

Reeve Langley, carrying a pistol, walking right toward me.

CHAPTER TWENTY-THREE

I scrabbled at my seatbelt, undid the lock, mind racing. Beretta. Somewhere in government hands. Felix. Back a few hundred yards at the compound. Tire iron for the Pilot. Somewhere in the rear. I slammed the door open, fell into the drainage ditch, and Reeve screamed "Freeze, Cole! Freeze, or I'll blow your goddamn head off right now!"

I turned, standing in cold water and mud.

Reeve came closer, stumbling, and now he was moving slow. His right hand held his pistol, his left hand was holding tight to the side of his pea coat, right on his torso. His hat was off, and his bare head and face were shockingly white.

Another man got out of the Range Rover, short and squat, holding a shotgun. Reeve turned to him. "George! You stay the hell right there! This one is mine!"

George stayed behind the open driver's door.

Reeve swayed and came back to look at me. I slowly walked up onto the roadway, hands extended.

"You look fairly peaked," I said. "Don't you belong in a hospital, Reeve?"

"Bah." He swayed again, spat on the ground. "Doctors . . . I get into a hospital, they see a gunshot wound, a whole lot of shit gets stirred . . . and I don't get to find you . . . and put you down. . . ."

He raised the pistol and fired it. I winced, closed my eyes. It was damn loud, and I could hear the sound of the empty cartridge casing hit the pavement.

But that was it. I was cold and scared out of my mind, but I was fine.

"Missed," I said, keeping still. "Think you can try again?"

"I . . . won't . . . miss. . . ." His face was raw with pure hate.

Another shot, but this time it was even more wide of the mark. There were *snick-snack* sounds as the round went through the woods.

"Bold talk for a bleeding biker, far away from home," I said, standing still, right in front of him.

"Fuck . . . you. . . ."

Another stumble, and his hand with the pistol weaved around and around, like the weapon was made of solid lead.

"Give it up, Reeve," I said. "You failed. Spectacularly. Sure, Will is dead, but you just hastened the process. No glorious tales of revenge there, Reeve. And his son Mark is still alive and well and going to get married soon. As for you, it's going to be a hospital room. And a prison term in our fair state, far from family and friends. And your bikers back west will eventually find out that it was an out-of-work magazine writer who took you down."

He made a noise of a bellow and a moan, and tried to use both hands on his pistol. But taking away the hand holding his wounded torso weakened him even more, and he stepped forward, stumbled, and fell to the pavement. I walked over and picked up his pistol, looked down at him. His face was twisted with pain, hate, and scorn as he looked up at me. I got down on the asphalt on one knee and said: "Reeve? Reeve? You hear me?"

A long, bubbling sigh that I took for a yes. I said "Remember back then, when we met, I said one of these days I wanted to visit Wyoming?"

A softer bubbling sigh. I leaned in so he could look up at me.

"I lied," I said.

Then he was quiet and still.

I got up.

The man called George was now near me, pointing his shotgun right at me.

"Hey," I said.

"Hey," he said right back.

I waited, not wanting to lift up Reeve's pistol, not wanting to give George an excuse. Finally, I said "Looks like we've got a situation here."

"Yep."

"Any suggestions?"

He looked down at Reeve's body. "He told me that you shot Billy, back up in Maine. That true?"

"No, it's not," I said. "An old man who once rode with him with the Stonecold Falcons, he shot Billy. He was trying to protect his son."

"What happened to the old man?"

"Reeve killed him."

George was squat, wide, with a thick heavy black beard and a bushy crop of hair. With a change of clothes, he could have easily gotten work in any number of Hollywood productions looking for a swordsman or axeman.

But right now I was focusing on his skills as a shotgun man.

"You telling me straight?"

"I am," I said.

Then he looked at Reeve, looked at me, said "Ah, shit," and raised up the shotgun so it rested on his shoulder. I slowly took Reeve's pistol and put it in my waistband, at my back. "Where's Billy now?" he asked.

"A funeral home up in Machias, Maine. The Washington County Sheriff's Department could probably get you the address."

"Ah, shit," he said, and he started crying, and he ran a wrist across his eyes. "What the hell am I gonna say to my aunt. . . ."

Then it was clear. "You and Billy . . . cousins?"

A nod.

"You were with the Crawford Notch Boys. You were helping out Reeve, weren't you."

"Yeah." Snot was bubbling out of his nose.

I looked at him more closely, and said, "You were the one back in North Tyler, when we were checking out the attorney's house. The one with the metal-detecting gear that walked by the Tahoe when Paula was in there by herself."

"Yeah."

"That's how you knew to come here to Milan. You slipped some sort of tracking device on the Tahoe. So you'd know where Felix was, and me, and Mark Spencer's girlfriend."

Again, the one-word answer: "Yeah." He wiped his nose and said, "That device . . . didn't work all the time. . . . And we got paid well, but . . . Reeve Langley, he was a cold-hearted psycho, that's what he was. Me and Billy, we wanted to quit, but we couldn't."

"Phil Tasker," I said, recalling the name of the motorcycle club's president. "He wouldn't let you quit?"

George shook his head. "No. Mister Tinios wouldn't."

"Mister Tinios?"

"Yeah. We got word from Phil, through Mister Tinios . . . no matter what happened, that we were going to stick with Reeve. We weren't gonna harm you. No matter how mean it got, we'd find a way to help you."

Back in Maine, at Will's house. The sound of the furniture falling.

Billy, knocking around a chair to make it easier for me to break free.

Billy, not tying the ropes as tight as he should have.

Billy, standing in front of me, pistol in hand, hesitating.

Hesitating until he was shot and killed by Mark's father.

Sweet Jesus.

"He did just that, back up in Maine," I said. "He saved my life."

George paused in his sniffling. "You telling me . . . you telling me my cuz, he died a hero?"

"That he did."

George pursed his lips, nodded a couple of times. "That's . . . that's good to hear. His family will be real proud to hear that."

I looked up and down the road and said "George . . . there might be some traffic coming along here, you never know."

"Christ, that's right," he said. "I stole this Range Rover back in Gorham, and there's a length of heavy chain in the back. Guess I could pull you out of that ditch if you'd like."

"That'd be great," I said, and then pointed to the body between us. "And what about him?"

A casual shrug. "We haul your Pilot out of the ditch, and we haul him in. How does that sound?"

"Sounds great," I said.

CHAPTER TWENTY-FOUR

The drive home to Tyler took over three hours, as predicted, and it seemed to go by quite fast, like the moment you jump out of a perfectly functioning airplane with a parachute and before you know it, you're on the ground, wondering, why in the hell did I just do that? On the drive south, I stopped only once on Route 16, in that town called Ossipee that seemed to sprawl over most of my long drive. I made my stop on a concrete bridge that spanned a fast-moving stream, and when I was sure no traffic was in view, I dumped Reeve Langley's pistol, and then went on.

I made a phone call to Diane soon after that, and she asked "Christ, you okay?"

"Just fine."

A burst of static and her voice faded ". . . no power and not much battery life, but Kara and I, we did okay and—"

Then her phone died. I called twice, it went straight to voicemail, and then I gave up.

My clothes and the Pilot's interior stunk of coffee, but I paid it no mind, the further south I got. Other traffic started to appear, from utility trucks from neighboring utilities coming in to help restore power, along with a number of National Guard vehicles moving along. Once I got into

Wentworth County, I got off I-95 and took a series of back roads to Tyler Beach.

It was a grim drive. Lots of utility trucks and workers—some from as far away as New Brunswick—were trying to make sense out of the twisted spaghetti of power lines. Houses with shingles torn off, a couple of homes with collapsed roofs. Going past an elementary school in North Tyler, sign outside saying EMERGENCY SHELTER HERE, the parking lot full and cars parked on the lawn. And along a beautiful stretch of farmland in North Tyler, within view of the ocean, scores of pine and oak trees upended and torn away.

When I got to Atlantic Avenue, the traffic was one lane only, which made it slow going to Tyler Beach, giving me plenty of time to think, which I hated. Lots of beach cottages were either crumpled or ripped apart, and a couple were even torn off their foundations and tossed across the road, into the bordering marshes. Along with the slow-moving cars and trucks, there were more National Guard vehicles and two television satellite trucks from Boston, here to record and report on the devastation, and I knew that later in the day, most stories would mention something about New Hampshire's Atlantic playground suffering a tremendous loss.

Near the border with Tyler, I saw an amazing sight, an orange State of New Hampshire plow truck, usually dispatched to handle snow and ice, but this time being used to plow sand and rocks that had been tossed up from the ocean by Hurricane Toni.

The Lafayette House came into view, looking like it had come through the storm just fine. Its near parking lot and the parking lot across the street, which I usually use, were pretty full, but I managed to find an empty spot. As I got out, a silly thought came to me: how well would I sleep tonight in the back of the Pilot, with all these cars and trucks parked nearby?

The sky was a sharp blue, with just a light cold breeze blowing through. The waves were roaring in, and to the south there were surfers taking advantage of the higher-than-usual wave action. Men and women, some wearing National Guard uniforms or utility work clothes, walked in and around the parked vehicles. Nobody paid me any attention. I started my long, long way down to where I'd once lived, and another thought came to me, that it wouldn't make any difference if I spent the night here or somewhere else, because now there was nothing left to keep watch over.

I put my cold hands in my pockets, kept my head down from the heavy winds buffeting me, and I walked and walked.

When I couldn't stand it anymore, I stopped and lifted my head.

And looked at my house and the near garage.

Still standing.

Still there.

I found it hard to breathe, and I whispered: "If this is a dream, old man, I sure as hell don't want to wake up."

Somehow I walked some more and was there, just staring, mouth agape. The converted shed that had served as a garage was standing free and new, freshly constructed. The burnt debris had been removed, as well as the charred corpse of my Ford Explorer.

"What . . . the . . . hell?" I whispered some more.

But my house. . . .

It was standing proud and new as well. No tarpaulins, no boarded-up windows, nothing. It needed some stain and I could easily make out the new construction from the areas that had earlier burned, but it looked good. Damn good.

I stood there for a few minutes and just bawled.

When I could move again, I went to the front door, and a stiff piece of white cardboard was there, wrapped in plastic, nailed to the wood. I tore it free, removed the plastic.

CONSTRUCTION AND REPAIR WORK COURTESY OF:
MASSACHUSETTS CARPENTERS LOCAL 114
MASSACHUSETTS ELECTRICIANS LOCAL 9
TYLER POLICE ASSOCIATION LOCAL 1212

Felix and Diane.

And I remembered something Felix had said earlier, how in his line of work, in order to get things done, you never knew who you would eventually have to talk to.

Felix and Diane.

With hands trembling, I unlocked the door and stepped in, to the smell of fresh wood and paint. The interior was pretty bare and no lights came on when I flipped a switch, which made sense, considering this whole part of the state was without power. I slowly walked through the downstairs, and the upstairs. I recognized the old wood, which I had purchased soon after the fire, exhausting my savings, but there were no bathroom or kitchen furnishings. The studs were bare as well, awaiting sheetrock and additional painting. Some of my belongings, books and furnishings, salvaged by Felix after the fire weeks ago, were in place. There was no bed or bureaus or office desk or computer, but my mind was already racing on when and how I would replace them, once the insurance money grudgingly came to me.

I went back downstairs to the nearly empty living room and to the sliding glass doors. The glass was still new, with stickers attached. I stood there and watched the waves for a while, and then I sat down, cross-legged, and then hugged myself, rocking back and forth for a moment.

My family had come through for me.

ACKNOWLEDGMENTS

As always, thanks to my patient fans and readers. I'm so glad you didn't have to wait so long for this one. My wife Mona Pinette was her usual keen self in reviewing my first draft. I'd also like to extend my appreciation to Claiborne Hancock, Jessica Case, and Iris Blasi at Pegasus Books, as well as Phil Gaskill for his copyediting skills. Special thanks as well to S. J. Rozan, Andi Malala Schecter, Sandy Balzo, and Deborah Rosan. I'd also like to urge my readers to consider donating to this special charity—www.hero-dogs.org—in memory of a departed friend.